ABSOLUTION

League of Vampires

RYE BREWER

ABSOLUTION

Ancient enemies, newfound coalitions.
Anissa's not about to take Jonah's decision to face his enemies alone. This former slayer isn't your average sit on the sidelines kind of girl.

New heroes, not so new archenemies.
Fane wants forgiveness and allegiance, but not at the cost of the ones he loves most. Certainly, not at the expense of an new soul that is joining his cadre.

Needs rarely line up with wants.
Philippa's feelings for Vance won't be the end of her, but will they be the end of a loved one

Cover Art by www.mirellasantana.deviantart.com

with Model Mirish – Deviant Art

1

JONAH

Images flashed through my mind, based on what Fane had told me.

His words rang in my ears still. *"It goes back centuries, the history I have with Lucian. All the way back to when I was a human, named Dommik."*

Dommik. When he'd been my father. Not Fane, the vampire legend that he was now

His words and those images in my mind mixed with memories of my childhood, back when I was human. We had been so happy. We were still happy after we'd been turned—and I could remember that clearly, like the end of one life and the beginning of another—but it was a different sort of happiness.

We couldn't live simply anymore. We had a clan to think about. A much bigger family than what we'd known before then.

And all because of Lucian's hatred and obsession.

The cool air suddenly felt freezing cold. Even the brand on my arm barely registered on my consciousness, which was saying something, seeing as how the burning was all I could think about when it first appeared and flared up, as if a design had been burned into my skin with a cattle branding iron.

There had been times when Lucian seemed fake, hadn't there? When his smile had faltered a little, or I'd seen emptiness in his eyes. That last meeting of the League of Vampires, the way he'd stood there like a deity, absorbing the appreciation of the vampires in attendance. False modesty.

I tried to tell myself I was only remembering things through the lens of what Fane —who I'd recently learned was my father —had told me. It was easy to do that, wasn't it? To let new information color memories? I had to be fair. Didn't I?

Yet... Lucian had turned my mother into a vampire. He set my family on its path, changed the direction of our lives.

Sure, I would be long dead by now if he hadn't, but I would've lived a human life. As complicated as humans thought their lives were, their issues were nothing compared to what we vampires faced. There had been times, especially after losing my parents, when I'd wished we'd never been turned. I wouldn't have had to live endless decades never knowing what happened to the people I loved most in the world.

Fane didn't try to comfort me or ask if I had any questions. He only stared at me the way a father would gaze at his son after missing so much of his life.

"I'm staring," he said with a slight smile. "I'm sorry."

"It's all right. It doesn't bother me." I studied him.

Funny how he resembled my father and sounded like my father but was different. Something about his eyes, maybe, or the way he held himself. A hardness? What had he seen since he left us?

"Where is the h—the girl?"

He'd almost called Anissa the half-breed again—I could tell —but stopped himself in time.

I decided to let it pass.

"With her father. She's safe there."

"You're sure about that?"

"Of course. I wouldn't want her to be anywhere I wasn't sure of her safety. I sent her there to be certain she's not part of whatever happens next."

The lines on his brow deepened when he frowned. "You do care for her, don't you?"

"You doubted it?" Anissa was part-vampire, part-fae and the most amazing woman I'd ever met.

"I didn't know if it was infatuation or real attachment."

"I'm not a baby anymore," I reminded him with a faint smile. "I've grown up a lot."

He nodded. "It's easy to forget that after all this time apart."

All this time.

Decades.

Even so, the memory of the pain remained fresh. I would never forget the way life had stopped during those first days, when my siblings and I realized our parents had vanished. No explanation, no clue where they'd gone. Nothing mattered, when all we could think about was our parents and what might've happened to them. We'd lived in a sort of limbo where the world kept turning, but we stayed still. And none of us had ever been the same after. Especially not Philippa.

Which brought me to the next matter at hand. "You have to see her."

His eyebrows shot up. "What? Who?"

I stood and stared at him. "Philippa. You have to see her."

He appeared defeated. "No. I don't."

"Then at least let me tell her you're still alive."

He shook his head. "Jonah, I already told you how dangerous that is. Remember? The fewer of you who know I'm alive, the better. I only stayed away this long because I wanted to protect you—I can't turn my back on the promise I made to myself. If all these years of hiding away were wasted and something were to happen to any of you anyway, I would never forgive myself."

I glared at him. "I understand. I do. I spent years as head of the clan. I know there are almost no decisions that are easy. There's always a drawback or a compromise."

"Not an easy lesson to learn."

"It isn't," I agreed. "I learned it the hard way, over and over."

He nodded with an understanding smile. "So you see, then. Being away from you all has been torture. It didn't get any easier as time went on."

There was pain written all over his face.

I tried to imagine having kids and forcing myself to be away from them. Not merely being apart, but with full knowledge they thought I was dead. It would crush me.

Then again, it had crushed *us*, never knowing for sure. Especially my sister.

"It didn't get any easier for us, either, you know. Especially Philippa." I stared hard at him to get my point across. "She changed. She'll never go back to being the girl she used to be."

A shadow crossed his face. "What do you mean?"

"You remember how she used to be—bright, fun, funny. Always teasing and joking. High-spirited."

"She was a joy," he murmured.

I knew he was thinking back on the way she could always make him laugh, no matter what sort of mood he was in. They used to go on and on for hours, playing word games, debating, challenging each other.

She was so quick, so wily. But those qualities were on the surface. She was a brilliant judge of character, too, even at a young age. It was what made her the ideal advisor for me—she would've been his advisor, if he had stayed.

"All that brightness and sweetness went away when you did. I'm not trying to heap guilt on you. I'm really not. But you need to know. She found a way to move on. We all did. We didn't have a choice. And it changed us all, but none of us changed as much as she did. She has an edge. She's jaded. She doesn't trust the way she used to." My eyes narrowed. "You owe her this much. She deserves to know you're alive."

He stared off into the distance. "You said it yourself—sometimes there are difficult decisions to be made. Maybe this will give her some measure of peace, but at what cost? Her safety? Her life?" He raised his hand, as if saying *halt*. "I can't allow that."

I shook my head. "I can't go back and face her—ever—with this lie hanging over me. I can't betray her that way. She still loves you so much. You were her hero."

"The me I used to be," he uttered. "That's not who I am anymore."

"Why don't you let her be the one to decide that? She'll be so glad you're alive it won't matter."

It seemed like he was almost ready to give in—I knew the look. He was fighting with himself.

I used the opportunity to gain the upper hand, perhaps twisting the knife a little. "I'll help find Gage if you go see her."

"What?" His eyes dilated—the sole sign of his surprise.

"I'll help, but only if you agree to see Philippa."

He folded his arms. "Blackmail?"

"If it works, yes."

He turned away.

I was getting more desperate. "What can I say to get you to understand how important this is? Please. All I can do is ask you to please do this. It'll mean so much."

"What if...?" His voice broke, and he cleared his throat. "What if she doesn't want to see me? What if she hates me for what I did? She always had a temper, and she wasn't good at letting go of a grudge."

I pressed my lips together to keep from smiling. "That's something that hasn't changed."

"Sometimes, I think it would be easier to remember her before, the way things were, when she didn't hate me."

"I never said she hated you. She doesn't hate you."

"You don't know that. It would be better for her to look back at me the way I was before. She will probably hate me when she finds out. I'm not sure you don't."

I ignored that. I wasn't going to tell him I hated him. I wasn't going to tell him I didn't.

Though I didn't.

With every passing day, I was learning we often had to make decisions that weren't always easy.

That hit home for me now, stronger than ever, knowing I'd sent Anissa to Avellane to be with Gregor, her father and leader of the fae, knowing she would be pissed. Hopefully, she didn't hate me—wouldn't hate me. But still...

He watched me, waiting for a reply, wanting to know.

I gave him one. "Anything is better than not knowing."

His gaze was steady. "Where should we meet?"

⚜

"It's been a long time since I've stood here." Fane walked to the edge of the roof after stepping through the portal behind me and gazed out over the city.

It was a night like any other—down there, at least.

Not where I stood.

He took a deep breath. "I've missed being here. That's for sure." He glanced at me from the corner of his eye and smiled. "I spent a lot of time looking over the city, thinking about things whenever I needed to clear my head. I didn't dare come back."

"I understand that."

"I hope your sister does, too." He seemed nervous for the first time since we met again.

He wasn't Fane at that moment. It was like being with my father again.

I looked around. Just because we were on the roof didn't mean we were safe from prying eyes. "You'd better stay out of sight up here. I don't want anyone seeing you—as either Dommik Bourke, previous leader of the Bourke clan, or Fane."

"Wouldn't it be better for me to wait inside, then?"

I shook my head. "I'll go talk to her first—to warm her up. Please, stay here. Don't leave."

"I'll be right here when you're ready."

I hoped he meant it. I would hate to go through what I knew Philippa was going to put me through for him to not be here when I came back for him.

There was noise inside the penthouse. It wasn't as empty as it was when I was last here.

I listened closely.

Philippa's chambers.

I hoped she was alone.

It occurred to me as I crossed the living area and walked down the hall that I hadn't seen her since leaving the league meeting.

I braced myself for what was to come.

She didn't notice me at first. Her back was to the open door. There was a backpack on the bed, open, and she was shoving things into it, right and left.

I caught a peek when she moved to the side.

Weapons. Several daggers, two handguns, two throwing stars.

She bundled dark clothes in there, too. Jeans, a sweatshirt, a sweater, tees—all in dark gray or black.

I hadn't known my fashion-conscious sister owned that much plain, dark clothing.

I cleared my throat, and she spun around.

Her posture was defensive, like she was ready for a fight.

I held my hands up. "It's just me."

Her fists dropped to her sides. "Oh, Jonah!" she breathed, and, in the blink of an eye, she was throwing herself at me and squeezing me around the neck until I could hardly breathe.

"Easy, easy," I groaned.

"Where have you been? I didn't think I'd ever see you again!" She pulled away, holding me at arm's length so she could take me in. "What have you been doing? Where did you go?"

"One thing at a time. What are you doing? What are you

packing for?" I glanced at the backpack. "I mean, it looks a little... stockpiled?"

"I'm so glad you're back. I have a million things to tell you." She hurried back to the bed and finished wedging clothes into it before closing the zipper.

"You picked the perfect time to return. I have an errand, so you can take back being the leader and keep these hooligans in line."

"Wait a minute. I'm not here to lead the clan."

She stopped and turned slowly toward me. "What's that again?" Her hands were planted on her hips, and her chin jutted out.

"I'm sorry, but that's not why I came back here. Besides, I don't think it's as easy as just walking back in and saying something like, 'Hey, I'm back.'"

She still appeared annoyed, but one corner of her mouth disappeared as she chewed on it. "I guess you're right. Well, I'm still glad you're here. I'm glad I get to see you and know you're alive."

Her words hit me like a ton of bricks. It hadn't been fair for me to run off without a word—the way our parents had.

"I'm sorry I put you through that. Really. Have you ever, I don't know, just got caught up in the moment? Did you ever do something you wouldn't think you were capable of otherwise?"

She sighed. "Yes. I can't lie." She glanced at her backpack.

I looked at it, too. "What kind of errand are you going on that you need all that? I saw the weapons, so don't pretend you didn't pack them."

She shook her head the tiniest bit, as if fortifying herself for the answer. "You're just going to try to talk me out of it."

"Depends on what it is."

"No, I know you. You'll try to tell me it's wrong."

"Which makes me wonder even more." I frowned. "Tell me."

"What if I told you it has to do with Gage? Like... finding him?" She slid the backpack onto one shoulder then leaned into it as she guided the second strap on.

"Hold on, hold on." I blocked the doorway. "Seriously? You think you're going to go searching for him?"

She blinked then regained her composure. "You think you're going to stop me?"

"No. I know better, and I don't have the time to waste,

either. I need you to stop and think about this first, is all. This is a big job, you know? It's dangerous."

"I know. Since when do I ever back down from danger?"

"Never. That's what's worrying me the most."

She tossed her red hair.

I watched it cascade over her backpack. How many times had I seen her do that when she was determined to do something?

Her eyes were piercing, the set of her jaw firm. "You're not the only one who's been wrapped up in doing things lately, you know. I've really surprised myself in the last few days."

I smiled. "I believe it. You always rise to the challenge."

"I have to go now," she whispered. "I'm sorry if you don't like the idea."

"There's something I need you to do first. It might even make things a little easier for you."

She raised a brow. "What do you mean?"

I took her by the hand and led her out into the main room, still dark and otherwise empty, toward the glass doors.

"Come on. Trust me."

"Is it Gage?"

"No."

She made a sound, something like a sigh of frustration—or anger. "Anissa? Is Anissa out there? Is she with you? Because I don't think visiting with her is worth spending time on right now."

When would she ever come around on Anissa? "Stop asking so many questions and come. Anissa is safe where she is."

"Wait." She stopped, still shy of the doors. "You left her somewhere? That doesn't sound like you. I thought you two were attached at the hip."

I rolled my eyes at the sarcasm in her voice. "Yeah, well, there are things going on right now she doesn't need to be part of. I don't want her getting hurt or... anything."

I pulled her again, and the muscles in my forearm flexed—which made my brand sting more than ever. I didn't bother saying anything about it to her.

I was already about to drop a bomb on Philippa, she didn't need to be concerned with the brand as well.

"Come on."

I walked her outside and hoped Fane was still out there.

The wind blew my and Philippa raised a hand to brush a thick, red strand from in front of her face as a dark figure emerged from the shadows.

I stepped back.

She froze, eyes trained on him as he came closer.

"I don't believe it." Her voice was barely a whisper.

"Philippa." His jaw clenched.

She shook her head. "No. This is impossible."

2

JONAH

I waited to see what she would do. It was like waiting for an animal to make a move—would there be an attack? Would it back down?

She threw herself at him, arms closing around his neck. "Is it really you?"

"It's me." He hugged her gently, like he was afraid she would break.

All sorts of conflicting emotions raced across his face before he pulled out of their embrace and stepped back. Their embrace had lasted the time it had taken me to blink. Not nearly long enough.

I groaned quietly to myself.

Then he turned to me. "All right. She knows. Can we go now?"

She stared. "Wait. What's wrong? You just got here."

"Yes, but we have something important to do now."

I winced. Didn't he have a clue how he sounded?

Her face worked as she processed this. "Are you serious? You're going to do this to me right now?"

I stepped forward, wishing he'd been a little gentler with her. Maybe bringing him home hadn't been a good idea, after all. It was one thing to think her father was dead, but another for him to reject her with no explanation.

I put a hand on her arm, wanting to comfort her—or maybe

keep her from doing anything rash. "I wanted you to see him. I didn't want to keep it from you that he was alive."

She glared at me like I was the one who had broken her heart. "You choose now to tell me? You're going to do this to me when there's so much going on? You bring him here like it's no big deal?" Then, she whirled on Fane. "And you! You just show up out of nowhere, after all this time? And you don't think to come to us and tell us you're alive? Jonah had to *bring* you here?"

Only she wasn't angry with him. She was hurt and confused. I could hear it in her voice and remembered feeling the same way myself at first.

He sighed. "Philippa, I can explain."

She held up a hand, and her head hung low. "Please. This is too much at once. I can't understand why this is happening right now. I mean, all this time? All this time!" Her head snapped up again, and she glared at him. "How could you not tell us you were alive? How could you let us think you were dead?"

"Please. I want to tell you everything, but you have to give me a chance—and we don't have much time."

"I don't have much time, either. Holy hell!" She threw her hands up and spun around then paced back and forth, shaking her head and cursing the entire time. "This is ridiculous. You walk back into our lives like it's nothing, you show up after all this time and I'm supposed to, what? Hug you? Cry? Tell you how happy I am you're alive even though I've spent all these years trying to get used to the idea of you being dead? Is that what you want from me? Is it?"

"I don't want anything from you," he said. "Anything at all. It means so much to see you like this... You look well."

"Yeah, so do you." She peered at me then back at him. "So? Are you back, as in back forever? Have you decided to be part of the clan again?"

"No, that can never be. I don't live in this world anymore." He glanced at me for help.

"Philippa... this is Fane." I held my breath and waited.

Her face contorted in disbelief as she shook her head so hard her hair flipped back and forth over her shoulders. "No. That can't be true. Not our father. Fane isn't a normal creature. I mean, he's practically a myth. This?" She gestured to him. "This is Dommik Bourke."

"It's true, Philippa." His voice was firm, sharp.

Her head snapped around to face him.

"This is who I am."

"How? How could you do that? How?" she shrieked. "You're somebody else now? You simply stepped out of your life and decided to be someone else? Like we didn't matter? And now you're, what? Some secretive nomad vigilante or whoever Fane is supposed to be? While we—" She clasped her hands in front of her chest when her voice cracked, then broke. "While we thought you were gone?"

He closed his eyes. "I can't make up for this, but it wasn't my choice. We had no choice."

"Mother?" she whispered through tears.

He shook his head.

Her body quaked with sobs she kept silent. After a few deep breaths, she spoke again. "Gage is missing. Things are crazy right now."

Fane nodded. "I know."

"You know? How could you?"

He smiled for the first time—a faint smile, but it was there. "I've been watching over things from a distance."

"Right. Because that's what *Fane* does," she muttered.

She was starting to slide off into anger again, which was nothing but a waste of time.

I intervened. "Okay. There's a lot we have to do, and we can't spend all our time with accusations."

"I agree," Fane said, his eyes still on her. "Tell me what you know about Gage. What have you've learned?"

"I found out why he ran away," she replied with her head high. "I have a reliable source who told me where I could find him. He was hiding at the league headquarters for a while."

Fane's expression hardened at the mention of the headquarters—as did mine, since I'd learned of Lucian's role in our family's history.

She went on, oblivious. "I went there and talked with him in the woods."

"Did anybody overhear you?"

"No, he insisted we go very far away. He said... He said he had a job to do. There were a lot of wild accusations." She shook her head. "I'm still not sure if he was in his right mind, honestly. Only now, he's gone again, and Vance has vanished, too."

"What has Vance got to do with it?" Fane asked.

I was on guard, too, seeing as how Vance was Lucian's son.

She lowered her gaze. "He was helping me for a little while, but my source tells me he's gone."

"And who is this source?"

"I can't tell you." She lifted her gaze to him. "I'm sorry. I owe them a lot and don't want to get them tangled up."

"Fine, then. I have my own contacts and can reach out to them." He faced me. "I want you with me on this."

"Wait! You're going to look for him?" Just like that, she turned into the little sister who felt left out when our father wanted to include her big brothers—but not her—in a mission. "What about me? That's what I was going to do."

"You stay here." He went to her, taking her arms in his hands. "I want you as far from this as can be. You have to stay safe—not only for yourself, but for the clan. Keep things together here."

Her shoulders slumped. "All right, I guess." Her eyes went to the backpack by her feet.

I felt sorry for her. She was all ready to go, and we showed up and changed her plans.

There were voices nearby, loud enough to hear. The three of us ducked into the shadows.

"Scott," I murmured. "Should we tell him?"

"That I'm alive?" Fane asked.

"No. Don't do it," Philippa whispered vehemently.

Both of us stared at her in surprise.

"How can you say that?" I asked. "How would you feel if you knew I was keeping him from you?"

"It's not about that," she said. "It's about Sara."

"What about her?"

"I don't trust her."

"Oh, come on." I rolled my eyes. "This again? What do you have against her? You really have to get over this."

"It's not personal, even though I don't like her," she said hotly. "I feel she's hiding something. And if that's true, she shouldn't know about Fane."

Fane nodded. "That's the sort of decision a leader makes. We have to think about all the possibilities."

My sister practically glowed at the compliment.

"Did you tell her?" she asked.

There was only one *her* she could mean—Anissa.

"No, I didn't. Well, I told her I met Fane, but I didn't say anything about him being my father."

"Right now, Gage is our top priority," Fane said. "He's in danger. Scott can wait." He glanced at me. "And then we can sort out the other things, too. After Gage is taken care of."

"What other things?" Philippa appeared hurt. "What else haven't you told me?" Her eyes darted back and forth between us.

He beheld me.

I stared back.

Neither of us said anything. I knew he wanted to protect her, and so did I.

"Great. Just great." She stepped back, away from us. "Go off and run around the whole world together. See if I care. I'll be here, holding down the fort, making sure you have a clan to come back to. I'm not special enough for you to clue in. No problem." She picked up her backpack and stormed off, back inside the penthouse.

I lunged forward, wanting to stop her, but Fane grabbed me and held me firmly.

"She'll get over it. It's for the best," he said. "I don't want her involved in what we're going to do."

"What are we going to do... now that you mention it?"

"You said you'd help me find Gage. First things first. We have to go now. We've spent too much time here already." He cast a portal. "Come on."

I turned to where Philippa had gone inside. I wished I had time to tell her I was sorry about excluding her.

We needed to be on our game, all of us, if we were going to get through what was coming.

She couldn't sulk or, worse, take things in her own hands to show us how valuable she was.

Fane might have forgotten how she could be at times, but I hadn't.

"Jonah. We need to go, now. Your brother needs us."

Right.

My brother.

The one in actual danger.

That pressed me into a decision, and I stepped through the portal.

3

ANISSA

It was weird, being back in the human world after running around between realms for so long.

Nothing was the same as it used to be while I walked in the city—once my city, not long ago, but yet forever ago—head down, hood up, fists jammed into the pockets of my sweatshirt.

It was as though overnight, I'd gone back to the person—the assassin—I used to be, dodging crowds of people on the street, doing my best to blend in, even as I walked with purpose.

People had no idea.

That was the funny part.

Those humans with their TV shows and lattes and little dramas. They didn't know how much went on right under their noses or over their heads. They were oblivious to what really made the world spin—and how close they'd come to extinction if the forces all around them decided to go to war.

Better to let them go on thinking they were the masters of their universe.

A light rain fell, creating a mist around me as I dashed up the wide stone stairs of one of the city's oldest and most ornate libraries. If I was going to find my best friend, Raze, it would be at the library. He never could get enough of learning about humans, and he knew better than to keep too many of their books in his rooms at the mansion.

Marcus, leader of the Carver clan, and his deep core of suspicion wouldn't allow for that. I had visited the library with Raze before and seen the way the college girls stared at him over the tops and sides of their books when they knew he wasn't looking. They'd whisper to each other about him while he sat there with his head buried, lost in another world.

Though I'd never wanted him that way, I used to sneer nastily to myself, knowing how fast they'd change their minds if they knew what he really was.

The inside of the building was a giant maze full of the smell of paper and people. I glanced around, wondering where he could be. He usually tried to find a quiet nook to hide out in, away from eyes and whispering voices.

I scanned the area, up and down the rows and stacks. It took me a few minutes, but eventually I spotted him, sitting alone in a leather chair, a thick book in his lap. His head was down, his eyes riveted to the page.

I couldn't help but smile a little. How many times had I seen him sitting exactly like that? The library could come down around his head and he wouldn't blink.

My assassin's mind woke up from its sleep—it had been weeks since my last mission—and reminded me that anybody could come up and take him out if they wanted to. He wouldn't fight back. Would he? The thought set my heart racing, although I reminded myself it was only a thought. Nobody would hurt Raze. There was no reason to.

Still, his absorption made it easy for me to sneak up behind him.

He didn't even flinch when I leaned in and whispered in his ear. "Read any good books lately?"

He jumped out of the chair. His book fell to the floor and slammed shut with a loud clap that attracted attention from all directions.

I ducked my head and heard him murmuring his apologies as he picked up the book and set it on the table.

"What are you doing here?" he whispered.

"I thought I would check around and remember what life was like before it turned into something from a TV show," I whispered back.

"What's that supposed to mean?"

"Since when do you sound so nasty with me? I thought you'd be happy to see me after all this time."

"Yeah, all this time with no idea where you were or what you were doing. I mean, come on, Anissa. I thought we were closer than that." He glanced around to be sure we weren't overheard.

I did the same.

"We are closer than that, but there's been so much. I'm sorry. I wish there was a way I could keep in touch with you while this is happening, but it's for the best you don't know much about it. Trust me. You're better off where you are now."

He rolled his eyes. "Yeah, okay. Easy for you to say. Meanwhile, I have to wonder where my friend is and if she's alive."

"I'm sorry. I really am." I reached for him and was startled when he pulled away.

He ran a hand through his hair. "I'm sorry. But you can't come strolling back in and act like nothing's wrong. I mean, after you ran off with *him*."

Him.

So that was what this was all about.

I let out a soft sigh. "You mean Jonah."

"Who else? You chose him and his clan over... over us." He stopped himself short, but I knew what he meant.

I chose Jonah over him. I knew it would come to this one day, that just being friends wouldn't be enough for him after a while.

It was inconvenient he chose this very moment to hurl it in my face.

"It's a long story—nothing I can get into right now. You deserve to know everything. But now isn't the time. I'm sorry, Raze. I wish I could tell you more, but I can't." I leaned against the chair, suddenly very tired. "I wish I had somebody I could pour this all out to. You have no idea."

He was quiet for a while. Then, "What's with your face?" He reached out to touch my skin. I flinched, and he pulled away.

"Sorry. It's not you. It's that they're not healed yet." I turned my face away to hide the worst of the scarring. It would be a little more time before my skin fully healed from being exposed to sunlight.

"What happened to you?"

"Like I said, long story. I'm all right now. Believe me, okay?"

"Right." He folded his thick arms. "You can't tell me what you've been doing, and I'm sure you're gonna tell me you can't stay around. Why are you here, then? What do you want from me?"

I hoped there would come a day when he wasn't so angry with me. I told myself there would be a time when we could talk it all out. I could tell him everything then.

"You're right. I need your help."

"I thought so. You can't tell me what you're doing, but you can ask me for help."

"Because you're the only one who can do this for me. Please. I need you." I forced myself to hold eye contact though he looked at me with hurt and disgust.

I hated to see him this way.

Then his shoulders slumped a little. "What do you need?"

Hope flickered in my chest. "I need you to go back to the mansion and into my rooms. There's a wardrobe in my bedroom. Behind the clothes, there's a hidden opening." I told him how to access it. "There's a shelf where I store my backpack. It has everything I need in it. Please. Can you bring it to me?"

"I guess so. You want it here?"

"Yeah, if you can. I guess I'm safe enough here for a while."

"It'll probably take a couple of hours. I can't simply walk in, take it, and walk back out. You know how it is. I don't want anybody following me."

Yes, I knew how it was. Marcus would be tighter than ever when it came to security.

"Okay. I'll be here. Please, hurry if you can." There was so much to do.

He would never understand how desperate I was at that moment.

All he did was nod and turn away, book forgotten.

I decided to flip through his book in the meantime. A history of the city. He was always fascinated with history.

I skimmed the pages—my thoughts elsewhere. The pictures of the men and women in horse-drawn carriages made me think of the early days of the clan, and my parents. I remembered the story my father told about how he met my mother and the happy times they spent together.

Granted, they weren't taking carriages everywhere, but they walked through the park and saw change taking place all around them through the time they were together.

Would it be the same for Jonah and me? Would we ever have time to be happy together?

No sooner did I have that thought than I became angry all over again. Jonah had pushed me away.

I flipped the page and decided to keep those thoughts at bay.

⟡⟡⟡

I FELT RAZE'S PRESENCE BEFORE I SAW HIM; I COULD SENSE HIM walking toward me. I looked up and almost cheered when I noted my backpack over his shoulder.

"Thank you, thank you, thank you a million times," I whispered as I took it with shaking hands.

"No problem. At least I did something to help you."

My heart sank a little. "I really am sorry. I mean it." I touched his arm.

"Yeah, well, as long as you're taking care of yourself."

"I'm trying to. This will help," I said as I lifted the pack onto my back. "Hey, you haven't seen my sister, have you? Or heard anything about her?"

"No. What, you don't know where she is?"

"It isn't that. I was only wondering if you'd heard rumors, that sort of thing."

He shook his head. "Nah. I mean, nothing worth paying attention to. You know how people talk. I figured she was with you."

"Yes and no." I'd find her back at Jonah's place. I bit back a sigh. And hopefully not run into him. Though a part of me wanted to. Then again, another part of me wanted to punch him for abandoning me with my father in Avellane.

It was better to leave it there with Raze. I stood on tiptoe to give him a peck on the cheek.

He gave me a sad little half-smile when I stepped back.

"I've gotta go." I squeezed his arm once before hurrying off, yanking the hood over my head again, prior to going back into the darkness.

The mist had stopped, and the air was dry. Good thing, too, since I needed to use the tools in my backpack and couldn't do it easily in the rain.

In minutes, I made it to a building a couple of blocks from

the Bourke clan high-rise. Was Jonah up there? My heart raced at the thought, but this wasn't the time.

I had work to do, so I pulled out the special boots and gloves I used for climbing and pulled them on in the darkness between the two buildings before I started my climb to the top. The special rubber I wore created a suction effect, letting me grip even the slickest of surfaces. It was forty floors to the top, and I made the trip in just a few minutes—not as convenient as an elevator, but I couldn't have everything.

Once I made it to the roof of the building, I made a plan for how I'd get to the Bourke roof. I needed several lengths of cable and the grappling hook, so I pulled them from the pack along with my trusty silver blade and sheath.

It felt right, tightening the leather holster around my waist. I slid another, thicker blade in there alongside the first. Just in case. I didn't feel so naked anymore, once I had my weapons securely in place.

The backpack would be safe in a tight space between two air duct vents, so I stashed it there before getting ready to make my sojourn. I'd be crossing high above two busy streets to get to where Jonah's clan lived.

Not like this was my first time, but I could never calm the rush of adrenaline just before I prepared to swing the rope above my head and toss the hook to the next building. There was always a chance the hook wouldn't catch or the cable would snap. Then where would I be?

A grim smile made its way to my lips, perhaps in defiance of the situation.

As always, the hook caught on the lip around the building's roof. I pulled it to be sure it was tight then latched my handgrips to the cable and held on as I kicked off the edge of the roof to glide to the other side. It was as close as I would ever get to flying.

I repeated the process to get to Jonah's building. Most of the windows were dark, making me wonder where the clan was. Usually, all lights were blazing away.

Fewer eyes on me, I told myself as I glided across to the rooftop.

I tucked the hook and grips in a dark corner. The roof was empty, the wind whipping through my hood and roaring in my ears. I was about to slip through the glass doors to the penthouse to do a little snooping when a portal opened.

Out of freaking nowhere, a freaking portal. Damn the luck.

I looked around, frantic, then ducked behind the chimney just before two figures stepped out.

I held my breath.

One of them was tall, with broad shoulders and a muscular build. His deep-auburn hair caught my eye.

Behind him was Jonah.

My breath hitched this time. I hoped I hadn't made a sound that preternatural ears could capture.

It took every bit of self-control not to scream Jonah's name.

He was safe, for the time being.

That had to be enough for me. If I could only touch him, hold him for a second. My arms ached for him.

But no. I couldn't let the other vampire know I was here. He was a powerful one, too, based on the aura around him.

It was stronger than any I had ever seen, and almost pure, deep indigo.

Who was he?

I bit back a gasp.

Could it be Fane? It all fit. A powerful vampire traveling with Jonah. But why were they still traveling together?

They exchanged a few words before Jonah left him alone, vanishing into the stairwell.

The powerful vampire paced back and forth with his hands behind his back, muttering to himself.

As though he was nervous, almost.

Fane? Nervous? Over what? Maybe it wasn't Fane, after all. Fane wasn't afraid of anything, or so the legends said.

Minutes passed before Jonah reappeared with Philippa.

To my surprise, she threw herself at the vampire, arms around his neck. Who was he, and why was she acting that way? He pulled himself away from her. Things got heated—of course they did, with her involved.

I couldn't help smirking a little. She seemed to be telling them both off, but I couldn't pick up a single word, not even with my vampire super-hearing, thanks to the wind blowing it all away.

Suddenly, all three of them moved into the shadows of the other side of the chimney I was hiding behind.

I held my breath, frozen in place.

What would they think if they found me spying?

Not that I'd meant to. It wasn't my fault they showed up as I got there.

Philippa stormed off into the penthouse, leaving Jonah and the other vampire on their own.

What a surprise, she was upset about something.

Jonah acted as though he wanted to follow her, which of course was what she wanted because she loved attention so much.

The other vampire threw a portal.

No!

I didn't want to lose Jonah again so easily. I wanted to jump out and tell him not to leave me. But I couldn't.

I had to watch while he stepped through the portal.

It closed right away, and, in seconds, it was like there had never been one at all.

I was alone again.

4

ANISSA

I waited for a while to be sure I was alone before stepping out from behind the chimney.

Philippa wasn't coming back out. I wondered what they'd said to get her so upset.

Not that it ever took very much.

Philippa was lurking around, angry. Nothing new there. If she was in the penthouse, I wasn't about to go inside. I knew everything I had to know, anyway—Jonah was off in another place, doing what he needed to do.

Well, maybe not everything. *Sara*, I thought with a silent sigh. I did wish I could get a look at Sara, maybe talk to her. Find out if she was happy or at least safe.

But, no, it was too dangerous to risk running into Philippa, having her tell Jonah I was here—loose from my father's grasp where Jonah thought he'd securely ensconced me.

I pulled out my gear and went back to where I'd left the cable attached to the roof when the faint sound of voices caught my attention.

I turned back toward the doors in time to see my sister step outside. There she was, as though she had heard me thinking about her.

She looked beautiful, better than she had in a while. There was no trace of the pain or torture she'd been through in

Marcus's prison. Her smile was radiant, her skin appeared smooth and fresh, her eyes were bright and clear.

Maybe that glow had to do with Scott standing next to her. It was obvious how crazy he was about her. She seemed to blossom under his attention.

No, it was deeper than that.

The aura I noticed around her before was as strong as ever. She held her head high and carried herself like a queen. That confidence was something new. That strength. Yes, she'd been brave before. That was what had gotten her imprisoned. But breaking a vampire canon by selling her blood had been an act of desperation. She'd done it for both of us. That wasn't the girl I was staring at now.

I wanted to call out to her, the urge strong enough to make me cover my mouth with my hand to shut myself up.

There was so much I wanted to tell her, but there was no way she would she be as happy as she was just then if she knew the truth about our mother and our half-brother.

She might want to come with me, and I couldn't run the risk of her getting hurt.

They finally went inside, and I waited to be sure they wouldn't return before zipping over to the building across the street.

I traced my steps until I reached the building I had climbed earlier. My backpack was still waiting for me, and I replaced the grappling hook and grips. I was closing it up when a hand clamped over my mouth.

Instinctively, I tore the hand away enough to open my mouth and bite down.

My attacker cried out in surprise and pain, and I whirled around to fight—

But then I recognized who was standing in front of me, shaking his hand, wincing in pain.

"Allonic?" All the fight left me. "What are you doing here? And since when do you sneak up on me like that?"

"I wouldn't have done it if I knew I would lose a finger," my half-brother muttered.

"I didn't bite you that hard."

"You have fangs, in case you forgot." His eyes glowed bright, and his gaze seemed to cut through the darkness and burn straight into my very soul.

"Sorry, I guess. You didn't have to surprise me like that." I looked around—he was otherwise alone. "So? What are you doing here? Isn't it dangerous for you to be out here? You don't exactly fit in." Even in New York, I doubted he would escape unnoticed with his supernatural amber-gold eyes and long robes.

"It's not difficult for me to find your location. It might have to do with the blood we share. The portal I used led me to this rooftop—just in time to see you gliding over here." He shook his head with something that looked like a smile. "That was pretty remarkable."

"You think so?" I couldn't help feeling a little pleased with myself that somebody like him—half-vampire, half-Custodian— would be impressed with me. "What's so important that you took the chance of coming here to find me?" Custodians were shades who kept the world's history in the form of memories— like from the very beginning of time—and lived in a hidden lair underground. Which is where I happened to discover Sara and I even had a brother.

"I have news."

Hair stood up on the back of my neck. News wasn't necessarily good. In fact, as of late, it was generally not good at all. "What is it?"

"Our mother wants to see you."

I wished I could be completely happy about that. Who didn't want to see their mom after years of thinking she was dead? All this time, longing for her, wishing she was with me. And I still wanted her. Part of me was still a little girl who wanted her mommy.

Then there was the part of me that had other things to worry about. Specifically, Jonah, who had dropped me off with my father as though I was a piece of baggage he couldn't be bothered to carry around. For example, where he was going with that other vampire, and why I couldn't tag along.

I was worried for him, traveling around with another vampire doing who knew what.

Not to mention Sara, who'd changed and was a woman I barely recognized now.

I shook my head. "I want to go. I want to see her. I do. But there are other things I have to take care of first."

He scowled. "Like what? Isn't seeing her what you wanted?"

"Of course, and it still is, but she did keep me waiting for a long time."

"She had her reasons."

"And I have mine. She'll have to respect that and wait a little bit until I get things in order." I chewed my lip. "Do you think she'll understand? I mean, you've spent a lot of time with her."

"I think she will. Though, you can't blame her for being impatient. She's wanted this for so long."

An idea hit me. "I think I know a way to make things go a lot faster." I smiled.

He read it right away. "Oh, really? You want me to help you now, after you almost bit off my finger?"

"Because you snuck up on me, but that's not the point. The point is, Jonah's doing something, and I think he needs help. He dropped me off with my father and disappeared."

"I'm sure it was for the best. He wants to protect you."

"I want to protect him, too. Why does it only go one way? Because I'm a girl, he thinks I need his protection and I'm not allowed to know what he's doing? Allonic..." I stared away, across the hundreds of rooftops. Jonah was out there, somewhere, far away. "I love him. If he's doing something important, I want to be there with him. I need to be. Do you know anything about it? Anything that would help me?"

"I can't tell you. I'm sorry. I'm a memory keeper. There are certain things I'm not allowed to divulge." At least he seemed sorry when he said it.

I could believe he meant it.

"I thought it was at least worth a try." I slung the backpack over my shoulder. "See you sometime... eventually."

He sighed, rolling his eyes like I would imagine a put-upon brother would. "Wait a second. Don't go alone."

I looked him up and down. "Oh? You want me to wait? You want to come with me now?"

He shrugged. "Yes, if I can't help you in any other way, I want to at least make sure you're not alone. Our mother would want me to." Again, with that put-upon air.

I bit back a smile.

"Thank you."

For the first time, I felt like he was really my brother. Maybe it was the way he'd mentioned our mother.

I wished I could hug him but wasn't sure how comfortable he'd feel with that.

5

PHILIPPA

I paced back and forth, muttering under my breath as I wore down the flooring in my room.

They think they can leave without me?

I didn't matter? I wasn't good enough to go with them? I wasn't valuable?

I didn't know if I wanted to tear something apart or cry, or both.

All those years without a father and it was like no time had passed at all. He always used to tell me how smart I was. He would even come to me every once in a while and ask if an idea he had sounded good to me.

And yet, otherwise, I was just a girl.

Jonah and Gage were the oldest boys. It had long been predetermined. Jonah would lead the clan, and, if he couldn't, Gage would. They got most of our father's attention. The three of them would go off to talk about clan business while I sat at home with nothing to do.

They got to have all the fun and all the attention.

I got to be pretty.

Lucky me.

I would never forget the way he'd pushed me away from him, as though I wasn't allowed to hug him anymore.

He was *Fane*.

I rolled my eyes.

Was being Fane so much better than being Dommik Bourke? Did it mean he wasn't our father anymore? Blood didn't mean anything? Or all the memories we'd made together?

I should've demanded they let me go with them. I should've forced them. I should've ripped them both apart. I should've done something, anything—it would've been better than feeling the way I felt now. Like I didn't matter.

Somewhere else in the suite, I heard Scott talking.

He would give good advice. He always did.

I only wished I could tell him about Fane, or our father. Or Fane.

I didn't know what to call him anymore. No matter the name I used, I couldn't give up what I knew. But I could still tell him I saw Jonah and he was well and going after Gage.

I laughed to myself; Jonah thought I was going to sit home and wait for him? No way would I let him go alone, especially when I had already seen Gage for myself. I could still remember how anguished he'd appeared and sounded when he told me Lucian set the Great Fire.

I wished I had asked Fane about that before he pretty much patted me on the head and told me to go play with dolls.

The sensible part of me spoke up: *No, that wasn't what he did.* He told me to lead the clan, which was still a big deal.

I couldn't lead the clan. I had other things to do, as in finding Gage. I would have to rely on Scott. He could lead.

I walked out to the main room and glanced around. The fire was still burning, and the lights were on, but the room was empty.

"Hello? Scott? Where'd you go?" I turned to go down the hall to his room. Sara was just coming out. "Hey."

She didn't seem mousy and nervous the way she used to. She looked glad to see me, as though we were old friends.

She had picked the wrong time to act that way. "What are you doing, walking around here like you own the place?"

"What?" She stopped short, and her eyes went wide. "I was talking to Scott."

First, I lost Jonah to her sister Anissa, and now I'd lost Scott to Sara. She was one of the reasons I felt separated from Scott. It was like he was somewhere else, in a different world, all because of her. He had no time for what he needed to prioritize on.

I felt so alone. It was all her fault. If I were to go searching for Gage, could I trust Scott to run the clan while she was in the picture? Would he be able to focus on what was really important?

"Why are you even still here?" I spat. "You're not in danger anymore. Your sister's out there somewhere. Why don't you go looking for her and leave us all alone?"

She frowned. "I don't think that's totally your call, Philippa."

"No? I'm acting head of the clan now, and I could have you out of here in no time. A snap of my fingers. I think you're forgetting who you're talking to."

She cocked her head to the side. "I think you're the one who's forgetting."

"Excuse me?" I had never seen this side of her before, and I didn't care for it.

A slow smile crept over her face. "Your brother wants me here, Philippa, so this is where I'm going to stay. I'm sorry if you don't like it. Maybe if you grew up a little and faced facts instead of being a brat and stomping your feet, you could get over it."

"How dare you? Who do you think you are, talking to me that way?" I bared my fangs and lunged at her without thinking about it. I needed to hurt somebody, and she was the closest thing to me just then. It would feel good, making her hurt as much as I did.

Then, something happened.

She raised her hands before I could reach her, and the room lit up bright white, as what resembled bolts of lightning shot from her fingers.

I gasped, stunned.

I had never seen anything like it before. In the blink of an eye, I was in a cage made of sizzling, crackling beams of pure electricity.

I froze in place, afraid to move a muscle.

"What is this?" I whispered.

That same smile sat frozen on her face. "Not so feisty anymore, are you? Doesn't take much to take the fight out of you."

I looked around. The bolts crackled and jumped, alive, ready to fry me if I touched them.

My heart raced double-time.

Who is she? How did she do this?

"From now on, I want you to back off, Philippa. I mean it. Don't force my hand." Her face changed, until it was a mask of

31

pure fury and her normally dark eyes flashed with a golden-yellow glow.

I felt as though I was in the presence of something much stronger than a young vampire. I realized I knew nothing about her at all.

Scott's door opened, and the bars vanished as quickly as they had appeared. Her face changed, too. Her eyes were dark again. She smiled as she turned in Scott's direction.

I, on the other hand, was sure I had to have been hallucinating.

"What's up, you two?" Scott glanced at me then at her.

She slid an arm around his waist.

"Oh, you know. Girl talk." She grinned at me like we had a secret.

Well, did have a secret. Only not the kind my brother would ever guess.

I still didn't know what to say or think. It was like she had a split personality. One second, she was casting bolts of electric current and threatening me, and the next, she was the sweet, smiling, affectionate girl my brother was falling deeper in love with every day.

He eyed me. "Did I hear you call me a few minutes ago?"

"Huh?" I thought I might be going crazy. What was happening to my family? Who was staying here with us? "Oh." I snapped out of it. "Yes. I did."

"What do you need?"

Both of them stared at me with the same wide, innocent eyes —except one of them wasn't so innocent.

She was silently daring me to tell him what happened. *Come on. Tell him. Tell him his girlfriend shot lightning bolts at you and see how long it takes for him to tell you you're insane.*

She knew I wouldn't, because there was no way he would believe me.

I could hardly believe it myself, and I could still feel the electric charge in the air. I had almost been electrocuted, but there was no way I could tell him. Especially not when she was standing right there.

"Are you feeling all right, Philippa?" She injected just the right amount of concern into her voice.

I could see through it.

I wished my brother could. Instead, he gazed at her like she was a saint. He couldn't know anything about what she was capable of, not if he looked at her that way.

"Me? Oh. Yeah. I feel fine. I mean, you know, considering." I was babbling. I knew I was, but I couldn't help myself.

Sara nodded then peered up at Scott. "I could use some air. Come with me?"

"Of course."

I could only stare, speechless, as the two of them walked outside. I had been surprised before—seeing my father for the first time in decades ranked up there—but this came close to topping it all. It was night and day, the change in her.

And I couldn't tell Scott. I didn't have the words.

It only hit me then, after they were outside, that I never got the chance to talk to him about leading the clan.

Then again, did I want him to, while she was by his side?

❧ 6 ❧

JONAH

A moment after stepping through the portal, we were back at the cemetery. I had started thinking of it as a sort of home base, since it seemed Fane was so comfortable there.

No matter how much time passed between one visit and the next, it never changed. It was always dark, almost pitch-black. The sky was starless and moonless although there were no clouds to block it. Where were we?

"Is this a real place?" I asked Fane.

The air didn't seem to move, I noticed, even though fog rolled along the ground at my feet. Sound didn't carry the same there as it did elsewhere, I realized. When I spoke, the words sounded flat. Deadened. As if I was in a padded room and the thick layers around us absorbed the echo.

Only we were outside. Weren't we?

The tombstones appeared real enough. The monuments and mausoleums were crumbling, but they were real. Or were they? Which part of the world were we in?

"It's a real place," Fane confirmed. "A real cemetery, though ancient. I wonder if you would believe me if I told you exactly how ancient. It's called Duskwood."

"Is it part of Earth?"

"Duskwood exists in an alternate world—dimension perhaps,

you might call it—with laws similar to but not the same as those of Earth. There's no day here. Only night."

"I guess that makes it safer for you to be here," I murmured. No day meant no sun.

"Exactly. It's become my refuge over the years, when there was no safe place for me." He made his way between the stone monuments, and I followed. He walked with a sureness I couldn't quite copy. His feet were used to the terrain, the rocks concealed by fog.

I had to keep looking down to be sure I wasn't about to break my ankle or go sprawling face-first.

"Did you stay here with Mother? Did you hide here with her?" I stared at his back as I asked the question and noticed the way he tensed. His shoulders practically touched his ears from the tension he was carrying.

"No. She was never here. Duskwood came after her."

"Do you live here?"

"Not exactly." He glanced at me over his shoulder. "You're full of questions."

"You have no idea the questions I have for you."

It didn't seem fair, the way he almost seemed to make fun of me for asking. Did he think he could walk back into our lives with no explanation? I loved my father, even if he had become Fane, and left behind so much of what made him who he was in his former life. Was I supposed to forget the strong, wise vampire I had looked up to over my entire existence?

"I hope we have the time one day to clear everything up... but that time is not now."

I told myself to suck it up and trust him to tell me everything in time. "Why are we here, then? Can you tell me that, at least?"

We came to a towering marble mausoleum that had to house the remains of hundreds, if not thousands. It was roughly the size of one of those supermarkets the humans were so crazy about, and three stories tall.

"This realm has become a refuge for more than just me. There are a number of us who use this dimension as sort of a meeting place—witches, mostly. We need Sirene if we're going to get anywhere."

"Wait. Sirene?" *The witch? Why did we need a witch?* "I thought she was one of your contacts."

"She is one of my contacts, and she has skills I don't. We'll need those skills if we're going to proceed."

"What skills? Wait a minute." I stopped walking around the perimeter of the structure, and Fane turned to face me. "Hang on. What is it she can do that you can't? What else are we going to need? You can already throw portals and travel through the passages. What else is there? How much more involved is this going to get?"

Traveling through passages—a series of interconnecting paths which occasionally use portals to connect—was such an asset.

He was impatient, if the scowl on his face meant anything. "I only have those skills because Sirene gave them to me. She has others she can't give to me. Those are ones she has to implement. Like the power to cast spells, for instance. That's not the sort of thing a witch can simply transfer to another creature. It's innate, born in them, though they often have to be trained in them. And those powers of hers might come in handy. If they're available to us, why shouldn't we use them? We'll need all the help we can get."

He seemed to know a lot about her.

I frowned. "What else can she do?"

He shrugged. "She can access creatures who have the Sight. It's a very powerful tool, the Sight. Seeing through others."

"What? I don't understand." I remembered how it felt to be taken over by the spiritwalkers and wondered if witches did something similar to those with the Sight—taking over their minds, seeing through their eyes.

"I couldn't say," he replied. "I don't know the all specifics of witches. They're a mystery to me."

"As they should be," I reminded him.

"Excuse me?" He glanced askance at me.

I was sure it wasn't my words but, rather, my tone that sent his eyebrows high up on his forehead.

I forged on. "Witches should be a mystery to us because it's against the law to consort with them. Or did you forget that, being away for so long?"

"Who said I consort with witches? Sirene is my contact, as I already told you."

I took a step toward him, then another. "You might be Fane now, but you're still my father, and I still know how you look and sound when you're telling me a half-truth. You wouldn't know so much about her powers, and she certainly wouldn't have given any of her powers to you unless you were more to each other than *contacts*. I'm not a child. Don't go thinking you can satisfy me with a few excuses."

"And don't go thinking you can speak to me that way and get away with it," he warned. "Do not forget who you're talking to."

"I don't know who I'm talking to. That's the problem. Are you my father right now, or are you Fane? Either way, you're someone who left me for a long time and forced me to take on a responsibility I wasn't ready for. But I did it. I held on to the clan even when Marcus Carver did everything he could to rip us apart. We grew, and we flourished, and I think that earns me a little bit of respect and a little honesty."

He eyed me up and down, thinking. "So, what is it you're asking me, Jonah?"

"I'm asking if you're consorting with a witch, though it's taboo. Is that what you've been doing all this time?" I couldn't keep the disgust and disappointment out of my voice. When I thought about my mother—my beautiful, sweet mother—it seemed unreal he would ever stoop so low.

Instead of answering me, like I'd expected, he threw himself at me and pushed me against the hard, cold marble.

With his face inches from mine, he snarled. "Who are you to judge what I do when you consort with a half-blood fae?"

When I was a kid, years earlier before he went away, he might have been able to get away with this. But I was much stronger now, and I shoved him away from me with my own fangs bared.

"Don't you call her that," I warned.

"Why? It's who she is."

"She's more than just a half-blood. And it's not her or me we're talking about right now. It's you, and the choices you've made."

He advanced on me again, like he was going to attack, when the fog swirled around us.

I felt another presence—calm, peaceful energy surrounded me.

I turned, as Fane did, to find Sirene walking toward us. With the fog around her ankles, it almost seemed as though she floated.

"Jonah. Please, don't do this."

"Don't do what? Ask my father what he's doing with you?" I glared at her. "That's a little too much to ask."

"It's never been my intention to take your mother's place in Fane's heart," she murmured softly in reply.

"No, only in his bed."

"Enough," Fane snarled, cutting off anything Sirene had been about to say.

It didn't matter, because something else registered on my senses.

Another presence.

It couldn't be. I looked around, but there were only three of us standing here. I cocked my head to the side and listened hard.

I heard it. Another heartbeat. Small, fast, but strong. There was only one place it could be originating from.

I turned to Sirene. "You're carrying a baby."

Her eyes widened in surprise, but she didn't tell me I was wrong.

I turned to Fane. "It's your baby."

They glanced at each other, then at me.

Fane nodded.

It felt like the world came crashing in around me. Not so much the baby, but the knowledge of all that had happened between knowing him as my father and meeting him again as Fane. He was a totally different being, no longer someone I felt I could trust.

What was worse, he'd become a hypocrite, which was never who he'd been before.

I wanted to yell at him and accuse him and reduce the monuments around me to rubble.

Instead, I scowled at him. "And you have the nerve to call Anissa a half-blood. To think I left her behind to help you find Gage."

I regretted it bitterly as I stood there glaring at him. He was a stranger. A stranger I couldn't trust.

"I'm outta here." I turned to leave—how I would get out, I had no idea, since I didn't know how to throw a portal. I just needed to get away from him, and her. I couldn't stand her eyes staring into me anymore.

"Jonah." Fane grabbed my shoulder, stopping me cold. "Have you forgotten the brand? What about the danger it could pose to your girlfriend?"

When he mentioned it, I felt the stinging on my arm, radiating up and all through me. It was like the brand pulsed along with my heartbeat.

In my anger, I had almost forgotten it.

I turned toward him but couldn't bring myself to look at him again. He disgusted me. I couldn't stop thinking about my mother and what he was doing to her memory by being with a witch.

How could he? He had told me he and my mother were in love, that their love was strong enough to destroy a lifelong friendship with Lucian and change our destinies. How could he forget all of that?

And he had the nerve to act as though he had the moral high ground. Calling Anissa a half-blood when his own half-blood baby was growing inside its mother's womb—a witch's womb.

"Jonah. Look at me, please." Something in Sirene's words, or maybe it was her gentle tone of voice, made me raise my head to meet her eyes.

There was kindness there. More than I had seen in a long time. Peace washed over me.

"Your father loves you," she said in the same soft, gentle voice. "He loves all of you. Let him, let me, let us both help you with your brand and to find your brother. Don't let what's happening now, between us, make you lose sight of what's important."

"And what's important?" I asked.

"Valerius. He's a powerful vampire. There's a reason he's put the brand there, and we need to find someone who can translate it."

She was starting to get to me, untying the knot of anger and betrayal deep in my chest.

I felt it loosening, softening. I wouldn't forget it—there were too many questions unanswered—but I was willing to let it go for the time being.

She was right. There were more important, immediate concerns.

I nodded grudgingly. "All right. What do we do now?"

7

PHILIPPA

I went back to my room and locked the door before Sara could come back. Was I going crazy? If I wasn't, I would be pretty soon if things didn't start making sense.

I had never felt so alone, not even in the days after our parents had disappeared. For all I knew, Sara had cast a spell over Scott and he would never be able to help me.

There were vampires like that, ones who'd learned how to control the minds of other vampires. I had never met one as far as I knew, but they existed. Was she one of them? It was possible —her sister was a half-blood, after all. Who knew who else their mother had consorted with?

I shuddered at the thought of exactly whom I had allowed into my home, the heart of my family.

And here, I was supposed to be leading the clan and taking care of us all. What a joke. I had never felt so out to sea with nothing to hold on to, and nobody to help me. Jonah was gone. I had no idea how to find him. Scott might be a lost cause. And Gage. Where was Gage? I was no further along with finding him than I was before, and I couldn't risk leaving the clan now. Could I?

My head spun with a myriad of thoughts.

And Fane. Our father. Whoever he was. I could've used his counsel about then. I could've used anybody, someone to listen and help me understand. I wasn't ready for any of this, but here I was, right in the middle.

I threw myself on the bed, wishing I could sleep. I missed sleep. I always used to feel better after a good night's rest, even when I was young and human and my problems had seemed so monumental. They always seem monumental to a kid, don't they? Like the world was ending because my hair wouldn't curl properly or the boy I'd set my cap for didn't return my affection. I chuckled half-heartedly when I remembered the quaint terms we used to use. So much time had gone by since then.

The whole world had changed, but some things stayed the same. Mother always used to say a good night's sleep made everything better, and it did. Until it didn't anymore, after she turned me.

What would she say if she was here? I squeezed my eyes shut at the thought of her. I had been so hopeful for a second when I saw Father—if he was alive, could she be, too?

But no. I couldn't be that lucky.

All I had was a father with more secrets than he'd reveal, one who acted like my very touch burned him.

What could've happened to change him so drastically? I'd heard stories in the past about vampires forced from their clans, who had to forget everything they'd ever known for the sake of their safety and their loved ones. I had imagined more than once my parents were going through a situation like that.

Nobody wanted to believe their parents would leave of their own free will. It was the fantasy of every abandoned child that their parents were out there, loving them, wishing they could all be together as a family. I wiped away a tear.

Was that what happened to him, after all? Or had he just found something he liked better?

My phone vibrated, and I reached into my pocket and pulled my cell out to see who it was.

An unknown number.

I frowned.

Normally, I wouldn't bother picking up... but then again, it could be Gage.

My heart leaped when I answered, my fingers crossed. "Hello?"

"Philippa?"

I knew the voice, but it wasn't Gage.

"Vance?" I whispered, sitting up.

"Yeah. I have to see you."

"Where?"

"Downstairs. The alley." Outside the tunnel, he meant.

I remembered all the times we'd met there back in the day, before he broke my heart. How many times had I run out to the elevator and jammed my finger on the button, like it would get me to the basement faster if I did?

"I'll be right down."

I hoped Sara and Scott wouldn't see me. I was more certain than ever Sara was bad news—I had only disliked her before, but after that little show she treated me to, I would avoid her like a plague.

She didn't need to know anything about what I was doing. I only hoped Scott didn't get in too deep before I figured out what she was really all about.

I opened the door slowly, as quietly as I could. I didn't hear either of their voices in the main room. Maybe they were still outside, or maybe they'd gone to his rooms on the other side of the hall. There was a light shining under the closed door. I assumed they were in there and hoped it was so as I tiptoed down the hall and out to the front door.

Once I was outside the penthouse, I dashed to the elevator and took it straight down to the ground floor.

Minutes after his call, I met Vance face-to-face outside the secret entrance.

He was pacing when I stepped out the almost-hidden door, but he stopped when he heard me. He wore all-black—turtle-neck, jeans, work boots, and a long coat which swept the tops of the boots. It suited him. He looked more handsome than ever.

I couldn't believe how good it felt to see him—funny, since seeing him had only recently turned my stomach. All the conflict I felt over him dissolved in the face of what was on my mind, so much so I went straight to him with my arms open.

He let out a little gasp of surprise. "Hey, hey. What's the matter?" Still, his arms closed around me. He didn't push me away.

This was exactly what I needed.

"I'm sorry. I'm so very confused and need a friend," I murmured, my head against his chest.

"I guess things aren't going any better than they were, then."

"Good guess." I straightened and shook it off. "Par for the course lately."

He looked me up and down. "If things are bad, it doesn't show on you. You're looking just as good as ever."

"Thanks." I folded my arms. "Do you ever switch gears?"

"When it comes to you? No."

"Is this why you wanted to see me? To make thinly-veiled come-ons? You could've done that over the phone."

"But you came running the second I called, didn't you?"

When I didn't smile, his smile faded.

"I was in the area and wanted to check on you. That's the truth."

"I guess that's pretty nice," I admitted. "Maybe. So, how are things going for you?"

"Pretty well. It's not easy work."

"I can't imagine." I remembered him telling me about joining the Vampire League's Special Operations team, and the top-secret nature of the work he'd be doing. I knew he couldn't tell me much. It was enough to see him safe. "Hey," I said, as a light-bulb went off in my head. "You've met lots of different vampires, right? I mean you've traveled a lot because of your father's work. Isn't that true?"

"Why?"

"Have you ever met a vampire with elemental skills?"

His brow furrowed as he frowned. "What do you mean?"

"One who could work with the elements. You know what I mean. The way some witches and other creatures can." I couldn't shake the memory of Sara and the lightning bolts. It made me shiver a little.

"Yeah, but it seems a strange question, that's all. No, I've never known any personally. I'm sure it's possible."

I could almost feel the electricity setting my hair on end. "Yeah. I'm sure it is."

More like, *I know it is.* All I needed—something else to be concerned with. one more thing to add to the list.

I had to change the subject before he asked more questions. "You're safe out there, right? You're not taking any big chances?"

He looked more mature, somehow, though it hadn't been that long since the last time I saw him. He'd changed. It had to be the responsibility he'd taken on.

"Nothing I can't handle." He grinned. "Dare I believe you actually care about me?"

I cocked my head to the side. "If I did, you just ruined it."

"Can I do anything to change that?"

"Probably not."

"What if I tell you I'm on a big, important, secret mission?" He took a step toward me, and I backed away until I was against the wall.

"Oh, am I supposed to get worried about you and realize I've loved you all along? Maybe beg you to come back to me in one piece?"

It was tough, sounding hard and cynical when he was this close to me. He left me breathless, weak-kneed, even with the entire world crashing in on me the way it was.

"That all sounds pretty good," he said with a little smirk— one that made him hotter than ever. There was no humor in his eyes, though.

"What is it? You're not really in any danger, are you?"

"It's Special Ops. There's an element of danger to it no matter what."

I wasn't used to him not being playful or flirty or sarcastic. Yes, he had changed.

"Don't take any unnecessary chances, okay? I'm being serious."

He snorted. "Yeah, well, when you're hunting for somebody like Fane, it's not easy to play it safe."

There is no way.

If he had told me that an hour earlier, I wouldn't have felt icy fear spread through my chest.

Life couldn't be this unfair, could it?

"You're hunting for Fane? I thought he was more myth than anything else." I fought to keep my tone normal, nonchalant.

His face hardened. "He's definitely real, and he's committed crimes against the league."

I gulped and fought to swallow around the lump that had appeared in my throat. "Like what?"

He frowned. "What's with the sudden interest?"

"Why wouldn't I be interested? It's sort of a big deal."

"You have no idea. I have to find him... and kill him."

Kill.

Double-gulp. There went that icy feeling again. I couldn't

breathe. "What's he done, exactly? All I've ever heard are stories, you know? Legends."

"They're not merely legends. They're very real. He's been feeding on humans for years."

"You're sure about that? That's a pretty big accusation."

I couldn't be too obvious. He'd see right through me—he always could. But I couldn't let him kill my father, either. No matter what he'd done, he was still my father.

"There have been several deaths," he said. "Not to mention the fact several missing persons have been noted. The entire agreement we have with the humans revolves around keeping up our end of the agreement. Without that, we might as well go back to the days when we were at odds with each other."

"You think killing Fane will somehow strengthen the agreement?"

"It can't hurt. Not if he's unwilling to follow the rules."

"How do you know for sure he's guilty?"

"Tips from reliable sources. He's been spotted."

How could I help my father? How could I keep him from dying? I tried standing up for him. "If he's gone rogue, he doesn't have a choice but to feed on humans, does he? When there aren't any options but to either feed from humans or die, what can you expect him to do?"

He was quiet for a moment. His frown deepened. "Why does it sound like you're defending him?"

"I'm not." I totally was, but he was my father for heaven's sake.

"It seems as though you are."

What could I say? There was no excuse.

Vance would never believe I had suddenly developed a soft heart for others—that was never one of my strong points. He knew me too well to believe that.

I opened my mouth, unsure of what would come out.

My phone vibrated.

Saved by the text, I thought as I slid it from my pocket.

Sledge: *There's been word about Gage.*

I looked at Vance. "I've gotta go. I'm sorry. It's important."

❦ 8 ❦

ANISSA

"I guess we'd better get going." I couldn't imagine Allonic scaling the side of a high-rise. How was I supposed to sneak him down to the sidewalk?

As it turned out, he had a better idea. "Here." He slid his cloak from his shoulders and handed it to me.

"What's this for?"

"Remember? To enable you to travel without using spirit-walkers. If you want to see your boyfriend, we'd better get moving."

It took a second to understand. "You're going to take me through a shade portal?"

He nodded.

"You just told me you couldn't disclose that information. Won't it get you into trouble?"

His smile was surprising. "I can handle a little trouble."

My heart swelled with affection for him as I wrapped the cloak around me.

I felt him take me by the arm to lead me into the portal—the sensation of going from one dimension to another without being able to see was unnerving, but not as much as it had been at first.

"You can take it off now."

I held my breath, wondering what I would see around me when I did. I couldn't have imagined what greeted me once my head was free.

"What is this place?" The air was cold, damp, and still. A fog rolled across the ground, and I could just make out the tops of crumbling headstones in the extreme darkness. I shivered—it was downright creepy.

"A cemetery, obviously."

"This doesn't resemble any cemetery I've ever seen."

The sky was so dark, so inky black, it felt as though we had left reality. Then again, maybe we had—or maybe this was reality, and what I thought was real was merely another, smaller dimension.

"Don't worry about it right now," he murmured. "Follow me." He walked toward a massive, marble mausoleum in front of us.

I hated the feeling of not knowing where I was stepping thanks to the fog, but following Allonic's footsteps helped. Like walking through the path someone else carved through a deep snowfall.

We rounded the mausoleum, and when we did, I barely made out the sounds of voices. The sound was flat, strange, but I recognized one of the voices right away.

I reached out and touched Allonic's arm in surprise. I hadn't expected us to go straight to him.

He only nodded. "I told you," he whispered.

Jonah sounded angry. I couldn't tell what he was talking about, or who he was talking to.

I stepped out a little, enough to see him in front of the structure. He was with the same tall, muscular vampire I'd seen him with on the roof, plus a beautiful brunette who definitely wasn't human. I couldn't put my finger on who or what she was, but I could sense the preternatural air about her.

The older vampire turned his head when he noticed me, which made Jonah swivel toward us.

His face was contorted in anger until he recognized me—then a smile broke over it, quickly followed by concern.

"What are you doing here?" he asked as he rushed to me.

Then his arms were around me and everything was all right because he was here, with me, no matter where "here" was or what he was doing with the other two.

I closed my eyes and let myself sink into his hug for a moment.

"How did you get here? How did you know where I was?" His

eyes were bright, sparkling even in the pitch-black. The warmth and excitement in his voice were heartening.

I had half-worried he'd be angry with me for unexpectedly appearing.

There was a noise behind me, and we both twisted around as Allonic stepped out from the shadows.

"Oh, that's how," Jonah said with a nod of his head. He didn't sound unhappy.

What a relief.

The older vampire approached, nodded, too. "Allonic," he said in a deep, sure voice.

Allonic nodded in return. "Fane."

Fane!

I knew it!

How did they know each other? Fane was rogue... But then again, there was much more to the hidden world than I had ever known. It seemed creatures crisscrossed everywhere—my mother with the shades, beings Jonah happened to know.

He also knew Fane, it would appear.

The world was much bigger and smaller than I could've guessed, all at the same time.

Fane and Allonic weren't friends. That much was clear. But they weren't enemies.

I heard respect in their voices and saw it in the way they held themselves when they spoke to each other—heads high, shoulders back, neutral expressions.

Interesting.

"Anissa," Jonah said, leading me to the other vampire. "This is Fane."

Why did I hear a challenge in his voice? There was no reason to challenge me to accept Fane's presence—no, he wasn't the optimal travel partner, but it wasn't my place to tell Jonah who he was allowed to spend time with.

Was he challenging Fane, then? Why would he do that?

Fane looked at me for what seemed a very long time. Finally, he said, "It's good to meet you."

"Can I have a minute alone so we can talk privately?" Jonah said.

He didn't wait for a reply before pulling me by the hand to a spot on the other side of the mausoleum, where we could be alone. The second we were, he took me in his arms.

I closed my eyes and rested my head against his chest.

"I've missed you so much," I whispered.

"I missed you, too." He pulled back, and I tilted my face up to his for a kiss.

It was electric, and I felt it right down to my toes. I had been so thirsty for his kiss. His arms were so strong. I didn't have anything to fear when he was with me.

He ran his fingers over my cheek. "You're a sight for sore eyes."

"You didn't have to leave me, you know. I could've been with you this entire time."

It reminded me of how irritated I was with him for dumping me in Avellane.

"It was too dangerous for you. I'm not sure it isn't still too dangerous." He stepped back. "What are you doing here, anyway? Why did you come after me? Did you trick Allonic or something?"

"I don't have to trick my brother into helping me," I retorted. I didn't much care for the insinuation I had to use trickery to get what I wanted. "I asked for his help, and he was happy to give it to me." I put my hands on my hips and glared at him. "While we're at it, what are you doing here? What is this place? And why are you with Fane?"

"You don't need to know. Did you ever think I was keeping things from you to keep you safe?"

"Oh, I see. I'm just the little woman and I need you to protect me and keep me in the dark. Is that it? I didn't think you were chauvinistic, but I guess I was wrong about that."

"Don't overreact. You're putting words in my mouth," he hissed. "And if it's not too much trouble, keep your voice down. We don't need everybody hearing this."

"I don't care if they do. I want them to know you don't think I can take care of myself. I want them to know you think I don't have anything to contribute."

"I never said that! Stop blowing everything out of proportion!"

"Then stop treating me like I'm fragile!" I bared my fangs. "I was taking care of myself long before I met you. I don't need you acting as if I'm going to break."

"If I could trust you to follow a request every once in a while, maybe I wouldn't be so afraid to include you in things!" His fangs were bared, too, and we faced each other down.

How had things turned so quickly?

"What request?"

"Let's see. When I asked you to stay in one place, but you decided to go exploring and got picked up by those shades at Sanctuary. Remember? It wasn't that long ago. And I went looking for you, which only put me in danger."

"You sound as though you resent me for that."

"I don't resent you, but if you want to know why it's important for me to keep you out of things, that's why. I care too much about you. You have a way of getting into trouble, and when I don't know exactly what we're facing in the first place—" He reached up to smooth his hands over his hair, like he was trying to calm himself down.

One of his sleeves slid up a little as he did, and I saw red marks on the inside of his forearm.

"Freeze." I held up my hands, eyes glued to him. "What is that? On your arm?"

"What?" He dropped his arms to his sides and his sleeve slid down again to cover what I'd seen.

"That mark. Like a brand. What is it?" I studied his face. "What happened to you?"

"It's nothing." Only he wouldn't meet my eyes.

"Don't lie to me. That's a brand. Was that on your arm when you decided to dump me with my father? What does it mean?" I had never seen anything like it before.

He sighed, shoulders slumping. "I don't know what it means. It appeared out of nowhere."

"Oh, Jonah." I reached for his arm without thinking about it, and he pulled away.

"Don't touch it, please. I don't know what would happen to you—and it still hurts, too. This is why I'm with Fane. One of the reasons, that is. He said he could help me find out what it means."

"Have you learned anything yet?"

He seemed reluctant to tell me more, but finally said, "I've heard a name in connection with it. Valerius."

I searched my memory but came up blank. "Who's that?"

"An Ancient. Nobody's heard from him in ages. This is his, or so I've heard."

"What does he have to do with you?"

His smile was grim. "Your guess is as good as mine."

Would it ever end? All the mystery and danger? I didn't want any of it. I wanted to live a normal life, though I was hardly normal.

It seemed like every time I turned around, there was some new challenge. And those challenges kept getting in between us.

"You shouldn't have pushed me away like you did. You can't just get rid of me like I don't mean anything to you."

"It was because you mean something to me that I left you with Gregor. I can't make it any plainer than that. Look at this." He showed me the brand again. It was angry, red, and it made me cringe just looking at it. "If this happened to me, what could happen to you? And how could I live with myself? I mean, I love you."

He reached for me, and nothing could've kept me from his arms. My heart softened. "Jonah, did you forget what I used to do before you loved me? Remember the work I did for Marcus? It's the reason we met."

"I know. You don't need to remind me."

"I can take care of myself, in other words."

"I know. I don't have to deliberately put you in harm's way, though, do I?" His lips were gentle on my forehead.

Something he said earlier came back to me.

"Hold on a second. You said the brand was one reason you were with Fane." I looked up at him. "What's the other reason?"

He frowned. "Gage."

🦂 9 🦂

GAGE

The first thing I registered was the smell of blood.

Human blood.

My nostrils flared. Immediately, my nerves seemed to sizzle with need. The need for blood. Real blood, not the synthetic version we fed from. Something to make my senses sing, to make me feel alive. The thought of it was enough to make me crave it with every fiber of my being.

The second thing I registered was I couldn't move. I was weak? I pushed the thought aside as I wondered about my location.

Where am I?

I listened hard for the sound of breathing but couldn't hear any save my own. I stayed very still, eyes closed, so whoever had me wouldn't know I was conscious. I wasn't sure what had happened, but it had been enough to knock me out.

When my ears didn't reveal anything, I relied on my sense of smell. It revealed a lot more about my surroundings, even if it didn't provide any definitive answers. I was out in nature, somewhere.

I took a deep breath through my nose. There was a dank, earthy smell. Moss? Leaves, for sure. They were damp, pungent.

I resisted the urge to wrinkle my nose. Clearly, the leaves had been rotting here for a long time. But where was *here*?

There was no light filtering in through my closed eyelids, so it was night—or I was inside somewhere. That didn't explain the odors around me, however. I couldn't be inside and smell so many outdoorsy nature scents. I concentrated harder and heard faint rustling noises in the distance. The woods?

I thought about my circumstances as hard as I could. What happened to me?

The longer I spent in my state of consciousness, the more aware I became of my injuries. I was definitely injured. Every inch of me ached or downright screamed in agony. I shifted a little, or tried to shift, to measure what was happening in my limbs. I could barely move at all, like I had been drained of life.

Drained!

I had been drained of blood—my life source—to within an inch of my life. That was the only way to describe it.

I must be dying.

I had seen vampires after they'd been drained before. Once or twice, during the Great War. I'd been too young to understand much of what I'd seen then, but it came back to me and I understood a lot better.

The complete weakness. The foggy-headed sensation.

I was sure if a wild animal came upon me right now, I wouldn't be able to defend myself. I'd have to let it kill me. It wouldn't take long, given the shape I was in.

Somebody had beaten me, too. Badly.

My ribs ached, my face hurt. I was sure there would be bruises all over me if I could see myself. Even if I hadn't been afraid to open my eyes, could I if I tried? Did I have the strength? Could I move my head to look down at myself?

What had transpired? I tried to push away the pain to focus on what I could remember. I had to try. Somebody—maybe several somebodies—had tried to kill me and had come extremely close. For all I knew, I might still die. It seemed I was teetering on the edge with every breath I took.

No matter how hard I tried, though, the thick fog surrounding my memory wouldn't let me remember. There was no way I could've naturally forgotten something like what I'd gone through. I must've felt pain, extreme pain.

There were only two reasons I could think of as to why my memory would be so difficult to access. Either another vampire had compelled me to forget, or a witch had cast a spell on me.

If my memory loss was the result of a vampire's actions, it

would mean breaking league laws that applied to what vampires were allowed to do to other vampires. Compelling was a weapon at its root, used to convince humans or other creatures to do our bidding. If a vampire had compelled me to forget, it had to be a very powerful vampire—and a very dangerous one to break that law so brazenly.

Or maybe it was a witch, after all. They didn't have the same laws we did. I didn't know any witches personally, but whoever had tried to kill me might be working with one.

I struggled to move again. I had to try.

Not knowing the extent of my injuries gnawed at me until it was impossible to stay still. I was on my back—the ground was hard and cold beneath me—so I rolled to the side. Or attempted to. I swallowed a groan as every part of my body screamed in protest, but I didn't manage to hold it in. Not entirely.

A low moan left my lips.

"You're awake."

I froze in place. I even forgot the pain, I was so surprised.

"I wasn't sure you'd make it."

A female voice.

She was on my left, not far from me. I turned my head—even my neck hurt, and my brain throbbed.

A human.

It was her blood I smelled, after all.

I could faintly hear it—through my own throbbing pain—as her blood was pumping through her veins, traveling through all of those vessels, keeping her alive.

Her blood was crying out to me. Making me want it. Making me crave it. I needed it desperately, required it to heal. I couldn't live without it. It was the only thing in the world, the only thing in existence.

That blood.

My mouth nearly watered, my body on fire with hunger for her blood.

She gave me a tentative smile. "How are you?" Her voice was like honey, sweet and warm, and anyone could see she was deeply concerned about me.

"I'm... alive?" I whispered. My voice was nothing more than a croak. I tried to speak again, a little louder, but I couldn't.

She looked me over with eyes the color of the ocean. "Are

you hungry? I'm sure you need something to help get your strength back." She held up a wrapped bundle.

I forced myself to keep my eyes open—my lids wanted to slide shut again, the exhaustion all-consuming—and watched as she unwrapped a small sandwich. My stomach turned at the thought.

Human food? I didn't need that. I needed something much more primal.

"Here." She crept toward me, slightly bent over.

I realized we were in a cave with a low ceiling.

She had to stoop to avoid hitting her head. She held out the sandwich and a half-full bottle of water. She couldn't possibly know who I was, what I was. If she did, she wouldn't dare be alone with me. Not even when I was on the line between life and death.

We might have forged a better relationship with humans and humankind, but there was still a long way to go before we could be considered friends.

I took a deep breath and gathered all of my strength. "I'm... not hungry. Thank you."

She frowned. "Are you sure? Maybe it doesn't matter if you're hungry. I mean, not if you really, really need to get your strength back. I don't know what happened to you, but it must've been pretty terrible. You need to recover." She came a little closer, just an arm's length from me.

If I'd had the strength, I would've reached for her.

"Please. Come closer."

She hesitated.

I stared at her, silently willing her.

She had such innocence about her.

I could tell she wanted to help. She wouldn't have dragged me wherever she'd dragged me if she didn't have a good heart. But she was starting to get a feeling about me. Her eyes weren't quite as wide or trusting. Her brows knitted together just a little as she turned over the questions she had about me.

Who was I, really? What had brought me here? She didn't know, and she was starting to wonder whether she'd gotten herself into a situation she should've avoided. It was written all over her face.

I didn't have a choice. It was either make her do something she didn't want to do or die. I had no doubt I would die, soon—

or it would take ages to heal. Much longer than I could afford to wait.

So, I reached deep down inside and used the skills I had developed over the years but had been forced to leave dormant ever since the treaty was signed by the league at the end of the War. I would use my innate skill to compel.

It was like flipping a switch, going from determining my own thoughts and actions to determining someone else's.

The next time our eyes met, I held on. I let my consciousness reach out to touch hers. She was like a scared rabbit inside, sure she should leave, wishing she had never found me.

She flailed around in her head, wondering why she was losing control of her actions. This had never happened to her before. She wanted to fight me off, but it wasn't possible. Even half-dead as I was, she was no match for me.

Come closer, I thought. *Closer. Until you're kneeling beside me.*

I can't, her thoughts said, and her eyes grew wider. *I can't do that.*

Yes, you can, and you must. I'll die if you don't. Come.

She still tried to fight.

I had to give her credit—even though my existence hung on who won out in our battle of wills, I could admire her strength.

Come. Now. Kneel beside me.

The last bit of her will drained away, and her hands released the sandwich and water bottle. She knelt at my side, hands in her lap.

Pull back your hair.

She was wearing a tank top under a short-sleeved shirt.

Release the top button on your shirt and open it.

Her eyes were blank as she moved, her fingers working the buttons. She opened the collar before pulling her long, thick hair to the other side of her neck.

I looked at the smooth expanse of skin and could just make out the sight of her pulse throbbing there. It was rapid.

She was so afraid.

I won't hurt you. I need to feed from you, but you'll be all right when I'm finished. Now lean over me.

She moved robotically, leaning until her throat was in front of my mouth.

The smell was overwhelming. It was all I could think about,

the scent of her blood. Like the most intoxicating perfume imaginable.

I bared my fangs and savored the last moment of anticipation before sinking them into her skin.

She gasped sharply, arching her back, then letting out a hissing breath through her teeth.

Oh, the sweetness.

I drank and drank, reminding myself every time more sweet, thick blood pumped out of her and into me that I had to stop myself before it was too late.

I wouldn't let her die.

Still, the taste of her and the way her blood set me on fire was too much to pull away from. Everything was sharper, more fully defined.

I couldn't believe the difference between the synthetic blood we'd been feeding on for years and the real thing. I could do anything—scale tall buildings, race a speeding train, pull a tree out by the roots. Anything. I was beyond super.

My brain raced in all directions, my head spun out of control. *Stop now. You have to stop. She's getting close.*

Her pulse started to weaken. The blood didn't flow so freely. She was struggling to stay alive.

Just one more drink… So good…

Enough!

Something stronger than my need screamed out in my head and was enough to force me to cease.

I pulled my fangs from her and hoped I hadn't waited too long.

She sank down beside me, her back to the wall of the cave. A thin trickle of blood ran from the wound in her neck. Her chest rose and fell—slowly, shallowly, but it did rise and fall.

It wasn't too late.

❧ 10 ❧

GAGE

I gave her a minute to recover, leaning against the rocks while I took the opportunity to check myself over.

The pain was a distant memory, erased almost completely.

I stared down at myself for the first time since waking in the cave.

My shirt was torn down the middle of my chest, hanging open. It was the same with my sleeves. They had been carefully torn to expose my skin—probably right before the silver had been placed against my exposed flesh.

The burns stood out, red and angry looking, the mark of a torturer.

Who would do this? And why? I still couldn't remember— the human's blood wasn't enough to break through the spell or compulsion that had been placed on me.

The human was watching me, eyes open—but blank. It would've felt eerie if there'd been any consciousness behind them. She was still in my thrall and too weak to do much of anything.

I glanced around. The cave went on behind me, on and on into the darkness.

In the other direction was the mouth of the cave. It was fairly dark out there, but there was a hint of light over the trees. It was nearly dawn. She had sat with me all night, it seemed, or else what had she been doing out in the woods in the middle of the night?

I took in her appearance. She was wearing hiking boots and long shorts with big pockets. She'd been hiking, maybe planning on camping. That would explain the sleeping bag. What were the odds she happened to come across me?

"Where are we?" I asked, hoping she had the strength to speak.

She took a deep breath and her brow creased, like she was concentrating on the answer to my question.

It would be a while before her thoughts cleared and she didn't have to consciously search for answers.

"I had been hiking all day, but it started to cloud up and I decided to go back to the car before the weather turned. I found you at the bottom of a gorge. At first, I was sure you were dead. I thought maybe you fell or rolled down the incline, something like that. But you didn't have any broken bones. It hit me. Somebody must have left you there. And you were still breathing—a little, but enough. I couldn't keep going when I knew you were there, all alone."

It was as simple as that for her. I had needed help, and she had provided it. I didn't know there were people like that in the world—especially not humans, whom I had never had much time or patience for.

"There was a storm coming, too," she whispered. "I dragged you to the cave. It wasn't too far. We made it in time."

"I am in your debt," I said. She had saved me twice—bringing me to the cave, then letting me feed on her—not that she'd had much choice with the latter.

"The sun is rising now. The storm has passed." She looked out toward the cave mouth. "When it's full light, I'll get you to my car. We can go to the hospital."

That couldn't be allowed to happen.

If either of us needed a hospital, it was her, but I couldn't let her go, either. It would not be a lot of fun, trying to explain the wounds on her neck.

If it weren't for her, I would've died overnight—or definitely once the sun rose, when I wouldn't have had the strength to get myself away from the sun, to the cave I hadn't known existed. I would've burned to death in minutes, no question.

Suddenly, she swayed. "I don't feel very well."

"Here. Lie down." I reflexively held my arms out to her.

She sank into them and curled up on her side.

I rolled my body around hers. There was something about her that inspired every protective instinct I possessed. That had never happened before. I'm typically more the take-care-of-myself kind of vampire.

"What's wrong with me?" Her already fair skin went almost dead white. "I can hardly move. I'm so tired. I feel sick. What's wrong?" By the time she finished speaking, her voice was barely a whisper.

"You'll be all right," I said with a hush, calming voice—at least, I hoped it was calming. "Give it some time. Rest. You'll feel much better once you do."

Her eyes slid shut.

I watched her pulse working in her throat to be sure she was still with me.

What was I doing? Holding a human in my arms, watching her sleep, making sure she didn't slip away. And what would I do if she did die, if she slipped into a great nothingness? I would have to let her go, wouldn't I? So, it would all be for nothing. Unless I turned her.

Her blood sang in my veins, and it was doing something to me. It brought up emotions I didn't normally feel. Normally, I couldn't stand humans. Selfish, blind, stupid, thinking they knew everything when they knew nothing about what went on around them. Nothing real. But they filled their lives with garbage TV, garbage movies, garbage food. Garbage, in general.

Yet, after all that, they held themselves up as being better than us. Superior. We were the bloodthirsty savages when they were the ones shooting and stabbing and raping each other left and right. Hypocrites.

But her. I glanced down at her aquiline profile.

She was different. She was gentle and thoughtful and concerned for others. She had stayed with me when she didn't have to. She could've left and called the police and had them come. But no. She had stayed and sacrificed herself for me.

And she was beautiful, too. So perfect. Like an angel, if angels existed. Maybe they did—she was sort of an angel, on second thought. My own personal angel. What had I ever done to deserve an angel such her in my life?

What was I thinking?

I jerked as though she'd burned me. What was I turning into? It had to be her blood, screwing with my thoughts. I was adopting human emotions, thinking sappy human thoughts. Only a sappy human man would consider staying with her. Watching over her, protecting her.

She was so weak and fragile. So easily broken. Somebody had to watch her and make sure she stayed safe.

It would be me. I would wrap her in cotton then titanium, if I had to, to be sure nothing could hurt her.

No. I shook my head and told myself to stop looking at her that way. I would stop looking at her entirely if I had to. Anything to stop the flow of thoughts I was drowning in.

She was merely a human. A stupid, loud, crass human. A consumer. Somebody who didn't give a second thought to the person living next door to her, I'd bet. Simply because she enjoyed occasionally walking out in the woods and had a conscience didn't make her anything special.

I would snap her neck.

Yes.

That was the only solution.

If she was dead, I could stop thinking those thoughts. I could go back to being myself and taking care of my life. I could stop wasting time thinking about her, watching to make sure she stayed alive. What a dumb, pointless waste of time that was. It would be so easy to kill her and free myself. Her neck was so weak, so easy to snap if I chose to do it. Yet another way humans were so far from infallible. Amazing they didn't fall apart.

Suddenly, my memories came rushing back—at least in part. Little bits and pieces began rising to the surface of my consciousness.

Being at headquarters, for one. I remembered hiding out in the basement, waiting for my chance to get...

I squeezed my eyes shut to make it easier to remember. It was awful, feeling as though I was out of control of my thoughts. Who was I trying to hurt?

Lucian. His face flashed across my mind—that haughty air of his. So superior, so full of his own goodness. So fake.

I meant to keep myself safe from him here, didn't I? Yes, because I wanted revenge for something and didn't want him to find me because he knew I was after him. He must've found out somehow.

What was it I wanted revenge for? Something terrible. I couldn't remember what exactly, but I could recall the feelings. The deep, intense hatred. Burning through me much as a blaze. *Yes! The Great Fire.*

And Philippa. She had come to see me. I had told her about what I was doing, why I was there, what I intended to do. She hadn't cared for it, but I didn't expect her to, either. I remembered the expression on her face—stricken, concerned, confused.

And then?

Nothing. Blank.

That was where it all ended, no matter how hard I tried to reach back. I remembered being in the woods, far from the cathedral. I remembered staring up at the stars through the tree branches. But that was as far as it went. My life might as well have ended there, since I could remember nothing about it until I woke up in the cave.

It might be for the best, I thought. *Who wants to remember the pain I must've gone through?* There were so many burns all over me. Why would I want to remember going through that? Not to mention the injuries to my face, the soreness in my back and ribs. Somebody had gone to great lengths to destroy me then wipe it all out. They didn't want me to remember who did it, I guessed. Or what they'd said while they were doing it. Maybe both. Either way, it felt like there was a hole in my life. Would I ever get to fill it in?

The girl stirred in my arms.

I held my breath and waited, but she didn't awaken.

Her breathing was soft, gentle. Like her.

I had to leave. To leave her alone before it was too late and I could never leave her. I could see how easy it would be to stay with her. Too easy. Just like it would've been too easy to keep drinking and never stop. Maybe that would've been easier, too. For both of us. Her life certainly wouldn't be easy if she had a vampire hanging on her every move.

Yet my arms didn't loosen their grip on her. I couldn't let go no matter how many times I told myself I needed to. It was crucial I let go. Except I couldn't. Not when she was so soft and fit so perfectly in my arms. She needed me, too—what if an animal came along while I was gone, and she was too weak to fight? I hated myself for even thinking such a thing, but the fear was there.

So, I decided to stop fighting it and get some rest while she got her strength back. I couldn't sleep, but I could close my eyes, relax, and savor the feeling of having her in my arms while I went into a healing stasis.

HOURS PASSED. WHEN I OPENED MY EYES AGAIN, SHE WAS still out—cold and pale, but not as deathly white as she'd been. Her pulse seemed stronger, too.

I couldn't believe I cared.

That heady, buzzy feeling was still there, but it wasn't as strong. I was getting used to the new blood in my veins. The high was wearing off. That wasn't a bad thing—I could control my impulses a little better when I wasn't half out of my mind.

I raised my head to look outside. There was still light, so I hadn't rested for too long. I couldn't leave until it was dark. What a shame. It meant I would have to stay with her, my arms around her.

But once the sun went down, I would have to live without ever seeing her again. Without touching her, hearing her voice, inhaling the special scent that seemed to envelop me. I would never smell a human again without comparing them to her.

She was special. I wondered what her name was. Would she wake up in time for me to ask? I considered going through her things but decided that would be an invasion. I wouldn't feel right, violating her that way. Even I knew how stupid that sounded, seeing as how I had drunk from her neck.

What was wrong with me? I wasn't in love... was I? No, that was impossible. It was also pointless. The minute the sun set, I was out of here. I would never see her again. It would be for the best. She was a weakness. She made me weak. I hated weak creatures. I'd hate myself for being weak.

Besides, I thought, *she would hate me if she knew who I was. What I am.* A stark thought, but a very real one. Who knew how she felt about vampires? She probably saw us the way all humans did. She'd never want to see me again. I wouldn't blame her, either. Not when I had almost killed her.

Her hair was so thick and shiny. It was mesmerizing. I

couldn't help looking at it. A beautiful shade of brown but shot through with strands of golden blonde and deep red. Whenever she moved, it seemed to change color. No way it was real, yet it made sense her hair was special. Everything about her was so special, not like anything I had seen in any human before then. Strange and special and wonderful.

What would I do without her? Nothing would ever be the same. Nothing would ever mean as much, either. I would go through the rest of my existence missing her, like a part of me was gone. A part of me I never knew was important before meeting her.

Had drinking her blood done this to me? Put me in this crazed state?

How had I gone so many decades never holding her? How had she lived without my somehow feeling her inside me, knowing she was out there somewhere? How had my soul not cried out for hers again and again? Or maybe it had. Maybe that was why I had never felt satisfied with my life. I always thought I was jealous of my brother, desperate to lead the clan. But it'd been her, hadn't it? I needed her. I hadn't known what to make of that need, so I'd attributed it to something tangible. Wasn't that it?

No. Impossible. I shook my head, warring with myself, tearing myself in two over the urge to let her go and the urge to soak in her presence as long as possible.

The light outside grew softer, fainter. It would be dark soon. I would have no more excuses for being here with her. I wished time would stop. I wished everything around us would stop, too, so I wouldn't have Lucian or the clan or anything to concern myself with but her.

"Thank you for saving me," I whispered, although part of my soul damned her for destroying me. I would never be the same. Nothing ever would, thanks to her. And I didn't so much as know her name.

I slowly, carefully slid my arms from around her. She stirred, and when she did, her smell met my nostrils again and set me sideways.

I left her there, lying as she had left me, with her head on the backpack and the sleeping bag beneath her. She looked so peaceful. There was even the littlest bit of color in her cheeks again.

I brushed my lips against her forehead, taking one more

chance to inhale her with all my senses. Her skin was soft and smooth and sweet, a little warm.

"Thank you," I whispered again.

Then I hardened myself and hurried from the cave.

I had to get away from her. It was better when I was not near her. Every step took me farther from her, and her spell over me seemed to weaken.

It was a relief, feeling like I could control my thoughts again. How had I ever thought it would be better if we were always together? I clenched my fists and told myself what a joke it was.

I had to get away, far away. I had to course. The forest seemed to go on for miles in all directions—I turned a full circle once I reached the top of a hill and saw how it spread out before me. I didn't know where I was, so I didn't know which direction to go. I only knew I had to get away from that cave and what was in it.

I was furious with myself for being so weak. I should've snapped her neck when I first had the impulse. I wouldn't miss her if I had.

I coursed before I could stop myself, gliding over the ground, through the trees.

The forest came to life all around me, living things stirring and running, startled at my presence. I ignored them. I ignored everything but the instinct to put as much distance as possible between myself and that cave.

I reached the edge of the forest and was about to cross into a long, wide field when a sharp, blinding pain in my arm stopped me.

I hadn't felt any pain since drinking the human's blood, and I froze with shock.

My torn sleeve revealed what looked like a burn on my arm. I t hadn't been there back in the cave—I would've remembered.

It almost sizzled, and I gritted my teeth as I examined it in the light of the moon.

It resembled a hieroglyphic. Or a rune.

Things I knew nothing of. It made no sense, and it hurt deeply. What was happening to me? Who had put it there? Why? What had I done?

I had no one to ask. I didn't even know where I was or how I'd ended up here. Forces I had no understanding of were working their will on my life without my consent and out of my control. I had to get back in control. I had to find a way to work against them, but how? How, when I didn't know who I was battling or what they were capable of?

I needed help. I couldn't go it alone anymore.

I glanced around again, but nothing within my field of vision gave me an indication of where I was. I'd figure it out, though. When I did, I'd find my way home. I had to get home to my family, my clan.

They were all I had. I'd be safe there. I hadn't felt safe since I left them.

It seemed like centuries since I'd walked out, sure I could do a better job of leading the clan than my brother ever could.

Funny, how important that had seemed. Funny, how childish it seemed as I stood here, confused and in pain, more alone than I'd ever felt before.

I took off toward what appeared to be a little town off in the distance, its lights glowing under the dark sky.

It was as good a place to start as any.

11

JONAH

Anissa frowned. "Gage? Is Fane helping you find him?"

"That's the general idea." I disentangled myself from her embrace. Not that I wanted to, but it was easier to think when she wasn't in my arms, making me want to kiss and touch her, and forget my father and her half-brother were waiting not far from us.

Not to mention the other one waiting. The witch.

Although I didn't want Anissa here because her safety was at risk, I was glad she'd taken the chance. How could I ever tell her to listen to me and take care of herself when I couldn't deny how good it was to have her with me? I couldn't keep from smiling when I looked at her, either.

She'd never follow my instructions if I forgave her for going against them so easily. But I couldn't help it. I needed a little comfort, too, and having her here was comforting. I was tired of feeling as though it was me against the world—more than the world, I reminded myself. I wasn't in the normal world as I stood in this cemetery.

At least Fane was here. He'd keep Anissa safe even if he didn't want to because that was who he was, how he was built. He might not have liked her half-blood status, but she was under his protection by virtue of being here. And she meant a lot to me.

If Sirene was telling the truth about him loving his children—

69

and why wouldn't she be?—he'd keep Anissa out of harm's way because I needed him to.

I brushed Anissa's white hair back from her face then held that face in my hands, cupping her cheeks.

If I dreamed, it would be her face I saw.

She had no idea how much she meant—words didn't describe it.

I wanted to tell her everything, especially the real identity of the legend she knew as Fane. That he was my father. I wanted to tell her about the baby, though there was still too much anger in me at the thought of it.

A baby. With a witch.

What had he been thinking? Didn't he care about anything that used to matter? How could he do such a thing to the memory of who he used to be? Would I have to treat the new baby as my brother or sister? It would be a long time before I'd do anything like that.

No, I couldn't tell Anissa about the baby because that would mean telling her Fane was my father. Someday, maybe, I'd be able to tell her. I hoped. I wanted to believe there would be a time when everything could come to light. It was exhausting, keeping track of what I could and couldn't tell, weighing the outcome, reminding myself of the danger. Always danger.

Then again, she could keep a secret. She knew how important it was. I hated keeping things from her. If we had a little more time alone, I might think about it—but we'd have to get back to the others soon before one of them came looking for us. Otherwise, I might be able to convince her to keep the news to herself. But there wasn't time for that.

"Come on," I murmured, taking her hand. "We'd better go back. They'll be wondering what we're doing over here by ourselves."

"I don't think they have to wonder," she whispered with a wicked grin.

I wished we had the time for a lot of things when she grinned up at me like that.

"Yeah, well, I don't want them looking at us funny, then."

She giggled.

We walked back together, taking our time with each step. The fog seemed thicker somehow. How did it move and roll over the ground when there wasn't any breeze to stir it around?

I would never understand all the rules of the different dimensions. I didn't know which one we were in.

Sirene smiled at us when we approached.

I willed myself not to smile back or acknowledge her. Simply because she was there to help didn't mean we had to be friends. She had no right looking at me that way, with that indulgent smile.

What Sirene and my father thought they had was nothing compared to what I had with Anissa. It irritated me she would think it was.

The brand seemed to alternately burn and itch, reminding me of its presence—not that I needed the reminder.

I rubbed it almost unconsciously through my sleeve, like someone with aching joints would rub them when they flared up.

I had almost gotten used to it, but when it suddenly itched or burned or when I stretched too much, I nearly couldn't stand it.

I glanced at Allonic. He was staring at my brand intently.

I saw what I thought was recognition in his eyes. He unnerved me, no matter how much Anissa liked him.

And I could tell she did. I was concerned that maybe she was starting to trust him.

He shifted his gaze away without saying anything about the brand.

I wondered if I'd imagined the look in his eyes. It must've been—my imagination was running away in all directions. Chalk it up to the stress I'd been under lately, I suppose.

"All right," Fane said. "Let's regroup. If we're going to find Gage, we should go where he was last seen."

"Where was that?" Anissa asked.

"League headquarters," Fane responded.

I definitely did not imagine his voice changing when he spoke to Anissa. It tightened. And he wouldn't look at her. My other hand, the one not holding hers, tightened into a fist. If she hadn't been there, I'd rail at him for being such a hypocrite. Then I wondered if it was something else. Maybe his problem with her wasn't because she was a half-blood. But what else could it be?

"Are we sure that's a good idea?" I asked, telling myself to ignore the way he treated her. "It's been a while since Philippa saw him there. He could've gone somewhere else by now. We might tip our hand if we all suddenly show up as a group."

"We don't have to announce our presence, though you have a point. It's something to keep in mind." He turned to Sirene.

I gritted my teeth when I caught the expression in his eyes.

How many times had he gazed at my mother that way? All that love. What was the point if he could forget my mother just like that? Had it ever been real? Was what he felt for Sirene real? It couldn't be.

Still, there was a glow on her face when she stared back at him that made me think she was sincere.

I wanted to tell her to stop wasting her time and find someone of her own kind—but wouldn't that make me as much of a hypocrite as my father?

"We could stop back at the penthouse to regroup," I suggested. "Maybe we shouldn't go straight from here to head-quarters. We might want to check with Philippa to see if her contact has any word of what things are like there. If security's tight, they're bound to see you."

"Also a good point," Fane conceded. "All right. We'll stop at the penthouse and see if she's around, then. We can't be too careful."

"Wait a minute." Sirene dug through her robes.

I tensed all over.

What was she doing?

I wouldn't put anything past a witch.

When she withdrew her hand and I saw the cell phone she held, I almost laughed.

"What are you doing with that?" I asked.

"What?" She glanced down at it. "You think witches don't need phones sometimes?" Her tone was playful.

I reminded myself—again—we weren't friends, but she was rather likable. "It surprised me, was all. Why do you need it?"

"I want to take a picture of the brand. I might be able to find someone who can interpret for us."

I pulled up my sleeve, bared my arm to her, and she took a picture. I reminded myself she was there to help, though I wished it was almost anybody but her trying to help me. I didn't want to feel indebted to her in any way.

"All right. Are you ready?" She regarded at all of us then threw a portal.

It shimmered blue, white, and purple, the light twisting and dancing.

"I'll never get used to this," Anissa whispered. "No matter how many times I do it, I swear."

"Just hold my hand." I took hers and squeezed reassuringly. "You'll be all right."

She nodded with her jaw set.

I turned to look back at Fane, and when I saw him touch Sirene's hand as a sort of parting gesture, it turned my stomach.

I clenched my jaw and reminded myself how important it was to find Gage. We could hash everything else out later.

Then I stepped through, bringing Anissa along with me.

❧ 12 ❧

PHILIPPA

I had to find Fane. But how? Finding Gage had taken a bit of a backseat when compared to finding Fane and letting him know the league's Special Ops had put a target on his back.

Every time I remembered the look of determination on Vance's face when he told me it was his job to kill Fane, it made me sick.

I couldn't let that happen, and I couldn't tell Vance who Fane really was. I felt helpless, which was not something I dealt with well.

What could I do? Once again, I was alone. I wasn't sure I could trust Scott enough to tell him what Vance had told me.

Plus, I didn't know if Sara would be with him. If she could throw lightning, what else could she do? I hated admitting to myself that she scared me half to death, but there it was. I had underestimated her. I reminded myself not to make that mistake again.

Maybe I could find Fane and Jonah, somehow. They were searching for Gage. I had told them about meeting with him at headquarters. Maybe that was where they went. Maybe I could find them there. Except, what if they came back to the penthouse and I wasn't here?

I tried calling Jonah, but the phone rolled over to voicemail. Where was he that he couldn't take my call? I couldn't imagine where Fane might have taken him. Did he not have his phone anymore? Had he gotten rid of it?

My heart ached when I thought of him. My father. What happened to turn him into who he had become? Hunting humans?

The legends surrounding Fane were impossible to keep track of. Some said he wasn't even real, just a made-up creature used to explain the crimes of other creatures. Some said he wasn't a full vampire, that he had some other magical blood mixed in which allowed him to jump dimensions and even go back and forth in time. It was laughable, the way imagination had taken off.

All many of us needed was the suggestion of a creature different from ourselves and we filled in the rest on our own. Some of us needed a vigilante, someone who would buck league law and live as they wanted. Some of us needed the idea of something bigger, braver than ourselves.

Some of us needed to believe our father was still in there, somewhere. To believe he only did what he did because he had no other choice. I didn't want to imagine what had happened to drive him to those lengths. It might've been the death of my mother. It might've snapped him in half. Or, he might've been scrambling to survive all those years because he'd seen what happened to her and knew it could happen to him. If only we had the time to talk it over.

I had so many questions, and all my father could do when I hugged him was pull away from me. I rubbed my knuckles over my eyes to wipe away my tears. I wasn't a baby. Crying wouldn't get me anywhere.

I had to try to find my father, and Jonah, too. He had to know the league's Special Ops team was after him—and Jonah needed to know traveling around with him was more dangerous than we could've guessed.

But how?

I went to the rooftop in the hopes they would come back. It was better than nothing. I stood there, wind in my hair, wishing and hoping they would appear. There were still a few hours left until the sun rose, and I walked the perimeter of the roof again and again, waiting, looking in all directions for a flash of light, a swirl of color.

Oh, please, please. Come back. I have to warn you.

What would happen if Fane was killed and I hadn't been able to do anything about it? I would never be able to forgive myself.

Although I wished with all my might, with enough intensity to make me feel a little weak, I was surprised when I got my wish.

Ahead of me, light started to swirl. A pin point at first, but it quickly exploded into a circle of light that touched the surface of the roof and spread up and out.

Fane was the first one to step through. I held my breath.

Then came Jonah... and Anissa.

I groaned.

And with them, someone new.

Tall, dark-skinned. He had a strange essence, something that told me he wasn't human. There was a preternatural sense about him, but I couldn't locate where it was coming from. Was he a vampire? No. I would've known right off.

Vampires didn't have golden eyes that seemed to glow like fire. Then again, there was something familiar about him, too. Maybe he was part vampire, part something else? Did he have fangs?

My attention turned to Anissa next. She was the one who started it all, wasn't she? It was all her fault. If she hadn't tried to kill my brother, none of this would've happened.

We were happy before she came along. We had lives, routines, things to be happy about, things to care about other than struggling to stay alive and keep each other alive. I had liked my life. It was fun, exciting, and there was nothing more important to think about than where we would go to party on any particular night. Jonah took care of the clan, and we enjoyed life otherwise.

But then she came along, and everything was ruined. She pulled us into Marcus's web.

And there she stood, next to my father, as she stepped out of the portal.

I should've been there. I should've been standing at his side, leading with him, traveling and fighting alongside him. Not her. She should not have been next to him.

No—he didn't trust me enough, didn't think I was worthy of that.

But she was? She was worthy? He trusted her? The little half-blood?

All of this went through my head in the blink of an eye—in the time it took the portal to close, in fact.

By the time it did, I exploded with rage.

All four heads turned in my direction as I flew at her, claws out, fangs bared.

Jonah tried to jump between us, but he was too late.

I took her throat in my hands and squeezed.

"What do you think you're doing here?" I screamed.

"Philippa! No!" Jonah pulled at me, while the tall, dark-skinned creature pulled at Anissa.

She clawed at my hands, but I had a strong grip.

"Why won't you go away already?" I asked, struggling to maintain my hold even with Jonah fighting me. "You and your electric sister! You're the reason this is happening! Gage was here with us before you came around! He left because of you, because of what you did to our clan and our family! Damn you both!"

"Philippa, stop this!" Jonah managed to separate us.

I lunged again.

This time, his arms were around my waist, holding me back. "Have you gone crazy?"

"If I have, it's because of her!"

Everything that had happened since the beginning flashed through my head.

Watching while Jonah and Scott planned to rescue Anissa and her sister. Seeing the rage all over Gage's face when he realized his twin would jeopardize the clan for a stranger.

Begging Gage not to go, not to split us up—things had never been easy between him and Jonah, but they were always better when we were together, acting as a team. How my heart had broken when he left, how I had practically about worried myself to death over him since then.

It was her, all her—her and Sara. Why did they have to come into our lives?

I threw myself at her again and managed to catch Jonah off-guard—I slipped out of his arms and clawed at her face, but she held up her arms in time.

"What right do you have to be here?" I roared. "What right do you have to be with my father, standing with him, working with him? You don't have that right! You're not his daughter! I am!"

It was like the whole world stopped.

Anissa's arms dropped from in front of her face, and her jaw hung slack. She looked at Jonah. "Your father?"

Fane was standing behind her, and, from the corner of my eye, I noticed him shaking his head.

I was still on the attack, my blood still boiling, and I took advantage of her surprise by swinging my fist and making contact with her jaw.

She reeled backward, saved from falling off the roof only by the arms of the dark-skinned one.

Then, it hit me.

She was surprised. She didn't know.

I told.

I told her.

I looked at Fane in horror, but he looked away.

No! I had pushed him even further away.

No wonder he didn't trust me. He would never trust me again.

Anissa steadied herself. There was a cut on her lip, slowly oozing blood. She didn't seem to notice.

"Is it true?" she asked Jonah, who stood there looking like he'd been hit by a train.

No, no! It wasn't supposed to be this way. My father wasn't supposed to be disappointed in me. None of them were. I was as good as any of them, as valuable to the clan and my family. They could trust me.

She turned to me. "What did you mean about my sister? You called her electric. What did that mean?"

I ignored her. I couldn't hardly remember what I'd said, anyway. It had all come out in a rush, as though my mouth had taken over for my brain.

I stood in front of Fane, willing him to look at me. "I didn't mean it. I swear. I'm sorry. Please, listen to me. Look at me. Please!"

A sudden creaking noise stopped me.

We all turned toward it. My heart was in my throat, desperation running through me.

What next?

What could possibly happen?

The rooftop access door opened slowly, its hinges screaming in the silence.

There was a light on inside, and a figure stood there, cast in silhouette.

🏵 13 🏵

ANISSA

I searched Jonah's face, confusion and fury fighting for control of my brain. Just when I thought I had things under control and we were on the same page, something else happened.

Nothing could've prepared me for what came out of Philippa's mouth.

Fane was their father?

When did Jonah think it would be a good time to tell me that? When would he ever trust me enough to share the truth? The full truth, not merely what he felt I could handle?

Never, that was when.

I would never know if he was being completely honest, or if he didn't trust me, or if he was sheltering me out of some misplaced chauvinistic impulse.

I felt foolish. He hurt my pride when he lied to me that way. I felt stupid for making it so easy for him to fool me.

I touched my mouth, noticing the blood for the first time. And that bitch, Philippa. How dare she touch me, much less hit me? What did I ever do to her?

What, because I was standing next to her father? No, she had always hated me—she was just waiting for a reason to hit me. She had been looking for one all along, and she'd finally had it.

I seethed—they were the same, the two of them, Jonah and Philippa. Both of them had secrets up their sleeves. Except with

Philippa, I knew what I was up against. I could handle a punch to the face. I could even handle strange, cryptic claims—what did she mean about Sara being electric? She had obviously lost her mind to jealousy.

What I couldn't handle were Jonah's lies and omissions.

Philippa was begging Fane to forgive her.

Fat chance of that happening. He wouldn't look at her. I could see his side of it, and I didn't blame him.

I was still furious with Jonah and with Philippa, my blood boiling until it bubbled over.

I dropped to one knee and slid a silver blade from inside my boot while no one was watching me.

In a flash, I jumped to my feet and laid the blade against Philippa's smooth, perfect cheek.

She screamed, a howl of excruciating pain as her skin sizzled with the silver blade's kiss. Her flesh corroded under the shiny metal, as though I had thrown acid on her.

She jerked away, holding a hand over the spot.

"Hit me again!" I screamed, lunging at her with the blade. "Come on! I dare you!"

"Stop! She's crazy!" Philippa was doubled over in pain, eyes wide and darting back and forth as she backed away from me.

I noticed then, for the first time, the open door and the figure standing in the doorway. I held the blade at the ready, waiting for whoever it was to come out.

I even forgot about Philippa.

The individual stepped forward—stumbled, actually, all but falling to the ground.

"Father?" Gage's voice was barely a whisper, almost carried away with the wind.

I gasped.

We all did.

He'd become a shadow of himself—there were scars all over his chest and arms. He was pale, weak, panting for breath. His eyes appeared glazed over, but I thought it was emotion more than exhaustion. He couldn't pry them from the sight of Fane—his father, I reminded myself.

"Anissa." Jonah pulled at my arm, trying to get me away from Philippa.

I shook him off.

He didn't have any right to touch me. Besides, I wasn't touching her, I was focused on Gage.

"Father?" Gage whispered again, staring at Fane.

Finally, Fane nodded.

Gage stumbled to him and almost collapsed before Fane caught him.

"Is this a dream?" he whispered.

"No, son. It's not a dream." He helped Gage steady himself. "It's real. I'm real."

Gage glanced around as though sure he would wake up from his dream at any second, like he was afraid of waking up and finding out none of it was real after all.

"What happened to you?" Jonah went to him, looking him over. "Who did this?"

"I-I don't know," Gage breathed. "I coursed here. A long way. I'm so tired, and I can hardly remember anything."

"Come on. Let's go inside. You need to rest." Jonah took him by the arm.

"What about Scott? What if he sees...?" Fane asked.

"If he does, he does. But we have to talk to Gage, and we can't do it out here on the roof. He can barely stand. We'll go to my rooms, better chance to have privacy there," Jonah said.

So, we all went inside, and Jonah helped Gage down on the sofa.

It reminded me of when we first arrived at the high-rise, Sara and I, and the way she had rested against the cushions.

I glanced around, trying to sense Sara, but I couldn't pick her up. She wasn't here. I would've felt it if she was, wouldn't I? I was starting to question myself.

Philippa dropped to her knees by Gage's side. One hand was still covering her cheek, where I had burned her, but that didn't seem to do anything to her joy at seeing her brother. "Where have you been? What happened to you?" She leaned against him, wrapping her free arm around him.

"It's a long story. I don't know all of it." His eyes weren't on her, though. They were on his father. It was clear he couldn't make sense of it.

I thought I could understand how he felt. I remembered when Allonic told me our mother was alive. How would I have reacted if she'd suddenly appeared out of nowhere, with no warning?

Then Gage gazed at Philippa. "Did you know he was alive?" There was no need to ask who he was talking about.

She raised her head. "No. Not until tonight."

He faced Jonah. "You?"

"Not for long," Jonah murmured. "It was after you left, for sure."

Fane cleared his throat and stepped forward. "I'm sorry."

"For what?" Gage asked. "Not that there's nothing to be sorry for, but I want to know what you think you should apologize for."

"I would've come to you sooner. You have no idea how much I wanted to." He looked over the three of them. "It was torture, every day. Every single day, I had to make the decision to stay away. Sometimes it was easier, sometimes it wasn't. Sometimes I considered locking myself away to make sure I didn't put you in danger by revealing myself."

"How would you put us in danger?" Gage turned to his brother and sister for help, but they stayed silent.

"Just know I wanted to," Fane said, sidestepping Gage's question.

Gage opened his mouth to speak, but something stopped him. He winced, touching his hand to his arm, his teeth clenched in pain.

Jonah stared at his arm. "Gage? What's wrong?"

"I honestly don't know." He lowered his gaze then moved his hand away from the spot he'd been gripping.

My eyes widened in shock when I recognized the same brand I'd seen on Jonah's arm. Identical, at least as far as I could see.

"You have it, too?" Jonah slid his sleeve up to his elbow and showed his twin his own brand.

Gage's mouth fell open. "Do you know anything about it? It showed up out of nowhere, earlier tonight."

Jonah shook his head. "We've been trying to find out. I wonder why you have it, too."

Allonic stepped forward. "Fane, I think—"

Gage made a strangled noise which shut Allonic up.

We all froze.

"*Fane?*" Gage nearly shrieked. "Did he call you Fane?"

Fane's shoulders slumped. "Yes. He did."

"You're Fane?" He shifted his focus to Jonah and Philippa again. "*The* Fane?"

I felt sorry for him. He had been through so much and was only trying to make sense of what seemed like an impossible situation.

Fane nodded, wordless.

"But... but... No! That's impossible. No. No way!" Gage laughed. "He's legendary. He's not even real, right? Like, half of what they say about him is probably made up. Right?" He searched his father's face, frantic for comfort, understanding, despite the situation being beyond all understanding.

"Son, there's so much I have to tell you and so little time to tell it. It can wait for now. Just know..." Fane took a deep breath. "Just know your father, the man you used to know, is dead."

"Don't say that," Philippa begged. "Please. You don't know how hard it is to hear." She was still at Gage's side, and he slid an arm around her shoulders.

I told myself I should feel for her the way I did for Gage, but I couldn't. Not when I still felt a rush of satisfaction when I saw the mark my blade had left on her skin.

"That doesn't mean it isn't true," Fane replied. "You can't keep thinking of me as the father I used to be. Too much has happened between then and now for me to ever go back to being who I once was."

"Fane, I'm sorry to burst in on this," Allonic said. "It's very touching." Was that sarcasm in my brother's tone? "But there's something I think I can help you with."

"What is it?"

I got the feeling Fane was glad for the distraction.

Allonic pointed at Gage's arm. "The brands. I can read them."

14

ANISSA

We all froze, surprised.

I bit back a gasp. "You can? You know what it says?" I took his arm.

He nodded. "It's actually very easy."

I snorted. "Yeah. Easy."

"What does it say, then?" Jonah bared his arm to Allonic. "Do they say the same thing?"

Jonah sat beside Gage. When they were together like this, I saw the resemblance more than ever.

Almost identical twins, at least on the surface. Somehow, their personalities made them appear different.

Jonah had confidence that made him carry himself a certain way, to where he appeared a little taller than his brother.

Gage usually had a chip on his shoulder that made his forehead crease in a frown. He never seemed relaxed or at ease, and somehow that gave the impression he was older than Jonah sometimes.

But when they were both sitting there together, staring up at Allonic as he studied their brands, they could've been each other's mirror image.

Allonic knelt on one knee by the couch, taking their arms in his hands. He nodded thoughtfully as he studied them, his eyes moving back and forth.

"Yes, these are virtually the same. They only change in that one refers to Jonah and the other to Gage. Otherwise, they are as identical as you two."

"What do they say?" Fane stood behind his sons, and while I knew he wanted them to forget who he was or what he'd once been to them, there was a still a paternal instinct in him that made him hover there, protective.

Allonic's voice was slow, deliberate as he explained. "You were right when you concluded this was the work of Valerius. He's marked them for protection."

"Protection?" The twins glanced at each other.

Jonah then lifted his gaze to me, but I wouldn't look at him. I focused on my brother, instead. It was childish, but I couldn't shake the anger I felt whenever I remembered all the chances Jonah had to tell me about Fane being his father. He'd deliberately hidden the truth, over and over.

"Yes," Allonic confirmed. "These brands provide direction. Valerius wants them to go to him."

"Go to him? Go where?" Gage asked.

"Wait a minute." Fane rested his hand on Gage's shoulder. It may have been an unconscious gesture, but I could tell it meant the world to Gage. "Why does he want them? Does the brand say anything about that?"

Allonic shook his head. "No, but I can help you with that. At least, I think I can, based on what I already know about twins."

"And that's what?"

"They're true twins, right? They were born human twins then were turned over at roughly the same time?"

Fane nodded.

"I thought so. Because of this, the powers they already possess as vampires are amplified. It's very rare for a pair of human twins to become vampires at all, and especially at almost the same time, the way they were first born as humans. Extremely rare." He studied the two of them. "You're special."

"Funny, but I would give my right arm to be normal." Jonah smirked.

"I've never felt special. I mean, I've never felt any stronger or better than anybody else." Gage looked at Jonah. "You?"

"Not really." He peered up at Fane. "Did you ever know this?"

"What parent doesn't think their children are special?" he asked. "But no. I've never heard anything about amplified powers."

"It's not common knowledge," Allonic admitted, "because these aren't the kind of powers either of you would use in regular life. They're powers an ancient, powerful vampire such as Valerius would find useful."

"He wants us to go to him so he can take advantage of our powers. Do we have a choice in the matter?" Gage asked.

Allonic hesitated, then shook his head. "I'm sorry, but as far as I can tell it isn't an option. The brands will continue to hurt until the pain becomes excruciating. You won't be able to think straight or function for the pain. Eventually, you'll lose your sanity."

I shuddered. I might be angry at Jonah, but I didn't want to see that happen.

"So, there's no choice," Fane mused. "All right. We'll take them to Valerius together."

"Are you sure that's a good idea?" Jonah asked. "I mean, this is dangerous enough. You don't need to expose yourself to even bigger threats."

"It's not an option," Fane said, almost dismissing Jonah out of hand. He returned his attention to Allonic. "So? What do you think?"

"I think it'll be a challenge," Allonic murmured as he continued to study the brands.

"Where is Valerius? Can you tell from reading?" Jonah asked.

"I think so. It seems as though he's in Sorrowswatch."

"Where's that?" Fane asked. "I've never heard of it."

"It's not far from ley lines I'm aware of in England." Allonic lifted his gaze. "I can get you there."

"What are ley lines?" Philippa had been quiet throughout my brother's explanation.

I noticed how she seemed to deliberately avoid looking at me —whether that was out of hatred or fear, I didn't know or care.

"They're invisible lines which run all over the globe. Along these lines, supernatural occurrences are more prone to take place, geographical spots with supernatural significance are likely to exist. In the places where they intersect, especially strong power resides."

"Like what?" she asked.

"Many human monuments, stretching back to ancient times. The Great Pyramids of Giza, for example. Machu Picchu. Easter Island. Stonehenge. All of these reside along ley lines, and all of them harken back to a time when mankind was much more in touch with the supernatural. One of the great misconceptions of humans is they believe they've gotten closer in touch with what's real as they've left superstition behind. In fact, they've dismissed that which is truly in control of their existence, in favor of that which will never provide answers."

"You know so much about this," I mused, admiring my brother. "Can you help? I can't imagine them going on their own when you already have knowledge that might help them."

He gazed up at me with a slight smile, an expression I was getting used to seeing. "That depends. Will you be involved?"

"Do you need to ask?"

"Anissa..." Jonah trailed off.

I shot him a *back-off* look.

If he knew what was good for him, he'd leave me alone. I wasn't in the mood to go around the block again in regard to whether I was up to the challenge of going with them. As far as I was concerned, he didn't get to tell me what to do again, not until he explained why he'd lied and especially not until he started telling me the whole truth.

Allonic nodded. "I can't imagine disappointing our mother by not helping out when I know you'll be involved."

Out of the corner of my vision, I noticed Philippa's eyes widen at the mention of Allonic and I having the same mother.

She must have been wondering who Allonic was.

It wasn't her reaction I was concerned with. It was the gleam in Allonic's eyes. I knew that gleam—I had seen it enough times in Sara's eyes, and always when she had an ulterior motive. He wasn't in this just to help me. What other reason could he have to go along?

Whatever his motivation, it didn't change the fact we needed him with us.

I nodded, then turned toward Jonah—he was still sitting there with his mouth open, like he wanted to come up with a protest but couldn't think of one fast enough.

"I'm going," I said, silently daring him to oppose me.

He held my gaze for a long moment, but I won when he looked away.

"I'm going, too." Philippa took Gage by the hand and smiled at him.

"What about the clan? You can't leave like this," Fane murmured.

"Scott can take care of things while I'm gone. It's decided. I have to do this." Her voice held the desperate edge of someone determined to prove herself.

I knew there was no sense in anyone trying to dissuade her.

Great.

All of us, traveling together.

No way that can go wrong.

🦋 15 🦋

JONAH

I t was all so surreal, sitting there with my brother. Our father stood behind us. We were almost a family again—except my twin brother was half-dead and claimed he didn't know why, and my father wanted us to pretend he was dead.

I looked at Philippa. Kneeling next to Gage, she smiled at him, holding his hand. Was she really that thrilled to be with our deserter brother again?

I told myself not to think the worst—she had been planning on searching for him after all, before I brought Fane here.

It seemed to me like she was making a bigger deal over Gage being back than she should have, almost groveling at his feet.

I couldn't help but wonder if that was because she wanted his protection, knowing she wouldn't get it from me. Not when I was as furious with her as I was at that moment.

I should've known I couldn't trust her. She was smart and wise, but she had no filter—and she never did know how to control her temper. I couldn't have guessed she would've blabbed while attacking Anissa, of course.

What brought that on? Not as though she'd ever liked Anissa, but something must've pushed her over the edge. I wondered what had been going on while I was gone.

And Gage.

I breathed out a heavy sigh.

I loved him, of course, but I couldn't forget his betrayal.

93

Whatever happened to him was his own fault for running off the way he did.

Considering his scars, I could tell he'd paid dearly. Did he learn his lesson? Could I trust him? I hated that I didn't know. He was my twin brother, someone I should've been able to trust implicitly.

I wanted to rant at Gage. *Look at what you did.* He'd torn us apart. And now, lucky me, I had a brand that matched his. Just one more thing to tie us together.

"What do you think Valerius will want with us when we reach Sorrowswatch?" I asked Allonic. "Is there anything in the brand about that? A clue?"

He scrutinized it again. "I don't see anything. He wouldn't make it obvious."

"Obvious?" I couldn't help chuckling. "Yeah, this is obvious. I can't make heads or tails of the symbols."

"And he knew you wouldn't be able to. Not everybody can. It takes knowledge of languages that are old and extinct."

Philippa spoke up. "Gage? What happened to you?" She traced his scars, grimacing.

"It's a long story," he muttered. "I wish I could say."

"What's that supposed to mean? Now's not the time to hold back on us," I told him.

Anissa snorted from where she stood behind Allonic. I didn't have to ask what she thought was so funny.

She would hold a grudge until the end of time because she felt like I was holding back on her. What would it take to make her understand I was trying to protect my father—and her? Fane was right. Knowing his identity was dangerous. And I could understand in part why he'd kept himself a secret from us. But now that Anissa knew, protecting her was my highest priority.

Gage glanced at me from the corner of his eye, and I saw a little of the old resentment there. "I'm not trying to hold back on you. I'm saying I really don't know."

"How can you not know? I mean..." Philippa studied the scars.

His face had been battered, too—his lip was swollen, his cheekbone and eye bruised.

Philippa frowned. "How could you forget something like this?"

"A spell," Fane said under his breath.

"That was my guess. A spell, or I was compelled."

"That's a pretty big accusation," I muttered.

"Do you have another explanation?" he asked. "I remember nothing, I mean absolutely nothing, after Philippa's visit to head-quarters. Everything after that is a blank slate. Not foggy. *Blank*." He regarded each of us, one by one. "If any of you has an expla-nation that makes sense, please, let it out. Because I would like to know myself. You don't know how it feels to not remember no matter how hard you try." He leaned his head back against the couch and covered his eyes with one hand.

Philippa had the nerve to scowl at me, like it was my fault he was upset.

I glared back at her. She had no right to the high ground.

Fane stood by the door, staring outside. "We need to get out of here. Not just to get answers, but to lower the chances of someone stumbling upon me. I've already taken too many chances."

I looked at him and wondered what it must be like to always be on the run. Never being in one place for too long. Not being able to spend time with his family.

"The sooner we get this taken care of, the better," I agreed, then turned to Allonic. "What should we do? Where do we start?"

"We need a witch to access the passage to Sorrowswatch. It'll help us avoid the need for spiritwalkers."

"I can access witch passages," Fane said.

Allonic nodded. "Yes. We Custodians are well aware of your skills, Fane. However, this is something beyond even your skill level." His voice was heavy with respect, and Fane seemed to take it well.

I, on the other hand, stared wide-eyed at the shade. The Custodians knew of Fane's skills? Of course—they knew every-thing, didn't they? I wondered what else they knew. Did they know all along my father was alive? Did Steward know and keep it from me? Funny how thoughts like that could color everything else. All the memories of moments spent with Steward took on a different meaning.

Fane shrugged. "We need a witch, then I'll have to get Sirene to help us."

I gritted my teeth again at the mention of her name. Why did she have to be involved?

"We have to go now, though. I don't want to wait around and run the risk of anyone else joining us. We already have enough in tow."

Fane nudged me. "Come on."

All eyes were on me.

"Okay. Let's go." I tried to take Anissa's hand, the way I had when we ported over from the cemetery, but she shook me off. I leaned in to murmur in her ear. "I'm sorry."

She shrugged. "So?"

That stung. She had never acted this way—at least, not since we'd gotten to know each other. She reminded me of the assassin I first met in the alley that night, outside the club, when she was supposed to kill me.

I refused to believe we had gone backward. "I want to talk to you as soon as we get the chance to be alone."

"Good for you. The odds aren't in your favor." She looked around at the others.

Angry or not, she had a point. That didn't mean I'd stop trying.

Fane threw the portal. "Hurry."

We took turns going through—Anissa went ahead of me.

I wanted to be sure she made it through safely before I went.

Just because she was hardly being civil didn't mean I loved her any less.

🕸 16 🕸

PHILIPPA

One minute, we were standing on the rooftop with Manhattan spread out in front of us.

The next, we were in the middle of a creepy, foggy old cemetery. Not simply old. Ancient. I was afraid the headstones around me would turn to dust if I touched them.

Maybe it was morbid, but I couldn't help trying to read some of the stones. Time had worn them down until the letters and numbers carved into them were indistinguishable. I crouched to get a better view.

"Don't waste your time."

I glanced up. That Allonic character was grinning down at me.

"What do you mean?" I asked.

"They weren't written in English, or any language used on Earth for hundreds and hundreds of years."

I stood slowly, glancing around. "Where are we? I thought we were going to England."

The air was dank and cool, but it didn't stir. It was strangely still. There was no sound of birds or bats or any other type of life. No stars, either. No sky? Only blackness. I couldn't understand what I was looking at as I craned my neck and a shiver ran down my spine.

"This is a pit stop," Jonah muttered darkly.

I hated hearing him like that, though I should've known. I let it slip about Fane being our father, and he couldn't forgive me for it.

Granted, his precious Anissa would've found out when Gage showed up even if I hadn't said a word. But no, he chose to hold it against me instead.

Meanwhile, I had a scar on my cheek from her blasted silver blade, but would he get an attitude with her about that?

No, he'd probably say it was my fault for going after her first, though, by the time she burned me, I was nowhere near her anymore.

I wasn't paying attention, which was exactly how she took advantage of me. No way could she have burned me like that if I had been paying attention.

Still, she's right and I'm wrong. She's perfect and I'm a nuisance.

I held back my anger and frustration.

"Come. This way." Fane pointed to a huge marble structure in the distance, and we slowly made our way through the fog.

Jonah and Anissa seemed a lot more surefooted than I felt—I stumbled more than once over the little bits of marble and granite sticking up from the ground, and gave Gage the heads-up so he could watch his step.

The stones must've sunk down over time. How many were buried there? Who were they? Why was this the meeting place Fane had chosen?

Allonic kept glancing at me with a curious expression.

Finally, I couldn't take it anymore. "Why are you looking at me that way?"

"Was I looking at you?"

"Yes. You were."

"I've never seen anyone so fascinated with a cemetery before, I suppose. I'm sorry if I was rude. I'm not used to the ways of vampires."

I couldn't help but laugh under my breath. "It's considered ill-mannered in just about every circle to stare," I explained. "Not just among vampires."

"All the same, I'm not used to being around so many other types of creatures. I've spent most of my life with the shades."

I didn't know much about shades, but I knew he wasn't telling me the whole truth. He wasn't all shade. There was something else inside him. Then, I remembered him talking about "their" mother with Anissa. He was Anissa's brother! I wrinkled my nose in distaste while he was turned the other way.

Yet another half-breed. Still, he didn't seem all bad, and he was our key to finding Valerius.

Once we reached the big, tall structure—a mausoleum, I saw, complete with carvings and an iron gate—a dark-haired witch emerged from the shadows inside. Did she live in there? Who lived in a mausoleum?

The place was getting creepier by the minute.

"This is Sirene." Fane introduced me and Gage.

I noticed he left Jonah out—but from the way my brother stared at her, it didn't seem like they were strangers.

What did he have against her? There was so much kindness in her eyes. No, we weren't exactly friends with witches, but I was willing to give her a chance if Fane considered her a friend.

Jonah obviously didn't feel that way.

"Allonic?" Fane turned to him. "Can we speak with you, please?"

Sirene, Allonic, and Fane, the three of them bowed their heads, murmuring together.

"Can I talk to you now?" Jonah was pulling Anissa around the corner.

From the way she resisted him, she didn't want to go.

What was her issue?

It seemed to me like she was always trying to make drama where there wasn't any. Wasn't what we were going through dramatic enough without her stirring the pot?

Still, it gave me the chance to talk with Gage more privately than we'd been able to since he showed up.

"Can I tell you something and trust you won't take it the wrong way?" I asked.

"That depends." Though exhaustion seemed to leak from Gage's pores, he managed a small smile.

"You look like hell."

"Now, why would I take that the wrong way?" He leaned against what appeared a coffin made of stone.

The way people chose to commemorate their dead was an endless source of fascination to me. Why replicate what was underground?

I glanced around to be sure we weren't overheard. "Okay. This is me you're talking to now. Are you sure you don't remember anything about what happened to make you this way?"

He rolled his eyes. "Philippa..."

"I'm serious. You know you can tell me. I understand if you wanted to keep it from the others for some reason, but we talked back at headquarters. You told me why you were there. So I already know. You don't have to lie or leave things out."

"I'm telling you, I'm not leaving anything out. I wasn't kidding earlier." He stared me straight in the eye. "I'm serious."

"All right, all right." I ran my hands through my hair, distracted, wondering what to make of it. "Do you think it was Lucian, perhaps? Maybe he found out why you were there, what you were thinking?"

"I don't know how he could've found out what I was thinking, since I never told anybody but you."

I frowned. "You can't think I would've shared that with anybody else."

"No, I don't think that at all. But that's my point. Unless he used his grudge against the family as a reason, I don't know how he thinks."

"That's probably a good thing." I smirked.

"Even so," he continued, "that's not proof. I can't prove who did it."

"What about getting away? Do you remember anything about that?"

"Not a thing. I woke up..." His eyes went a little unfocused for a second. "I woke up in a forest. In a cave in a forest, that is. I don't know if whoever did it to me dropped me there, or if I escaped somehow and found it myself. Although, honestly, I was in such bad shape, I can't imagine finding my way anywhere. I could barely lift my head when I first woke up."

That was strange. He could barely lift his head, but he'd somehow healed fast enough to get home in pretty short order?

He hadn't been missing for all that long after I met with him. The sort of beating he'd taken, complete with burns all over him, should've taken days to recover from before having the strength to course.

I stared at him, hard, trying to figure out what he was holding back. I came close to asking why he wasn't being completely honest, but decided to let it go. There was no point in starting an argument so soon after being reunited.

Instead, I glanced over to where Fane was talking with the witch and the shade. It was the first time I'd had a chance to really take a look at him without him knowing. It was easier to observe him that way.

"Does he seem different to you?" I whispered, pointing toward our father.

"Different how? His face is the same. I recognized him right away."

"I did, too. I don't mean that way. It's more the way he carries himself. He seems a lot older than he should, too."

"I guess he's seen a lot," Gage mused. "Certain things age us faster than others, I suppose."

"You must be right." Except for his face, I wouldn't have guessed he was my father at all.

My father was always confident and sure of himself, but there had also been a twinkle in his eye. Good humor. He loved a joke more than just about anybody I knew. He loved to banter, too, and I used to love getting into little wars of words with him, debating and teasing and trying to make him laugh. And when he did laugh, the sound would fill whatever space we were in. He was larger than life in every way imaginable.

Fane, on the other hand, was terse. He used few words.

I couldn't imagine Fane laughing, ever. The weight of the world was on his shoulders. He had skills I had no understanding of. So many secrets. There was no joy, no spark, no vitality. He was a survivor—all the joy had been rubbed away, just like time had worn down the stones in the cemetery.

"What do you think about him now?" I asked Gage. "What's your gut reaction?"

"I was overjoyed when I first saw him, if that's what you're asking."

"And now?" I forced him to meet my eyes, dipping my head to follow his gaze until they locked. "Now what do you think?"

He shrugged. "Now I have questions. A lot of questions."

"Yeah. Me, too."

🕷 17 🕷

ANISSA

The second we were out of sight of the others, I pulled my arm from Jonah's grasp.

"What is wrong with you?" I hissed through clenched teeth. "Why are you hellbent on making a scene in front of everyone? Especially your sister?"

"Why are you hellbent on starting a fight with me?" he hissed, just as sharply.

"Because, no matter what we go through or what I do to show you I'm trustworthy, you still lie to my face. Continually. Why do you do that?" I wanted to hit him—anything to vent how I was feeling. "I mean, you tell me you want to protect me or something, right? How can I trust you to do that when I can't even trust you to be honest with me?"

"That's exactly why I held back. To protect you. And while we're throwing accusations around, why do you insist on making it so hard to keep you safe? You question me at every turn. You make my life impossible."

"Oh, well then." I took a step back. "Don't bother yourself anymore. I don't want to make your life any more impossible." I turned to go back to the others and find some way to get back home, but he stepped in front of me.

"No. Not until you listen to me for once."

"For once." I laughed, not bothering to hide the scorn on my face.

"Yeah, for once. Really listen. Don't run away before I get a chance to explain to you."

I was fine until I met his eyes. I was always a fool for him when I caught sight of his eyes.

And he probably knew it.

"Fine. I have nowhere to go, anyway. Not without help."

Still, I stood at a distance. Every moment that passed only made my fury more real, almost strong enough to taste.

He lied to me. He didn't think I mattered enough to tell the full truth to.

I felt like such a fool for ever believing him.

He took a deep breath. "For one thing, it wasn't my secret to tell. It's Fane's."

I rolled my eyes, though he had a point. "That's pretty convenient."

"Second, there's a reason why he's been in hiding all this time. I believe him when he says it's dangerous for us to know he's Fane. You don't know how much I wanted to tell you, but when have we had more than a few minutes alone since he reached out to me?"

"Keep talking." I hated the way he melted me down even when I was determined to punish him for lying.

He might not have come right out and lied, but a lie of omission was just as bad.

"I had to ask myself if telling you this secret would put you in danger. Fane isn't exactly revered. There are groups who want him dead, and I doubt they'd stop with killing only him if they found out he had a group of other vampires around him who knew his identity. Think about it. Why did he adopt this identity? What has he seen? What secrets might he know, and what did he have to do to survive over the years?" He paused for effect. "What did he reveal to us that we might tell others?"

The whole cold truth hit me.

We could die just for knowing Dommik Bourke isn't dead.

"And while I trust you not to give away his secrets, I know there are people out there who won't stop at anything to get the information they want. I shudder to think what they would do to you to get answers. Remember what Marcus did to your sister? I bet that's child's play in comparison."

I shuddered—the memory of Sara's agony was etched in my mind and heart. I would never forget the screams, the torture on her face. She had transformed into a soulless monster, unable to think or reason or feel anything but soul-searing hunger. It was living hell.

And yet, there was a flaw in his logic. "Simply being in Fane's company marks me for punishment, right? No matter whether or not I know who he is, his enemies will see me as a threat. Why would it matter if I know who he is, then? I'm already in trouble."

He sighed. "Don't remind me, okay? I can't help that, but I don't want to make things worse, either. I'm scrambling around, trying to do damage control. I can hardly keep track of who knows what anymore or who's a bigger threat to us at any given moment."

I felt sorry for him as he leaned against the thick marble wall, although I was still hurt and angry. I hated thinking of myself as a burden, but that was how he'd made it sound. Like I was just one more thing for him to worry about.

He already had his clan and his father and the brand on his arm, not to mention his missing brother—who at least had reappeared now.

"Would it make things easier on you to share with me? I might have a perspective that helps you. You never know."

He tilted his head to the side, staring at me. "Maybe."

"You can trust me to keep it between us."

"That's never been an issue," he snapped. "Stop making it about that. I'm telling you, it's the rest of the world I don't trust." His eyes glowed with a light I had never seen.

"Okay, okay." I didn't like him taking that tone with me, but we could talk about it later—when I wasn't concerned he would try to rip my head off.

"This is all about Lucian," he murmured. "He's the reason my family turned vampire. He's been bent on revenge against my father for centuries."

My head spun from that little bit of information.

Lucian.

I had no problem believing it, even without explanation. How I'd always felt Lucian didn't mean half of what he said. The coldness in his eyes. How he obviously loved the attention while he pretended to be humble. As though he only cared about the league and the vampires he led.

"Why?" I breathed.

He told me the story of his father's youth as a human, how he and Lucian had been best friends. I could almost see all of it—the way Elena and Dommik fell in love and brought on Lucian's jealousy. Obsession leading him to turn Elena, and love leading her to turn her husband—not to mention the love it took for him to want to turn.

By the time Jonah finished, there were tears in my eyes.

"I wouldn't put it past him," I muttered when he went silent.

"He'll stop at nothing to destroy our family. Do you understand now how serious this is?" His eyes searched my face. "You can't have a more dangerous enemy than Lucian. It gets no worse than him."

I looked around. "I don't know. There are so many other dimensions, places I never knew existed until now. It might get worse than him, right?" I tried to be lighthearted, but there was no helping Jonah at that moment.

He was way too far gone.

"And to think," he murmured, "all this, even after our mother's long gone. He won't stop even now. For all I know, Lucian's the reason she's gone. Fane won't tell me anything about that."

"I'm sure it's too painful for him and he only wants to spare you the same pain. You can't blame him for that."

His expression hardened, and his eyes seemed to go dark. "No, I can't blame him for that. But I can blame him for forgetting about my mother and getting himself involved with that witch."

I gasped then paused to absorb and sort this out. "The witch? You mean, Sirene?"

His nod was grim. "Yeah. Her. The one carrying his baby." He might as well have been talking about garbage, he sounded so disgusted.

I covered my mouth with one hand to stifle another gasp, louder than the first one.

A baby?

"But she's... She can't!"

"No kidding," he growled. "A witch, and after he was with somebody like my mother. He really fell far, didn't he?"

I cringed. "I don't mean it that way. I mean she'll die. It will kill her."

"What?"

"Don't you know? A witch can't bear a vampire's baby. She'll die."

And she was so beautiful, too. How terrible. To think of her knowing the danger she was in, but carrying the baby anyway. Probably loving it more than herself. And the poor baby, never having its mother because she wouldn't live through the childbirth.

And Fane. What would it be like to know his baby killed its own mother? Would he feel guilty over it?

I wasn't sure what I expected from Jonah. Maybe sadness. Concern, at least.

Instead, his eyes turned hard. "Why should I care what happens to that witch?"

If he had hit me, I wouldn't have felt more surprised. Who was the stranger standing in front of me?

"How can you say that?" I whispered.

"Easily. What, you think I should care that my father—who hasn't been there for his kids in decades, in case you forgot—got a witch pregnant, and now she's going to die? He said it himself. He's different now. He's the sort of vampire who consorts with a witch. He's made his bed, and he can lie in it."

"But... the baby. It'll be your brother or sister, and it'll grow up without its mother. Doesn't that matter to you?"

"I've spent all these years without my mother. Am I supposed to feel sorry for *it*?"

He talked about his own sibling as a thing. He even sneered when he did it.

Nothing I said would get through to him.

That much was clear. He was determined to hold a grudge.

And it made me wonder about him. How well did we really know each other? I was so sure I understood what happened in his heart, wasn't I? So, who was I looking at? Could someone who loved me have so little compassion?

It was as if I didn't know him at all.

Maybe I didn't.

"Do you ever feel we never really got the time to get to know each other?" I asked.

He frowned. "Where did that come from?"

"I'm just wondering. We haven't had a whole lot of time to get to know each other well. It's easy to feel we're deeply connected when everything around us is so crazy. Isn't it?"

"Sure. I guess so. I keep wishing for the time to simply be us, if that's what you're talking about."

"It is, in part." I lowered my gaze to the ground—or, rather, the fog swirling around my legs. "I'm not sure what I mean, I guess. It's not easy to say."

How could I tell him I didn't know how I felt about him anymore? I didn't want to look at him. He'd shown me a side I didn't want to see again. Where was the kind Jonah I fell in love with?

"What's the rest of it?"

At least he didn't sound hateful or cold anymore. That was a plus.

I willed myself to lift my head and meet his eyes. "I'm sorry. You don't know how hard it is for me to say this. It's just... I don't know about us right now."

His eyes widened. "You can't be serious. Since when? Is it because of the whole Fane thing?"

"It's bigger than that. I don't know you. I don't know what to think right now." It had been too much of a tornado of emotions, accusations, and now his coldness.

I took a step back, then another.

"Where do you think you're going? You're not leaving, are you?"

"No, no. I just..." I wrapped my arms around myself to keep from shaking. I didn't want us to be over, not when I didn't know how I could survive without him. He was the best thing that ever happened to me. Only I wasn't sure I liked him very much.

"I can't believe this," he murmured. "You can't mean it. You're—"

"I'm not saying I want us to be over. I'm only telling you I'm not sure what's going to happen to us after this. Maybe we need more time to get to know each other, I don't know. I feel different all of a sudden, and I thought you should know. I'll still go with you to be of any help I can. I won't desert you now. But once this is over, I'm going to see my mother. And I'm taking Sara with me. I'm sure they'll want to see each other, too. I'm letting you know, so you're aware of my intentions."

He opened his mouth then closed it.

The look on his face was enough to rip my heart apart. I wanted to take it all back, beg him to forgive me.

I hated to think I'd hurt him, especially when he was already going through so much.

He surprised me then. "If that's the way you think it has to be, I won't beg."

And just like that, everything was different.

❧ 18 ❧

ANISSA

The air between us felt colder, somehow. I wished we had found a better time to talk things out—we were about to go into something neither of us had a clue about, and I had made things weird.

Allonic cleared his throat loudly before turning the corner and revealing himself to us. "Fane wants to speak to everyone before we move on."

Jonah made a strained sort of choking sound, like a cross between a snort and an exasperated sigh.

I didn't bother glancing back at him.

They were waiting for us, grouped together at the gate to the mausoleum.

Philippa's eyes were cold, full of judgment and accusation. All I felt when I looked at her was fatigue—I was so tired of fighting. What would she think of what just happened between me and her brother? Every marching band in the city would have to clear their schedule to perform in the parade she'd throw.

Fane waited until we were gathered together. He scanned us all with a critical eye, his gaze lingering on his children before he spoke. "There's no reason to sugarcoat this. What we're about to go into... it's dangerous. We have no idea what we'll find, or who. We'll have to be on guard at all times. We'll have to keep our eyes open, as well as having each other's backs. We have to protect each other once we start moving."

He regarded his kids again. "It's important for us to work together. As a family."

"How can you say that?" Jonah asked. "You tell us you're gone —the man who was our father, I mean—but then you tell us we have to work together. Which is it?"

"Right now, we have to be as united as possible. This isn't the time for bringing up hurts and slights."

"That's not fair," Philippa said. "Please, don't belittle what we've been through."

He nodded slowly. "You're right, of course. The reason I brought you all together like this before we got started was answer a few of the questions you have. I want to remove as much of what stands between us as possible."

"What about our mother?" Gage sounded stronger than he had since he first showed up on the roof.

Philippa nodded. "Yeah. What happened to her?"

The pain etched on his face was very real.

I remembered what Jonah had just told me about the love between his parents, and what it had meant to them. Elena had turned Dommik so they could be together, instead of running away in shame the way Lucian had expected her to do. They had loved each other enough to build a life together and have children and walk into an entirely new life side by side.

"All I can tell you is she didn't make it. I know you want to know more, and I wish I could tell you—believe me, I do. Only it's not something you want to hear. Trust me. And it's not something I feel I can share. That's the most I can say."

He stared at them as though offering a challenge. Would any of them dare press him on it?

I studied them out of the corner of my eye and could tell they were torn between needing more and wanting to stay out of a fight. They might even have been trying to respect his wishes.

When none of them spoke up, he went on. "It's been many years since I lost your mother. I've always carried her memory with me, and I always will. She was the center of my world for a long time, and I'm sure nobody gets the chance to find love like that more than once. That sort of instant, soul-encompassing love."

He glanced at Sirene, and I realized where he was going. I peered up Jonah, standing on my right. His face was a mask of pain and anger. Was this the best time for Fane to announce an addition to the family? I wasn't sure. Not if he really wanted his family to feel united.

"However," he murmured, "someone else has come into my life, and you deserve to know about her."

Philippa gaped openly. "Her?" She pointed to Sirene.

"Yes," he said. "Sirene."

"Tell them the rest," Jonah muttered through clenched teeth. "They should know everything."

"What?" Philippa asked, looking from Jonah to Fane. "What's he talking about?"

Sirene nodded with a sweet, gentle smile, and my heart ached for her. She had to know what was in store for her.

Fane appeared pained but managed to keep his composure. "Sirene is carrying my child."

Philippa let out a strangled sound I had never heard from her before. I couldn't tell if she was upset for the same reasons Jonah was. Was it disgust? Heartache for her lost mother's memory? Knowing Sirene wouldn't live through it? All three?

Gage, on the other hand, didn't make a sound. He only frowned.

I wondered what he was thinking. Did he feel the way Jonah felt? Meanwhile, I could almost see waves of emotion radiating from Jonah. He didn't know how to feel, I realized. He couldn't be on his father's side for fear of betraying Elena's memory. Once he had time to absorb the news and process it without the rest of the world falling in around us, he would do the right thing.

I reached out and took his hand in mine. I still loved him. I couldn't help feeling for him. He glanced down at our hands, clasped together, but didn't say a word. He didn't let go, either.

Fane cleared his throat. "I'm going with you because I want to know what the brands mean. I need to know what's happening to my sons."

Jonah shifted from one foot to the other, as though uncomfortable.

Fane continued, "I want to be there to free you from any danger the brands might mean, too. I have skills which might come in handy."

"And then?" Philippa didn't sound like the petulant party girl anymore.

"And then, we'll come back. I'll go to the penthouse to see

Scott—I have to see him at least once—but after that, I'm gone. This time, it has to be forever. We don't have a choice."

"We don't have a say in whether or not we can see you again?" Gage asked.

Fane practically snarled. "What about this don't you understand? I know you want us to be together again, but it's impossible. Things have changed. I didn't want it to be this way, but sometimes things have to be the way they are for a reason. It wasn't in our control whether or not we could stay with you kids, and this isn't in my control, either. All I can do is keep you safe for as long as I can. Let me do that."

"This this about Lucian?" Philippa asked.

All eyes fell on her, including mine. How did she know?

"Yes. If he knows you know Fane—and Fane is me—there's no telling what will happen. He's the most dangerous vampire in our world, at least when it comes to our family. He'll stop at nothing to make me pay for what happened a very long time ago."

"Haven't you paid enough?" Philippa's eyes filled with tears.

"I'll never pay enough for him. It will never end." He stared at the three of them. "I'm sorry. This has nothing to do with you, but he's making you pay, too."

"We can handle it," Gage said.

Fane smiled a little. "Yes, it looks like you've handled it well so far." He gestured to the scars on his Gage's chest. "I won't let that happen again. You won't have to pay the price for what I did anymore. You'll all have to go on like you never saw me once we return from Sorrowswatch. That means telling no one you know about me."

Philippa glanced at me. "No one?" I glared at her until I realized it wasn't me she was talking about. She seemed nervous, distracted.

"No one. It's unfortunate that so many others have found out about me already, but there's nothing we can do now."

Philippa chewed her lip over her father's words. What was she so edgy over?

"Understand, that this isn't the way I want things to be, but it's a way to keep Lucian from you. And to keep him from getting any closer to me."

Philippa shook her head. "But, Fath— I mean, Fane. He's already close to you. You're in more trouble than you know."

❧ 19 ❧

ANISSA

"What's that supposed to mean?" Jonah asked. "What are you holding back?"

Philippa didn't look at him. She only had eyes for her father. "I've been meaning to tell you."

"Tell me what?" Fane asked.

"Lucian has a Special Ops team with one mission. They have to find you... and kill you when they do." She seemed to almost crumble under the unspoken pressure from her brothers.

Their eyes practically bored holes into her.

She sucked air in. "They're close, or they were from what I last heard."

"How do you know about this?" Gage asked.

"It doesn't matter."

"It does," Jonah said. "How can you say it doesn't? I mean, do you know whether your contact knows what they're talking about? Can you trust them? Why would they even tell you?"

"Stop questioning me," she warned before crossing her arms over herself. "I can't tell you, all right? But yes, my contact is reliable. They wouldn't lie to me. They don't know who Fane is to me, and that's the only reason they shared information." There was still an edge to her voice, as always. Like she dared any of them to try to get more out of her. But under that pointedness, there was something else.

I wondered if I was the only one who heard it. A vulnerability. Softness. I remembered the way she was when we first met. The ultimate party girl. All sharp edges. Defiant.

There was an intensity to her that hadn't been there before, too. Like the attack on the roof—I was sure she'd thought about ripping my throat out before. Her animosity had been barely concealed. But she hadn't gone through with it until then. Claws around my neck. Eyes that spat fire. She'd wanted to kill me. Nothing less.

What happened to her?

Fane held up his hands to quiet his sons, who hadn't stopped asking questions even though Philippa had told them to. "Enough. Don't worry about the Special Ops team. They're nothing."

"Are you sure?" Jonah asked. "You want us to believe Lucian's Special Ops team isn't a threat?"

"This isn't the first time somebody's tried to find me. I've always managed to stay safe before now. Staying out of sight is something I've become pretty good at." He glanced at Sirene, who'd been standing off to the side the whole time.

She smiled.

"We've worked hard at keeping him out of sight," she said. "That's why we're here right now. No one can access this realm, since they can't use witch passages."

"All I have to do is get back here and know you all will stick to the story that you've never seen me. Not since I first disappeared."

"We'll do everything we can," Sirene confirmed. "You don't have to worry."

I could tell from the expressions on the Bourke faces this wasn't enough to convince them. It was easy to feel sorry for Sirene—she was only doing her best to work as a member of the team, but the three of them weren't impressed because of Fane's relationship with her.

Allonic cleared his throat. "I don't want to intrude, but..."

Fane looked relieved for the interruption. "You're right. We need to move out. Are you ready?"

My brother turned to Sirene, who nodded. The two of them stood together.

"You can't do this alone?" Gage asked.

"No. It takes more than my powers alone," Sirene explained as she raised her arms.

When she did, I caught sight of the swell of her belly under her robes. My heart ached for her. How much longer did she have? Was she afraid? It didn't appear that way. She seemed calm, even happy. She was clearly concerned for Fane and the rest of us, maybe—which only made my stomach turn when I remembered how cold Jonah had been earlier. He didn't care about her, the baby, or anything that related to her.

Allonic raised his arms, too, and the two of them closed their eyes.

I was sure none of us breathed as we watched.

There was a feeling in the air, something different. It stirred for the first time since I'd arrived here and felt cool against my skin. A point of light appeared in the air in front of where the two of them stood and slowly grew. It was hypnotic.

I watched with awe as it swirled and danced. The extreme darkness all around it only made it seem brighter.

Fane took a step forward. "Sirene can only hold it by herself for a few moments, so Allonic will be the last to go through. Let's hurry. We'll need him to conserve as much strength as possible."

Jonah nudged me forward.

I looked back at Sirene before stepping through. I felt sorry for the little half-blood baby growing inside her. Life was difficult enough for a half-blood vampire, but to grow up without a mother's protection? I'd never forget those early days after we were sure our mother had died in the Fire. We'd been so scared and alone, and nobody wanted anything to do with us because of Mom's relationship with my father. I didn't know that at the time, which only made things worse. Why were the other members of our clan rejecting us? It wasn't our fault Mom died.

It shouldn't have surprised me Jonah was so disgusted by Fane and Sirene, since vampires hated mixed blood—except I'd thought he was different. I didn't think he would be so cruel.

When he said he didn't care about Sirene or her baby, I remembered the backs that had turned on me when I needed help the most.

"Go on," Jonah said, giving me a little push. We walked through together. I wondered if I would ever see Sirene again.

Then we were on the other side.

The first thing I noticed was the sound of running water, all around me. Over me, to the sides, everywhere. But the ground was dry.

"Get out of the way of the others," Jonah muttered as he pulled me off to the side. He was rougher than he needed to be. Still holding a grudge, I guessed. Two could play at that game. I yanked my arm out of his grip and ignored him as I turned to examine the walls. They were cold, solid, and very smooth. Immediately, it reminded me of the underground system of tunnels Allonic and Steward called home.

"So dark," Philippa whispered when she came through.

So dark... So dark... So dark... Her voice echoed over and over until it mingled with the sound of moving water.

"I wonder how old this is," I whispered. I ran my hands over the walls and couldn't feel evidence of any tools having been used to carve the tunnel.

"Ancient." Fane appeared behind me. "Many thousands of years."

"How far do they run?" Gage asked. I could just make out the shape of him in the dark—even with our enhanced vision, it wasn't easy to see.

"All over England." That was Allonic. He leaned against the wall to catch his breath.

I touched his shoulder. "How are you? You didn't tire yourself out too much, did you?"

"I don't think so." His eyes glowed. "It's been many years since I had to throw such a complex portal. I enjoy a challenge."

I smiled. "You did a good job." I leaned closer. "Do you think Sirene will be all right back there?"

He nodded. "She has a lot of support. Unlike vampires, witches don't leave each other alone in situations like this."

I hoped the baby would find a home with them, then, since it didn't seem likely the vampires would care very much.

Jonah and Gage winced and groaned in unison, and the sound of their pain echoed around me until I couldn't hear anything else.

Fane went to them. "The brands hurt more now that we're closer, don't they?"

"You could say that," Jonah replied. His teeth were gritted, his voice tight.

Allonic stood up straight. "We have to move. And I'm sorry,

but the pain will only intensify the closer we get to where Valerius is waiting."

"Wonderful. I can't wait."

Philippa took Gage's hand and leaned against his arm for a second. She was more affectionate than she used to be, too.

I guessed almost losing her brother made her appreciate him a little more.

We started walking down the endless tunnel, and, as we went, I looked from side to side and saw more offshoot tunnels than I could count. They must have stretched all over the country. How Allonic knew where we were going was a mystery to me, but we had to be headed in the right direction since, as hard as Jonah tried to hide his pain, I could just make out the sound of him drawing in sharp breaths.

"Are we walking under water?" I wondered out loud.

"There are rivers and streams all throughout the countryside. They're all around us, even in the areas where humans built over the natural landscape." Fane made a derisive noise. "They insist on ruining everything that's natural."

"You never seemed to mind the city very much," Philippa reminded him. "In fact, you used to love standing on the roof, looking out over the skyline."

"And?"

"Do you think those buildings always existed?" She was teasing him.

I could hardly believe it, until I heard him snicker. It was the first real, comfortable moment I had witnessed between them. I wondered if that was the way they were together before he disappeared. I never had that sort of relationship with a father— the thought of joking with Gregor was almost enough to make me laugh, it was so absurd.

It had been the same with Sara's father, too. He was always good to me, but we weren't friends. I envied Philippa for having that and understood why she'd miss it.

We trekked for what had to be miles. I wasn't used to traveling at normal speeds for such a long time—we coursed for a good reason. This walking was exhaustive.

But Allonic couldn't course, and the rest of us weren't sure where we were going. We needed him to guide us. There were a lot of twists and turns, rights and lefts we took at what felt like random intervals.

Allonic called out directions as though he'd been there a million times, totally sure of himself.

Still, it was exhausting, and the pain was taking a toll on Jonah and Gage.

Jonah started stumbling a little, as though he couldn't concentrate on putting one foot in front of the other when he had other things to think about.

I took his arm when it seemed he couldn't keep going anymore.

"Let me." Fane took my place and helped Jonah keep moving.

I stepped aside and tried not to watch. It felt like I was invading their special moment.

Allonic was in front of me.

I fell in step beside him. "Why are we hiking all this way?"

"What would you suggest?"

"Getting a portal directly to Sorrowswatch instead of slogging on for hundreds of miles?"

"It hasn't been hundreds of miles. Besides, we can't portal directly. There are many layers of enchantments over Sorrowswatch. It's impossible to open a portal there."

Which probably meant we'd have to walk back out to where we started. I hoped Jonah would feel better after we finished, or else there was no way he'd make it.

Gage was in terrible shape, too.

We continued on, moving as fast as we could, considering two of us were in agony. I took comfort in the thought that the worse the pain, the closer we were.

Some comfort that was.

❦ 20 ❧

JONAH

The pain was almost blinding. If I could've cut my arm off to end the burning sensation, I would have. Except it was starting to spread throughout my body. Every step was agony.

"We're almost there," Fane muttered as he helped me stay on course. "Just hold on."

I could make out the shape of Anissa next to Allonic. She had tried to help me. She didn't hate me, not that I understood why she would, if she did.

I had not done anything to hurt her, had I? I couldn't think clearly, but even so, I couldn't remember anything. She was the last person I'd ever want to hurt. I went out of my way not to hurt her, although she always found a reason to be mad when I meant well.

I looked to my right, where Gage and Philippa walked together. I still had a hard time getting over what he'd done when he ran away, but at least he was feeling the same pain I was. That sort of made up for it. We could work the rest of it out somehow.

"Talk to me," I groaned as Fane helped me through the tunnel. "Tell me something. Anything. I need to stop thinking about how this damned brand burns."

"What do you want to hear about?"

"Anything. I don't care. Give me something to think about

other than this." I held up my arm, and that slight gesture was enough to make me grit my teeth.

"Your sister got me thinking about when your mother and I first came to the city," he said. "We could always see it across the river, you know. We watched it grow bigger and bigger. Sometimes, we'd go over if we needed something—parts for our farm machinery, that sort of thing. Neither of us really cared for the hustle and bustle. She was a farm girl at heart, and farm work was in my blood. I had grown up thinking people who lived all crammed together were insane. Why would you do that if you could live out in the open? Feeling the earth between my fingers, smelling the fresh air—especially right after the rain? That was the best." He sounded like his old self when he talked this way, animated and happy.

"Only, we couldn't once we turned." His voice went dark.

I wished he would keep talking about the farm if it meant he would sound happy again.

"We tried to live our normal lives, but there isn't much work a farmer can do when he can't go out in sunlight. Granted, by that time there wasn't much work I had to do on my own. We had hands to help with the grunt work, so to speak. But those hands needed supervision. They wanted to see me during the day, outside. That just wasn't possible. I'll never forget the first time I tried. You think you're in pain now?" His laugh was grim. "It was the same with your mother, too. Do you remember any of those days?"

I tried to think back. I only vaguely remembered life before moving to the city. "Gage and I used to chase the chickens around until Mom would just about lose her mind. She said we'd worry them so much they'd never lay eggs again. I remember being barefoot a lot of the summer, too. That was fun. We'd try to catch fish with our bare hands. Remember that, Gage?"

He snorted. "Remember the time you fell into the creek face-first when one slipped out of your hands?"

"That was closer than you ever got to catching one."

We both laughed a little. Those were good days. I'd always thought we were lucky to grow up where we did, when we did.

Fane chuckled. "It was difficult for me to take the four of you away from there and move to the city. We spent many nights talking straight through to the dawn. Of course, we didn't sleep anymore, so we could do that easily." He sighed. "We couldn't hunt freely, for one thing. News traveled fast. If there were people passing through the village, for instance, everyone knew about them. If they disappeared, everyone would know that, too. It was a struggle in those days. We knew everyone for miles around, and they knew us. We had to live someplace where it would be easier to hunt and get away with it."

"So, you moved across the river. I remember that. None of us understood why. I cried every night for a week," Philippa admitted.

"We knew you did, and we wished there was something we could do for you. But it was the only way. We trusted you'd understand one day. It wasn't only survival, either. We needed others like us. We couldn't survive on our own. There were things we needed to know. We needed support. The only way to find it was in Manhattan."

"How did you find others like you?" I asked. "I mean, it's not like you could go to the internet to find others with similar interests."

"We learned to look for certain traits. Pale skin, bright eyes. I'm sure you've noticed how we carry ourselves differently from humans, too. Over time, it was easier to recognize those like us. We found that, most of the time, they were happy to make connections, too. Many of them were unorganized, moving around on their own. I decided to band us together. One thing led to another, and, after a few years, we met the members of what's now the Bourke clan. When I took over leadership of the clan, it took our name."

"Did you ever regret turning? Becoming what you are today?" Philippa sounded a lot more subdued than usual.

"Never for a minute. If I hadn't, it would've meant saying goodbye to Elena. I couldn't do that. I didn't want the four of you to be away from her, either. We were a family."

Philippa let out a sort of choked cry, but we all pretended not to hear her. It was easier that way.

"Do you ever regret our decision to turn you?" Fane asked.

We were quiet for a long time, all three of us. When neither of the other two spoke up, I decided to.

"We were a family. If any of us had chosen not to turn, that person would've had to live without the others. I don't think any of us wanted that."

"And we didn't want to leave any of you behind," he agreed.

Suddenly, the pain broke. One second my arm burned the way it would as if Anissa's silver blade was pressed to it, then the next... nothing.

I stopped dead in my tracks.

"Gage?"

"You, too?" He was looking at me.

"What is it?" Allonic stopped short and turned to us.

"The pain's gone. Absolutely gone." I flexed my arm in amazement. It was enough to make me want to drop to my knees and thank whoever made it stop.

Allonic's eyes glowed like fire. "I had suspected that would be the case but didn't want to get your hopes up in case I was wrong."

"What happened? What changed?" Anissa asked him but stared at me.

"We've crossed the boundary and are now in Sorrowswatch. There was a chance the brand's spell would last until we reach the very spot where Valerius waits, of course. I couldn't be sure."

"It doesn't matter much to me either way," I admitted in relief. "I'm too glad it's over."

"Do you think we're very close now?" Fane asked.

Allonic nodded. "We'll have to be careful now. We could come upon the chamber at any point."

"Chamber?" Philippa asked as we set off again.

"I doubt he's waiting for us above the surface," Allonic said. "We could come upon him at any moment. Where we stand, this spot, is where the brand leads to."

I looked around and noticed the tunnel had widened. The ceiling was higher than before, too. "Is it lighter in here, or am I imagining things?"

"I thought so, too," Gage murmured.

We all moved with a lot more caution than we had before. Since I didn't need his help anymore, Fane took his place beside Allonic. He wouldn't let his kids go ahead of him. No matter what he said, I couldn't believe he wasn't still the same person he used to be.

Anissa fell back a bit, and I walked next to her. "You okay?" she whispered.

"Better than before." Which was an understatement.

Allonic stopped short with his arms spread.

We all paused behind him.

"What is it?" Fane asked.

"We've arrived," Allonic announced.

Glancing around, I didn't see anything different from what I'd seen all along. "Where?"

"Here. Straight ahead."

A rock wall stood before us, but Allonic stepped forward with his hands out and touched the stone. It seemed to dissolve under his hands.

"Holy hell," Philippa whispered.

Why any of us were surprised by anything like this anymore, I couldn't say.

I tried to see inside the chamber Allonic had revealed, but the opening was too small to allow a very good view. Anissa took my hand as we walked through the doorway, and I didn't let go. None of us knew what we would find on the other side.

There was more light in there, though I couldn't tell where it was coming from. The sound of water went away and left a sort of deafening silence in its place. An enchantment, I guessed. The chamber reminded me of a church I'd been to back when I was young, before turning. The ceiling stretched up beyond us, up and up. I never would've guessed it would be so large.

"Where are we? I mean, what is this place, really?" Anissa turned in a full circle, looking around.

Allonic shrugged, but I wasn't sure it meant he didn't know or didn't want to say.

Something along one wall caught my attention A huge glass box. The light reflected off it, so I couldn't see what was inside. It sat straight up, on its end, just like in those mummy movies.

"What is that?" I couldn't help but walk toward it. Something about it drew me closer.

Philippa and Gage followed me.

"Wait." Fane drew up behind me. "Don't make any fast moves. We don't know what we're dealing w—"

He went silent before he finished speaking.

I knew why.

I couldn't find any words.

None of us could.

It was a sarcophagus. There was a body inside. It had been decades since I last saw her, but I would've known her red hair and creamy-white skin anywhere. Not to mention the nose that was so like mine, and the light scattering of freckles Philippa had inherited.

"Mother?" Philippa breathed.

"Impossible," Fane murmured.

But she was there, in front of us.

We all saw her.

Then her eyes flew open.

❧ 21 ❧

JONAH

Philippa's scream was loud, echoing off the walls. "No! It's impossible!" she shrieked. She clawed at my side.

I put my arm around her. I could barely move or make any sense of it.

Gage rounded on Fane. "You said she was gone!"

"Because she is, son." He took Gage by the shoulders. "This has to be an illusion. Don't allow yourself to be taken in by it. Be strong. All of you!"

"Jonah?" Anissa's voice was barely a whisper.

I put my other arm around her.

"I don't understand. That's your mother?"

"If it's not her, maybe she has a twin none of us knew about."

Philippa, meanwhile, sobbed against my chest.

I couldn't blame her. It was unsettling, seeing somebody who looked just like her. But Fane was right. It couldn't be her, even though her eyes were so much like Mom's. Everything about her was.

The sarcophagus opened, and I jumped when *she*—I couldn't think of her as anything else—stepped out. She wore a long, flowing white gown that just brushed the floor and made her hair resemble fire.

"Who are you?" Fane asked. "I know you're not Elena. You can't be Elena. Who are you?"

She gazed at all of us with a blank, flat expression. "Please, do not raise your voice in this chamber."

The fact that it didn't sound at all like our mother was a relief. If she'd had the same warm, sweet voice of my mother, I might've lost my mind. I wouldn't have been able to take it. It would've been too cruel.

Philippa stared at the woman with our mother's face and body. "Who are you?"

"There is no time for that," Mom-not-Mom said. "We've been waiting a long time for you. I'm glad you're finally here."

We? She'd been alone in there, or so it seemed.

"Come. Follow me. Valerius awaits." She swept along the floor.

We didn't have a choice but to follow, and, at this point, I was too curious not to.

"You look like my wife, but you don't sound like her," Fane said as we walked. He still appeared horrified. For once, his steely exterior cracked a little.

When Allonic spoke, it was almost a surprise. He had been silent up to that point. "It's Nivia," he whispered.

She whirled on him, and the gown whirled with her. "Very good, shade." She stood in front of a small, stone door.

Nivia?

I glanced at Anissa, at my family. The same confusion was on all their faces.

"Come." She pushed the stone door open and stepped into a small room.

"But Nivia is dead," Allonic said as we followed her inside.

"Not exactly," she murmured. "I'm in this body now. I've needed it, in order to watch over my beloved."

"Your beloved?" Allonic asked.

Instead of answering, Nivia—whoever that was—raised an arm to motion to one corner of the room.

All of us turned to look.

A tangle of roots had overtaken the corner, filling it completely. Tree roots, thick and white, crisscrossing over each other, forming a sort of tomb.

In the center was a white-haired man.

He was old.

Ancient. His skin was as thin as paper, his cheeks sunken and gaunt. He didn't move. It didn't even look like he breathed.

He was in a state of living stillness—alive, but not alive.

"Valerius," Allonic announced.

Nivia nodded. "My love. My consort, now and forever. I have been keeping watch over him for longer than you've lived." Then her eyes landed on me and Gage. "You're here. Finally."

Fane stepped forward. He had shaken off the shock of seeing our mother again and had composed himself. "Why are you in my wife's body?"

Her thin shoulders rose in a shrug. "My soul needed a vessel, and this body was available." She raised her arms to the sides, flexing her fingers. "I could've done much worse."

"How did you do this?" Allonic asked.

"He arranged it." She looked at Valerius with an expression that could only mean love. Adoration, even. Complete devotion. "It was after I died and before he became trapped in this... this hell. Motionless, surrounded by roots."

How had that happened? And why? I glanced at Anissa to see how she was taking everything. Her expression was one of complete awe.

Nivia smiled at us. "I can't tell you how relieved I am you're finally here to free my love."

"That's why we're here?" Gage asked.

"How is that possible?" Fane's voice overlapped Gage's. "Why did Valerius brand my sons?"

She drew a deep breath. "I suppose it would be best to start at the beginning. You'll understand better then, why we've gone to these lengths."

She stared at Valerius again. "I was born a shade, many centuries ago. Valerius, on the other hand, was a member of the fae. We fell in love, even though we knew it was a terrible mistake for us to be together. There is no stopping true love, however. Neither of us could fight what our hearts wanted."

Her eyes went unfocused, like she was looking at something very far away. "When my father found out, his fury was other-worldly. He killed my love. My Valerius. I was certain I would die with him. There was nothing worth living for without him. Father didn't care. Our love disgusted him. Valerius did not deserve to live, and I barely deserved protection from my father anymore."

"And yet, Valerius lives," Allonic murmured.

"Yes, because I made a deal to bring him back," Nivia replied.

"I found a witch and a necromancer who were willing to barter. They brought him back to life—or, rather, a sort of life." Her expression darkened.

I had stopped thinking of her as my mother, but when she looked like that, I couldn't help but remember the way my mother would look when I was in trouble. It was uncanny.

"I didn't know the necromancer would turn my love into one of the undead. I had him back, but the creature he'd become was possessed of a severe bloodlust."

"A vampire." The words were heavy as they fell out of my mouth.

"Yes. The original Ancient." She shook her head sorrowfully. "I still wanted him, of course, even though I had no idea what to do with him once I realized what he was. It didn't matter, since his soul was still his. He still loved me. Enough that, when my father had me killed for bringing him back, Valerius used his powers to resurrect me, as well as created a cadre of vampires to attack the shades in revenge. Those vampires became the Ancients."

My head spun from everything she was sharing. I had always wondered who the original vampire was, how they had come about. How we had spread throughout the world.

"Once the war with the shades was over and I was safe, Valerius rarely created more vampires. They'd served their purpose. However, there were a few exceptions. One of them was—" She appeared ill. "Lucian."

Philippa went stiff.

Gage let out a growl.

Fane didn't move a muscle, but the tension in his frame gave him away.

"It was Lucian who put my love in this hell," she said, her voice deep with rage. "He weakened him by feeding him a victim whose blood was laced with silver flakes."

"Sick," Anissa whispered.

I agreed with her. Only a monster would even imagine something so twisted.

"He was in agony," Nivia mourned. "And weak. So weak. Too weak to fight back when Lucian then imprisoned him here. He couldn't dig his way out of his tomb. So many layers of roots, thick and strong. It's been hundreds of years since Valerius has fed. He's been starving all this time."

I couldn't imagine. When she'd used the word "hell," it hadn't been an exaggeration. Every moment of his life must've been hell.

"Where were you when this happened?" Allonic asked.

She closed her eyes. "I was in another body then, the body I'd taken over after I first died. Lucian locked me away, far away. There was nothing I could do. It took me ages to free myself. After that, I needed to find a new body. Which I did." She ran her hands over her sides and hips.

A twinge struck my heart. My mother's body. What happened to Mom?

"How are we supposed to help you?" I said instead of asking about my mother. "Why did Valerius bring us here?"

"The blood of true vampire twins carries indescribable power," she explained.

So Allonic had been right about that.

"That's it? He'll drink our blood?" It seemed a little too easy —not that letting an Ancient feed off me sounded easy.

"That's all."

"Why did you wait so long?" I asked. "We've been vampires for a very long time."

She nodded. "And it's been torture, waiting all these years. But the timing had to be just right. All pieces had to be in alignment."

What pieces? But I had the feeling that explanation would only lead us down yet another road full of more questions than answers.

"Why were we branded?"

"How else could Valerius be sure of your protection, while at the same time ensuring you could find your way here?" She shrugged like it made all the sense in the world—and, in a way, it did. I wondered why they'd had to hurt so damned much, but that was another story.

"What happens after he drinks our blood?"

Gage and I looked at each other. I could tell from his expression he wasn't a much bigger fan of the thought than I was.

Her smile was beatific. "He'll be restored. Valerius will return to me, as strong and powerful as he once was, and he will seek his revenge against Lucian."

"What about the other Ancients?" Fane asked. "You said

Valerius stopped creating vampires after the first group, but where did they go?"

"They're everywhere, all over the world," she replied. "Some choose to live in anonymity while others possess positions of power. But none of Valerius's other vampires sought out power the way Lucian did. It twisted and warped him."

She wasn't kidding.

He had wreaked havoc on so many lives, and I wondered how many we were unaware of.

Her gaze fell on Allonic, who returned her gaze. "You are a shade, the way I was born. At the same time, you are not. How is this so?"

"My father was a shade. My mother was—is—a vampire."

"And of what line was your father?" she asked.

"The Archein, the first line of the shades. I'm the son of Traxon."

"Traxon?" Her eyebrows shot up. "Does this mean you rule?" It surprised me she was aware of the name, being locked up in a sarcophagus as she'd been.

He shook his head. "Ressenden would never allow a half-blooded shade to rule. Only a pure-blood is allowed to do that."

"So, who does rule now?"

"A blood relative," Allonic said with a shrug.

I wondered why he was being so evasive.

"This is very nice," Fane interrupted, "but it's not getting us anywhere." He stalked over to her and stood face-to-face.

Philippa shuddered, seeing the two of them together.

When Nivia wasn't speaking, it was so easy to think of her as our mother.

"I want your assurance my sons will not be harmed when Valerius takes their blood. I want your assurance their blood is all he wants."

"Do not be alarmed. All he needs is their blood. Nothing more."

"What about his body?" he asked. "He's withered and decayed over the centuries. What will become of his body?"

"Oh, not to worry. I've already obtained a host body." Her tone was chilling. She lifted a hand to point to another corner of the room.

For the first time, I was aware of a body slumped there.

Chained to the wall.

🕯 22 🕯

PHILIPPA

I squinted to make out the body in the corner. There was enough light to make out the thick, heavy chains around the wrists and ankles. I could see arms, legs, and a head hanging low.

A dark head.

Then, slowly, the head lifted.

I blinked hard, stunned.

Then a shriek nearly tore me in two as I ran to Vance.

Jonah tried to hold me back, but I shook him off and fell to my knees.

"Vance! Oh, no! Not you!" I whirled on Nivia—the mirror image of my mother. "Let him go! Release him immediately! I will not allow this!"

"That's impossible," she replied in the voice that was so not like Mom's. "The chains are enchanted, so he cannot escape, and there is no way I'll release him. He's too important. I've already explained to you how important he is."

"No. This can't be happening." I looked at him again, sure my heart was breaking.

Not Vance.

I wouldn't watch him being forced into something against his will. Just seeing him looking so pathetic, chained to a wall, made me want to tear Nivia's throat out.

"Vance?" I reached for him. My hands ached to touch him. How could I ever have hated him? Was I insane?

He glanced around. When he laid eyes on Fane, they went wide with surprise. Then, he saw me.

I expected him to be happy to see me.

Instead, his eyes narrowed dangerously.

"You? You're with him? You did this to me!" His voice was weak, but there was enough power behind his words to chill me.

"No! I didn't do anything!"

"You're the only one I told about my mission. The only one. You never told me you were collaborating with Fane!" He almost spat his words at me.

"I didn't even know him yet! Vance, I swear, I didn't betray you. I would never do that. Please, believe me."

I would've done anything to make him understand, but the anger in his eyes told me my words fell on deaf ears. He didn't want to understand. I tried to put myself in his place—how would I feel if I were chained to a wall? Would I be reasonable?

"So, this was your contact?" Jonah asked. "This is how you knew?"

"You told them?" Vance asked.

Just when I thought he couldn't sound more disgusted with me, he did.

"I didn't mention your name, as Jonah said. I never told them how I knew. But, Vance—"

"Don't bother trying to explain. I have bigger problems right now."

"Enough." Nivia's voice cut through the air like a knife. "I've waited too long for this. Valerius has as well."

"No!" I jumped to my feet. "Don't do this!" I turned to Fane. "Please. Don't let her do this."

Meanwhile, Nivia produced a bronze goblet inlaid with jewels, along with an old knife. Its handle was heavy, carved ivory. "Send your sons forward."

"Sons?" Vance asked, but I brushed it off.

"Please, don't let her," I begged my father. "Please."

He hesitated then looked the boys. They glanced at each other, and only someone who knew them the way I did would have noticed the tiny nod they exchanged.

"No way," Gage said. "You can't make us do it."

"Maybe I can't," she said.

Suddenly, both of them doubled over in pain. Their faces contorted in agony—meanwhile, even from a distance, I could see the brands growing bigger.

Jonah yelled, and the veins on the side of his neck popped out as he went rigid all over.

Gage dropped to his knees, rocking back and forth, gripping his arm.

Anissa appeared stricken as she hovered over them. "Do something!" she shouted to no one in particular.

I knew how she felt for once. I was totally helpless.

"This can stop very easily." Nivia's words carried above the overlapping voices. "It doesn't have to be this way. You can make the pain end right now."

I glanced at the Ancient, asleep, almost too weak to breathe. But he still had the ability to put my brothers in agony.

How powerful would he be when he had his full strength?

"It's... killing me..." Jonah gasped.

Anissa turned toward Fane.

He was barely holding himself in check.

"Make it stop, please!" Gage begged.

I could just make out the sound of sizzling, and it turned my stomach.

"It can stop easily," Nivia almost shouted. "All you have to do is give me your blood."

Anissa bent over him. "Jonah, please. Give her what she wants!"

I didn't know what to think. They would use Vance. I looked down at him.

He was still furious with me, though what was going on around him shook him up. He grimaced when Gage screamed in agony.

It was a knife to my heart to hear him.

"All right! Please, make it stop." Jonah struggled to his feet and went to Nivia.

Gage did, too.

I knew it was the last thing they wanted to do, but they didn't have a choice. I watched as Jonah took the knife from Nivia's outstretched hand and sliced into his wrist.

Gage did the same.

They both held their wrists over the goblet. With the pain no longer an issue, they breathed easier.

"That's enough." Nivia's eyes were wide, and her nostrils flared as her chest heaved up and down. She had been waiting a long time to do this, and her excitement was obvious. I looked down at Vance again, and he stared up at me. I couldn't imagine what would happen to him.

Nivia raised her arms, along with the goblet, and chanted in a language I didn't understand. Maybe it was from back in the time when she and Valerius were what they were before.

We all watched, frozen.

Once the chant ended, she bent to put the edge of the goblet to Valerius's mouth.

I gasped when the glowing began.

It was almost blinding. It started at his mouth then ran over his face, down his neck, and through his body. His skin smoothed as his face filled out. He wasn't gaunt anymore, or even old. The centuries fell away, and he became a rugged young man—though his hair was still long and white—a fae trait.

Nivia let out a cry of joy.

"Whoa," Gage whispered, holding a cloth over his wrist to staunch the bleeding.

It wouldn't last long. We healed quickly.

Nivia bent to stroke Valerius's face. "My love. You've come back to me after all this time. Speak to me, please."

"I'm here."

Only the voice didn't come from the body in the roots. I jumped up, away from Vance, when I realized the rumbling voice had come from him.

It was like seeing Mom for the first time all over again. The body was Vance's, even though the face looked slightly different. The features were the same, but the way he held his head wasn't the same at all. He stood, and the shackles around his wrists and ankles released without his doing a thing.

"No," I whispered. "This isn't real. This is impossible!" Rage boiled over as I threw myself at Nivia. "Get him out of Vance's body! Now!"

Fane caught me and pulled me away just before I had the chance to sink my claws into her.

"Easy," he said. "Don't do something that will get you killed."

"But Vance!" I screamed. I struggled against his arms, but Fane was much stronger than me.

Nivia's expression didn't change. She didn't even flinch. "I can't remove my love from this human body until I bring together a witch and a necromancer to reverse the spell."

I collapsed against Fane. It was too much to handle, all of it. Like a nightmare for the first time in all the years I had been a vampire. If I could still sleep, I would swear it was a terrible dream.

"Do not lose sight of what is important," Nivia said. "The body I've chosen for Valerius is the perfect vessel for the tasks ahead of him. Do not worry. I don't care for this body at all." She went to him, running a hand over Vance's shoulder then down his arm.

Bile rose in my throat.

She smiled eerily. "I can be patient. So can Valerius."

Vance—no, Valerius—looked at her.

"I liked your old self better," he said in the unsettling voice that didn't belong to Vance but was coming from his mouth. "I don't know how I feel about this new body of yours."

"As long as it allows us to be together again, my love."

The two of them gazed adoringly at each other while the rest of us looked stunned, disgusted, or angry. An overwhelming aura of power surrounded them.

Fane's arms relaxed, and I broke free.

I ran to the old body, the one Valerius had been trapped in for so long. It was still surrounded by roots.

"Please, wake up!" I screamed. "Please, get out of Vance! Leave him alone! We'll get you out of here so you can use this body instead!" I pulled at the roots, thinking I could break them, but they were stronger than steel.

It didn't matter, anyway. He never flinched.

"He's not in there," Nivia called out. "Your words are wasted."

I turned to her with a snarl and flung myself at her. If I couldn't hurt Valerius, I would hurt her. Before I could reach her, she held up a hand, and a force like a shockwave hit me and knocked me to the floor.

"Fine! He can't stop me, can he?" I scrambled to my feet and went back to the unresponsive body. I would show her how it felt to watch somebody she loved getting hurt.

"You can't!" she cried out. "If you harm his body, his soul can never re-enter!"

That stopped me.

"You're lying," I spat, claws raised. I couldn't reach much, but I could reach his face if I needed to.

"Philippa, stop this. What if she's telling the truth?" Fane's voice was low and soothing.

He thought he could calm me down that way.

All he did was stop me. I was not calmed.

I couldn't hurt Vance, either, as much as I wanted to. Anything to get the Ancient out of him. Where was Vance in there? His soul had to still be inside. He had to be aware of what was happening. Just thinking about it was excruciating.

I stepped away from the roots. There was nothing I could do. I had to watch Vance being used.

It seemed Allonic didn't feel the same way. He pushed past me and attacked the root tomb.

I had no idea he was so strong—his hands tore at the roots around Valerius's throat and threw them in every direction.

"Stop that! What are you doing?" Nivia screeched when Allonic's fangs appeared.

He plunged his head down to meet Valerius's neck and started drinking.

Everything happened at once after that.

"No!" Vance roared. He clawed at Allonic, but couldn't pry him away. "Get away from my body!"

Nivia jumped on Allonic's back to help. "Get off him! Stop this!"

She and Vance attacked Allonic, who wouldn't let go no matter how hard she kicked and he clawed.

Gage and Jonah took hold of Vance, pried him away, and slammed him into the wall. He bounced back, hissing and snapping his jaws with his fangs extended.

Gage swung at him and made contact with his jaw while Jonah went for his midsection. Vance laughed and threw them away from him. They hit the floor but leaped to their feet and attacked again.

Vance flicked Gage from him like he'd flick a fly, but Jonah was stronger. He couldn't shake him, so he did something else.

Vance sank his fangs into Jonah's neck. Jonah slammed his fists into Vance's face and shoulders, but there was no freeing himself.

"No!" Anissa screamed. She ran, jumped, and landed on Vance's back.

I wondered for just a split second what she could do to someone so strong before she slid the silver blade from her boot and plunged it into his back.

Vance let go of Jonah, who slid unconscious to the floor.

"Get it out!" he shrieked, but he couldn't reach the blade—and even if he could, he couldn't touch the silver handle without it burning him.

I watched in horror as he started withering before my eyes—his face contorted into a mask of pain and horror, frozen that way, as a strange almost gray color started spreading over his skin.

"What's happening?" I realized he was petrifying, and it had something to do with the blade in his back.

I reached for it before I could stop myself and closed my hand over the handle. The metal seared my skin, making me scream, but I still tried to hold on. Except, I couldn't get a strong enough grip to pull the blade out. It was eating my skin away and not allowing me to keep a firm grasp on it.

"Help him!" I shrieked at her. "Get it out!"

She was on the floor with Jonah, cradling his head in her lap. He was still unconscious from the effects of being bled.

"Forget it! I don't care what happens to him!" She looked down at Jonah, stroking the hair back from his forehead.

"No, no!" I took Vance's face in my hands and wept as he turned to stone in front of me. Then I searched the room for Fane. "Make her help! Please!" I begged.

In that moment, he was my father, and I was his little girl, and I was begging for him to help me.

"What am I supposed to do?" He appeared completely out of his depth. "I can't make her do anything!"

Nivia's roar of rage and terror when she stopped fighting Allonic long enough to see what was happening with Vance split the air in two. "This must not be!" she roared. "If he dies, Valerius dies with him! Lucian will be unstoppable!"

Fane's eyes met mine then darted down to Anissa. "Take out the blade. Please."

I was surprised when he said please, but it got through to her.

She rested Jonah's head on the floor with a heavy sigh and did as he'd asked, pulling the blade out and dropping it to the floor with a look of disgust on her face before going back to Jonah.

His eyes opened, and he gazed up at her.

Nivia went back to Allonic, who was still crouched over Valerius. "You must stop. Please. Before it's too late!"

Allonic rose with blood dripping from his lips.

I wondered why he'd done it, but didn't have time to think much about it since the petrification was reversing and Vance started sliding to the floor.

I caught him and lowered him along with me, holding him tight. He was still in there somewhere. I knew it. I didn't want to let him go.

"Vance. Come back to me," I whispered as I stroked his face with the backs of my fingers. "Please. I need you. Come back."

His eyes flickered open. For just the splittest of split seconds, he was Vance again.

I knew him.

Then, his expression shifted.

"Nivia?" It was Valerius's voice.

I winced and looked away. He still wanted her.

My love, calling for my mother. No, not my mother—a creature who was using my mother's body.

I let him go.

Nivia didn't hear him.

Though Allonic had finished bleeding Valerius, she attacked him with claws bared.

He ducked her swinging arms and picked up the blade Anissa had dropped to the floor. With one swift motion, he plunged it into Nivia's chest.

"No!" Four of us screamed at once.

Seeing her... her body... getting stabbed... though it wasn't her, it was still her. Just as seeing Vance with the blade in his back had been too much to take.

Fane rushed to her and took her in his arms as her knees gave way. She scrambled to pull the blade out, but couldn't.

"Elena," Fane said. His body shook. He stroked her face the way I had just stroked Vance's.

Seeing them together, even the way they were, was like going back in time. I had wished with all my heart to see them again. But not quite like this... Still, it was something.

Jonah got up with Anissa's help. "She's not Elena. Remember that." He touched Fane's shoulder. "It's not our mother. It's not Elena."

"I know," he muttered. But he wouldn't let go of her as she sputtered and struggled.

I was so busy watching I hadn't noticed at first that Vance had gotten to his feet until he stumbled across the room. With a shredded piece of his shirt wrapped around his hand, he went straight to them and pulled the blade from Nivia's chest.

Then plunged it into Jonah's back without a word.

Fane let go of Nivia as he turned to Jonah.

Vance caught her and lifted her in his arms.

He was a blur as he coursed out of the chamber.

❧ 23 ❧

PHILIPPA

Anissa's horrified scream rang through the chamber.

Just the way Vance had, Jonah's body started to petrify. It must've had something to do with where the blade had slid home—I'd never seen anything like it happen before.

I struggled to my feet and went to him.

Anissa pulled the blade from him, but it was too late. He was already dying.

He dropped like a rock, frozen from the waist up.

Anissa's eyes were wild as she looked up at Allonic. "Help me!" she sobbed. "I can't let him die!"

"Give him your blood," he ordered. "Quickly!"

She reached into her boot for another blade and slid it across her wrist. Like magic, the thin red line pumped rich, red blood. She held it to his lips.

She was defying league law. We all knew it. None of us said a word about it. As if I was going to criticize her for trying to save my brother's life. Not a chance.

At first, he didn't move. The blood ran down his chin.

"Drink!" she urged. "Come on! Drink!"

His mouth moved. His throat worked. It was happening. He was drinking.

I let out a cry of relief as I watched—but then nothing changed. He was still immobile.

"Why isn't it working?" Gage asked.

"We have to do something else," Fane growled.

"Wait." Allonic held out his arms to block the rest of us from going to Jonah. "Just wait."

Slowly, slowly, he started coming back to us. His skin went back to its normal color. His face moved. His shoulders. His arms and hands.

I closed my eyes and leaned against Gage for a second.

The way he trembled showed me he was as overwrought as I was.

When I opened my eyes, I saw Jonah roll onto his side and start gagging. Thick, black blood poured from his mouth as he vomited. His entire body clenched as he expelled it. Once it subsided, he sat up and opened his eyes.

"Oh, Jonah." Anissa threw her arms around him, while the rest of us gathered close.

"Are you all right?" I asked. Fane helped him to his feet.

"I think so?" he murmured. "That was... different."

Anissa stepped back and took Allonic by the arm. "Why did you do that?" she whispered.

I was sure she thought none of us were paying attention, but I was.

"Do what?" he asked.

"Feed off Valerius. You don't need to do that to survive, the way I do. Why did you do it?"

Good question. It didn't seem to make a difference on the surface. It didn't change anything.

"Valerius's blood is concentrated, more powerful than any other vampire's."

"Right..." Anissa prompted.

"He's an Ancient, and a fae. That's a special combination, especially strong. And I'm descended from the Archein."

"Yes? And?"

I glanced at them.

Anissa's hands were on her hips as she glared at her brother.

He shook his head. "Now's not the time. We can talk about it later." He stared at me—he knew I was watching—and I shifted my gaze away.

They rejoined us.

As usual, I had more questions than answers.

I turned my attention back to Jonah, who was looking more like himself. "My brand is almost gone," he said, lifting his arm.

Gage did the same. They were barely visible anymore.

"Do you feel them?" Fane asked.

They shook their heads.

"I wonder if that's really all Valerius wanted from us," Gage muttered. "I feel like we got out of that too easily."

Jonah snorted. "Maybe *you* did."

"You know what I mean."

Fane broke in. "I have to wonder if sharing your blood with him tied you together somehow."

He glanced at Allonic, who shook his head.

"I don't know the full repercussions, especially when dealing with an Ancient—the original Ancient, at that. He probably knows enchantments none of us have ever heard of."

"I hope it's not the case," Fane said, but there was no hope in his voice.

I looked around at all of them. They were all forgetting one very important thing. "What about Vance?"

"What about him?" Fane asked.

The rest of them stared at me like I'd suddenly started speaking another language.

"Well... I mean, what do you think I mean? We have to go after him! We can't let Valerius inhabit his body that way! We need to go after him!"

"No, we don't," Fane said.

"We do! Somebody has to help him! I'll go by myself."

"No." Fane stood in front of the doorway, blocking me.

Allonic spoke up. "There's another way."

"Oh, what?" I whirled around with my arms crossed. "You didn't know what we were getting into when we got here, but now you're going to tell me what's going to happen in the future? That makes a lot of sense."

It didn't seem to faze him. "Valerius will come back for his body. When he does, Vance will be free."

"I don't understand. If he wants his old body, why did he take Vance?"

Allonic shrugged. "Who can say? Maybe a younger, stronger body would work better. Maybe Vance's body is specific to his goals."

"Maybe they know who he is to Lucian," Jonah mused. "They're using Vance to get closer to Lucian."

That made sense, at least. And I wanted to see Lucian pay for everything he'd done. That would take an eternity.

"What about my mother?" I asked Allonic. "Will Nivia leave her body? What happens when she does?"

"I don't know." He shrugged again, appearing sorry. "Since I don't know what happened to her, I can't say."

I thought back. The only thing Fane had ever said was that she was gone. Not that she was dead. Maybe something else had happened besides death?

He stayed silent on the matter. Instead, he said, "We should go. Who knows what else is down here?"

I looked back at Valerius, still entombed. "What about him? His body is unprotected now."

"So?"

Fane's tone surprised me.

"So? So somebody should protect it." Why was that not as obvious to him as it was to me?

Fane sneered. "Both he and Vance can rot in hell as far as I'm concerned." He sounded like he meant it, too. "We're leaving, right now."

"No. I'm staying with him." I went to the body. "I won't leave him here."

"Are you out of your mind?" He stared at me like he thought I was. So did the rest of them. "You can't stay here. I won't leave you so far away, alone. You must be kidding."

"I'm not."

His eyes hardened. "I forbid you to do this."

"Forbid?" I laughed. "Who are you to dictate policy to me now? You think you can walk back into my life, tell me you're not my father anymore, then tell me what to do? You don't get the right." I hardened my face to match his. "You don't lead the clan, and you don't lead me."

I didn't know what to expect from him—so when he rushed at me and took me by the wrists, the surprise gave him an advantage. I struggled, baring my fangs and hissing.

"Stop it, both of you!" Jonah's voice was strong, but it was only in the background of my mind.

I was too busy wishing I could hurt Fane the way he'd hurt me.

"Let go, damn you!"

But he wouldn't. He was too strong for me, no matter how I kicked at him. It didn't take long before I was exhausted, out of breath.

I stopped fighting.

"You're not staying here alone," he said again. "I won't leave you here unprotected, handling who knows what all by yourself. You are coming with us." He pulled me closer until we were eye-to-eye. "You don't have a choice in this, Philippa."

My chin trembled, and I cursed the way I cried whenever I felt as overwhelmed as I did just then. Crying was a sign of weakness, or I had always thought of it that way.

Only when I was as full of rage and helplessness and despair as I was at that moment, crying was the only thing I could do. "I can't leave him, Dad. What if Vance comes back for the body? What then?"

His expression softened a little, but his hands didn't release my wrists. "This is the way it has to be."

"Wait a minute." Jonah approached. "I think I have an idea."

"What is it?" I dared to hope.

"What if we take the body with us? We can keep it safe somewhere nearby instead of leaving it here. This way, if Vance comes back, we'll know."

"Where could we leave it?" I asked.

I looked at Fane.

"Not in Duskwood," he said.

"Oh, come on. I thought you said it was safe there. Don't let personal issues get in the way now."

He shook his head. "I can't say for sure that somebody or something won't get through when I'm not around."

"The only option we have is to take the body back home," Jonah decided.

"Sure. We'll leave him in the living room, in front of the fireplace," Gage muttered. "How about we mount him like a trophy?"

"I don't mean there," Jonah fired back.

"So where?"

He appeared guilty all of a sudden. "I have a vault."

My eyes widened. I glanced at Gage, who was just as surprised as I was. "A vault? Since when?"

"Since always. It doesn't matter." He faced Fane, who probably knew about the vault. The whole head of the clan thing. "We can leave him there. Nobody knows about it."

"Okay. That works. As long as he's not alone." I never thought I would care so much about the body of an Ancient I'd never met.

Everything hinged on him.

We went to the roots, which had been impossible for me to tear up earlier. But Allonic had managed to rip some of them out, and that seemed to weaken them.

We worked together to free the body then Fane lifted it.

"He weighs next to nothing," he murmured, slinging Valerius over his back. "Let's go."

We retraced our steps through the tunnels and through the portals, all leading to the rooftop outside the penthouse.

By the time I stepped through, I was sure I had never been more exhausted in all my long life.

And I couldn't stop thinking about Vance.

Where was he?

What would he do?

24

JONAH

H ome had never looked so good.
We stumbled into the penthouse without checking first whether Scott was there. I guessed he was out somewhere, doing clan business. The place was empty, the fireplace dark and cold.

Fane lowered Valerius into an overstuffed chair then stretched. He'd been carrying the body for hours.

"I need to get back," he said with a grimace as he rolled his head on his neck. "I can't stay around here. You remember what I told you."

"What about Scott?" Gage asked. "You said you were going to meet up with him."

"I also said I can't let anyone see me with you."

"Can you wait a little while?" Philippa asked.

She appeared completely worn out, physically and emotionally. There were dark circles under her eyes.

I had no idea she still cared so much about Vance. They'd been over for ages. But the way she'd attacked Nivia and fought Fane to stay in Sorrowswatch told a different story.

"I can't." Fane glanced around, saw how disappointed that made us, and he melted a little. "Maybe I can come back when you have Scott with you, and we can all go to Duskwood. It's safer there. But I need to go, right now."

"How will we know how to reach out to you?" I asked as he walked to the doors leading outside.

"Don't worry. I'll find you." With that, he was gone. I looked at my brother and sister, and it was clear we were all wrung out. Seeing our mother... and the way he held her...

"I should go, too." Anissa's voice behind me was a surprise. For a second, I almost forgot she was there. "And I'll take my sister with me."

That got Philippa's attention. She seemed happier than I had seen her in a long time.

"She's probably with Scott," I reminded her.

"Yeah. I know. I'm sure they haven't gone far. When I tell her our mother's waiting, she'll come with me."

I left Philippa and the others to look after Valerius while I pulled Anissa aside. "Are you sure you want to go alone?"

"I won't be alone. I'll have Allonic with me. He proved himself back there, didn't he?" She looked impressed, proud. Maybe a little concerned, too.

"Are you all right?"

She nodded. "Yeah, I'm fine. Maybe I just need a break from all the excitement, too. I mean, it's been a lot."

"Tell me about it." I could still remember the sensation of turning to stone while the silver infected my blood. I still wasn't sure what Vance did to me with that blade, but I never wanted to feel it again.

"Are you all right?" she asked. "I mean, are you feeling yourself?"

"As much as I can be, I guess. I wish I could sleep."

"Me, too," she smiled. "I would sleep for days. But we can rest. You should. Get your strength back, regroup. We'll all get through this."

She took a step back, away from me. I grabbed her hand to hold her in place. "Hey. Wait a second. I have something else to say."

"What is it? I think your sister is in a hurry to get Valerius to the vault." Sure enough, Philippa was pacing the floor, biting her nails. She would have to wait a minute.

"I wanted to apologize for not telling you about Fane—my father. I'm sorry. I didn't know you would take it that way."

"I know you didn't," she murmured. Emotion washed over her face, but she didn't say anything else.

"Are you still, you know..." I trailed off because I didn't want to say it out loud.

"Unsure about us?"

"Yeah." It broke my heart to think it.

She nodded.

"But what about everything that happened back there, in Sorrowswatch?" I remembered being in her arms. I remembered her screaming for help when Vance stabbed me.

She didn't sound like a girl who didn't have feelings anymore.

"I haven't stopped caring about you," she whispered. "I never will. I just don't know if you and I are what I thought we were. So much has happened. I need time to think, you know?"

I couldn't deny how much it hurt, so I didn't bother. "I understand."

It was all I could say, although it didn't seem to scratch the surface of what I was going through. How was I supposed to be without her? It felt like couldn't remember a time when she wasn't in my life, even when I had lived for decades before we met.

"Be careful with yourself, okay?" She reached up to touch my face.

I told myself to remember how it felt, in case she never came back. I couldn't believe she wouldn't, but there was always a chance she would decide we didn't have a future.

"You, too."

Allonic joined us. "We should go."

She was right, he had proved himself—but I still I wondered why he'd fed from Valerius. It didn't seem to do anything to help us, and he appeared the same. Valerius's body, on the other hand, looked almost as feeble as it had before Nivia gave him our blood.

"There's only one thing," he said. "I can't go through the building to leave, but we can't port without Sara."

"Oh. Right." She chewed her lip, frowning.

"I can show you a back way to leave through," I offered.

"I still don't think it's safe for me to go through the high-rise —I don't mean any offense," Allonic said.

"None taken."

He looked at Anissa. "I'll find you when you have our sister. We'll portal out then." Allonic nodded to me, as though bidding me farewell.

"Take care of her," I said.

"I will." He went out to the roof, and I just made out the flash of a portal before the light went out.

He was gone, too.

She looked as resolved as ever, so even though I wished she'd change her mind, I led her out to the hall and to the back stairwell.

"It's a lot of stairs to the ground floor, but it's better than getting spotted alone on the elevator. Nobody takes the stairs."

"Thanks. I'll go look for Sara in her room... or Scott's first." She gave me a half-hearted smile. "See you soon."

"I hope so." I watched her disappear through the door and felt like I was losing part of myself. It took all my self-control to keep from following her. How could I survive not knowing whether or not she was all right?

The sound of a throat clearing, and a hand on my elbow shook me out of it, and back to reality.

I still had issues to take care of.

Philippa was standing behind me. "We need to get to the vault. What happens if Scott comes and finds him?"

"Right, of course."

We went into the penthouse. Valerius was still in the chair, sitting upright. He might as well have been dead. He barely breathed and didn't move at all.

I lifted him with Gage's help while Philippa kept a lookout in the hall. She gave the all-clear, and we carried the body out to the elevator. Philippa inserted her key into the lock above the panel, turning it into a private elevator. It removed the chance any curious clan members would come across us.

"Where to?" she asked.

"The sub-basement." I hadn't been down to the vault in a long time.

Years.

"How come you didn't tell us you have a vault?" Gage asked.

Maybe because I never trusted you. "Dad told me not to tell anybody, not even family members."

It was tough, working alongside Gage, and remembering all the grief he gave me for so long over wanting to lead the clan. There was still just the slightest bit of resentment in his eyes, too. I was used to that.

"Why is there a vault in the first place?" Philippa asked.

"In case there's something that needs hiding. You know. Like the body of an Ancient." I left it there.

Fact was, I didn't know why we had a vault. I had never used it, even though Dad had more than once. We had lived in relative peace for so long, I hadn't worried about it.

The sub-basement was dark except for the few utility lights strung up at intervals along the hall. It was dank down here, cold, and it reminded me of the tunnels leading to Sorrowswatch.

Only I knew where we were going, and, instead of running water, the buzz of generators filled the air.

The door leading to the vault looked like any of the other metal utility doors on that floor. I used my key and swung it open.

"It's... just a room." Philippa stepped inside what resembled a mostly empty supply closet.

I went around her and pushed in on the specific cinderblock which sprung the lock and opened the hidden door behind a set of metal shelves.

"Help me move these."

We pushed the shelves aside then I opened the inside door.

"Nobody would ever find this," Gage marveled as he walked in, still holding Valerius across his arms.

"It's perfect," Philippa agreed.

I felt the same way. "And now you'll know he's safe."

Gage lowered Valerius into one corner. "We can always try to make him comfortable, too. Maybe bring down some pillows, blankets. Whatever you think he'd need."

I could see why Gage was coddling our sister like he was.

She had a sort of crazy glint in her eye, like she was obsessed with looking after him.

I could sort of understand why, even though I still didn't get the whole Vance thing.

"When did the two of you..." I glanced and Gage, and he shrugged.

So he didn't have a clue how to approach Philippa, either.

I continued, "When did you get back together?"

"We didn't," she whispered. "I don't know that we ever would. But that doesn't change how I feel."

"I'm really sorry." I folded my arms around her, from behind her, as she stood there, watching Valerius. Watching for what? I had no idea. He wasn't going anywhere.

"It'll be okay. Vance will come back for the body. I know he will. He has to." It sounded like she was trying to convince herself, not me.

"I'm sure he will." I wasn't sure of any such thing, but I had to say something; she needed encouragement.

"Come on," Gage said. "We don't want to run the risk of anybody randomly showing up down here."

"Nobody ever comes down here," she whispered.

"Yeah, well, there's a first time for everything." I let go of her. "Come on. I can't wait to take a shower."

Everything else would have to wait a while, even the stuff with Gage.

"And when Scott shows up later, without Sara, after Anissa finds her, we'll have to catch him up on some of this," Gage reminded us.

We walked out together, and I turned to wait for Philippa to come out, too.

She didn't.

"Philippa? Come on."

Gage and I glanced at each other.

A sneaking suspicion started growing in my chest.

She shook her head. "I can't."

I nearly groaned in frustration.

She was clearly determined to keep me out of the shower. All I wanted was a shower. And maybe to lock myself in my room for a year.

"What are you saying? We can talk it out upstairs. This isn't the place for you to hang out, you know? Come on. You'll feel better once we're home."

She shook her head again and didn't turn toward us. "No. I can't leave him. Not for anything." She went to him and sat on the floor with her back to the wall. "I won't leave as long as he's here."

"Now what?" Gage asked.

I shrugged. "I wish I knew."

❦ 25 ❦

JONAH

The club was on fire. Not literally, but almost. I didn't think I had ever seen it so packed, so full of energy. And why not? We had Gage back, and everybody knew it, so everybody in the clan wanted to party like they were the ones who'd personally rescued him and brought him home. Far be it from me to stop them.

That didn't mean I had to join them, though.

While the rest of the clan's members danced and thrashed around under swirling, multicolored lights, my siblings and I sat on the deck. It was cooler out there, the air fresher. And we didn't have to scream to be heard. The conversation we were having wasn't exactly the kind we could scream in public, so taking it to a private corner was for the best.

Philippa's eyes swept back and forth under lowered lashes. She thought we didn't know how desperate she was to get away from us, but she was wrong.

"Philippa, relax," I murmur, touching her bare arm. She flinched as though I'd burned her, so I pulled my hand away.

"That's easy for you to say," she muttered darkly.

"Come on. Jonah's right." Gage slid an arm around her shoulders, and this time she didn't act like she was repulsed or in pain. "It's bad enough we had to talk you into coming out, but you can't act like this. Somebody's going to notice and know something's wrong."

"Something is wrong," she reminded him then turned to me. "If I asked you to leave your precious Anissa behind—"

I held up a hand to stop her. "Don't go there," I warned.

"Well? Isn't that the truth? You would never leave her in some dark, cold vault where she couldn't protect herself."

"But Philippa, you know nobody can get in there but us. Nobody knows it exists but us, and nobody except for me and D — Fane know the access code. And now you know it, too. But that's all. He's as safe as he would be anyplace else. Safer, even."

"You can't sit in there with him forever," Gage reminded her in a quiet voice. He always could get through to her better than I could. "You would waste away, and we won't let that happen."

"You don't know how this feels," she whispered.

"You're right," I said, and I tried hard to make my voice like Gage's. "What's happened lately… I can't wrap my head around half of it. And just when I think I have things under control, something else happens and I question everything I thought I knew all over again. It's insane. I'm exhausted," I admitted.

"Me, too," Gage said. "But we're all together now, and we always work better as a team. We'll look back on this one day, and we'll laugh about it."

I met his eyes, and he shrugged.

Sometimes, he could lay it on really thick. But it was the sort of thing Philippa needed to hear. She visibly relaxed, which helped me relax a little. But only a little.

"Shh," she said, shaking Gage's arm off. "He's coming back."

The three of us pretended to be talking about something else, anything else, as Scott returned to the round table the three of us sat at.

I hated lying to him, even lying by omission, but he didn't know yet about Fane.

We couldn't even use his help in keeping Philippa out of the vault, where Valerius's body still rested, because it would've meant going into the whole story about where we got him and what happened before and after that—eventually, all roads led to Fane.

I still had to work at it to stop thinking about him as our father.

I exchanged a glance with Philippa and Gage as Scott sat down. They agreed it was best for Fane to announce his presence personally. It just wouldn't be the same coming from one of us, or all three of us. I hoped Fane didn't take his time about it, was all.

The more time went by, the more lying we had to do.

And the worse I felt.

He looked miserable as he sank into his chair with an ungraceful thud, tossing his phone onto the table in disgust.

I glanced around, and guessed it was my turn to ask, "What's up?"

His mouth was drawn into a thin line, and worry lines creased his forehead. "She's not answering her phone."

"Sara?"

He stared at me like it was stupid to ask. "Yeah. It's not turned off, but it keeps going to voicemail."

"I wouldn't worry about it too much," Gage offered.

"You don't know her," Scott reminded him.

Philippa made a sort of strangled noise like she was trying to hold something back, but couldn't quite manage it.

I rolled my eyes at her, but she didn't react. It was obvious she'd never liked Sara, but she'd been more negative toward her than usual over the last few days.

I couldn't figure out why, and she wasn't telling. I wondered if she would ever get over her hatred of Anissa and her sister, then doubted it. I had known my sister long enough to know she didn't get over things easily. If ever.

I turned back to Scott. "You know, Anissa was looking for her. I bet they're together someplace and she just can't get to her phone. I wouldn't worry too much about Sara—Anissa would never let anything happen to her."

Again, I couldn't be completely honest with him, and it killed me. I was no good at keeping secrets from my siblings. I could keep information to myself if it was for the good of the clan, I had been doing it for decades, but lying to my brother was something else.

It would be as simple as telling him Anissa wanted to take Sara to see their mother for the first time since the Great Fire. But I couldn't because too many other random bits of information were tied up with that. He had missed so much.

He didn't look convinced. "Where did Anissa go, anyway?"

"Oh, you know. People to see, things to do. Sometimes, I forget she had a life of her own before we met." The words rattled off exactly as if I had practiced them in front of a mirror.

I hadn't, of course. It surprised me how easy it was to come up with a half-truth.

He was too worked up over Sara to notice how lame my explanation was, anyway. Good thing, since I didn't want to talk about it.

I didn't know until she told me she needed her space how much I needed her. It was one thing to know the sun would burn your skin, but it was another thing to feel that burn. It was the same thing with her, only worse.

I didn't know there was such a hole in my life until she came along and gave me what I'd been missing all along. Somebody to love and protect, someone to fight for. Without her, I felt rudderless. I had no desire to go farther along the path we were on, with all the secrets and revelations and danger to us and the clan. What did it matter, really?

My mood fell even lower than it already was. We must have been the most somber table at the club. One good thing about everybody else having such a good time was that none of them noticed. And if they did, they didn't care.

I caught movement out of the corner of my eye and turned in time to see Scott go stiff. "What's up?" I asked.

"Excuse me." He hurried away in the direction of the bathroom.

Philippa frowned. "He's worrying himself sick over that—"

"Watch it," I warned.

"What? I'm not allowed to have an opinion now?"

"Keep it to yourself. Please. There are bigger issues at hand right now. You know that." I gave her a meaningful look, and she turned away.

It was ridiculous of her to be so consumed by jealousy, or whatever it was she held against Sara, when Valerius's body was in our vault.

"Yeah, bigger issues like this." Gage tapped the inside of his forearm, and I knew what he meant.

"Does it still burn?" I rolled my sleeve up to my elbow, keeping my arm under the table so no one but us could see.

"No. Yours?"

"No." I turned my arm, studying it. "But they look the same. They haven't faded a bit."

"At least the pain's gone. I thought I was gonna go out of my mind."

"Tell me about it," I said with a grimace. "And there I was, thinking I had a high tolerance for pain. This was blinding."

"I wish it would go away." He chuckled, and I understood why he did. If we didn't laugh, we would lose our minds. It was just one more thing to be concerned over.

"Quick. He's coming back." Philippa waved her hands under the table, so Gage and I unrolled our sleeves and buttoned them before Scott saw us.

"You feeling all right?" Philippa asked him.

"Oh, yeah. It's one thing after another, you know?" He shook his head.

The three of us exchanged looks that said, 'If he thinks things are bad now, he's in for a rude awakening.'

I hoped again his awakening didn't take much longer. I wasn't sure he would forgive us for withholding the truth so long.

❧ 26 ❧

GAGE

"Does anybody want a drink?" Philippa asked as she got up from the table.

I was worried about her; she put a little effort into her appearance for the sake of looking good in front of the rest of the clan—we had to put on a united front and all that—but I could tell she was suffering.

There was no light in her eyes, no energy in her voice. She might as well have been dead. I told myself to stop being so morbid, but it was hard not to be after what I had been through.

I was about to ask her to grab a chalice of blood for me when something hit me. Not a thing, though it might as well have been since the sensation was something like hitting a brick wall would be.

My head spun. I was almost dizzy. I scanned the area for the source of it.

Her.

I had to find her. I knew it was a her—the girl from the cave who rescued me. How, I couldn't say. Instinct.

Something about the girl I had caught scent of told me I had to find her.

"Excuse me." I got up without looking at the rest of my family and ran down the metal staircase leading straight to the street from the second-floor deck I had been sitting on.

My head swiveled back and forth, my nose searching for her

scent. She was out there. She had reached me from two stories away.

I hurried to the corner, almost pushing humans out of the way to get there in time. The conflicting odors of their colognes and perfumes and deodorants and hair products screwed with my head, but there was one scent stronger than any of them.

Blood.

I had smelled blood.

Blood I had to have.

There.

To my left.

Halfway down the block, in the middle of a group of girls dressed up like they were out on the town and living it up.

I followed her, single-minded, homing in on her scent as I drew closer and closer. I caught a flash of dark-blonde hair, long and wavy the way the girls liked to do it—funny how trends seemed to double back on themselves, a creature alive as long as I had been knew how often that happened over the decades.

I heard a voice as familiar to me as my own.

"I don't wanna go!" She was laughing when she said it, but I could tell she meant it. She was only pretending to joke around for the sake of her friends. I could tell the insincerity from the scent of her.

"Come on, Carissa. Don't be a pain in the ass tonight. We've been talking about this all week!" This came from a brunette in *her* group.

Carissa.

The girl who saved me in the forest is named Carissa.

I decided I didn't like that mouthy, tall, dark-haired girl with the poker-straight hair and the big ass, teetering like a horse on stilts in a pair of ridiculous shoes. She was pushy.

"Yeah, I know, and I've been telling you all week I don't want to do this. Why don't you ever listen to me?"

"Because she wants to get laid by a buff, hot, steamy piece of man meat tonight!" Another girl, this one with hair even redder than my sister's, shrieked with laughter as the dark-haired girl took a swipe at her.

A third girl, the short, plain one, who seemed to be along for the ride—every group of friends had one—piped up. "I'm practically drooling over the descriptions on the website. Have you seen some of the pictures of the guys who go there? Oh, God!" She fanned herself.

Carissa gave her a wink and linked an arm through hers. "I hope you can handle all that hotness in one place," she said, and I liked that.

She was a nice girl, encouraging the friend who would most likely go home alone.

I kept my distance, following along as they and a few others made their way another three blocks to the club. They talked and shrieked and giggled the entire way there.

When they arrived and I saw—and smelled—what the big deal was about, I froze.

They were going into a shifter club. And not just any shifters, either.

Not the werewolves I was used to. That was clear. I wondered about this different breed of shifters, but not for long. My mind was preoccupied with Carissa.

Who the hell were these girls, and what were they thinking? A human girl had to be crazy to go into a club with a bunch of shifters. Didn't they know what they were getting into? How they could be ripped apart? It wasn't a good idea to even let a werewolf get too familiar in a social setting, since they could claim a human as their own and basically stalk her until she either gave in—or else.

I shuddered to think of Carissa going into a place like that.

What was worse, I couldn't follow her.

They would kill me the second I walked through the door. I wanted to go to her, order her not to step foot inside, tell her she would regret it for the rest of her short, vulnerable life.

Except...

Either she had incredibly sharp instincts, or she was smarter than the rest of them. She hung back, closer to the curb than the velvet rope designating the line to get into the club.

I realized none of them knew what kind of club it really was. They just thought it was a meat market.

But she must have sensed differently.

"What's the matter with you, Cari?" The tall girl took her arm and tried to pull her—playfully, or at least pretending to be playful.

"You know I don't do this sort of thing," Carissa said, pulling away.

"What sort of thing?"

"You know." She looked around like she was embarrassed. "I don't go to clubs and pick up guys just to sleep with them."

Tall Girl's hands found her hips, and she cocked one of them out to the side.

I knew that pose. My sister gave it to me at least once a week.

"What's that supposed to mean?"

"Nothing! Nothing!" Carissa sputtered, waving her hands. "That's great for you, if that's what you're into. I'm not trying to comment on anything else but that. It's just not for me, is all. I would feel too... awkward."

"Believe me, you'll get over that real fast." The other girl laughed.

"I don't know." I noticed then, too, Carissa was dressed differently from the other girls. They wore tight, short, low-cut dresses—even the bigger girl—while she wore a sleeveless dress cut across her clavicle that almost reached her knees. And what most women would never understand was she was much sexier than the ones with half their body hanging out.

I looked up at the door to the club, where a trio of males was walking up red-carpeted stairs to get inside. Werewolves. No, shifters, I corrected myself. The hair on the back of my neck stood up, and my fangs threatened to descend. Only they weren't the sort of werewolves I was used to. Instead of a bunch of hulking thugs wearing grungy clothes, half-covered in fur, these shifters were classy. Sophisticated. They didn't stink of dirt and grime. They wore Rolex watches and tailored dress slacks, polished shoes, and sunglasses even though it was as dark as night could get. I still didn't trust them.

I could almost understand why human women would want to go there. Almost.

The girls watched the shifters enter the club, then just about dissolved into the sidewalk.

"Oh... my... God!" Tall Girl looked and sounded like she was either going to have an orgasm or a seizure. "That's what I'm talking about! You mean to tell me you're gonna stand out here —*alone*—and miss out on that?"

Carissa hesitated, shifting her weight from one foot to the other. She didn't look anywhere near as sure of herself as she had before.

I could sense she was starting to buckle, as I could smell her rich, fragrant, sweet blood.

Don't do it. Don't you give in like that. You know there's something wrong, don't you? You can sense it. You're smarter than your friends. They're not like you, those men.

"I really don't feel comfortable, you guys."

I could sense her friends losing their patience—I could see it, too.

"You're all going to hook up with random guys and leave without me, and I'll be all alone."

"Come on, Cari! You're being ridiculous. You know you could pick one of those guys if you wanted to. Jesus Christ, you're ruining the whole night." Tall Girl tottered over to the red carpet. "I'm going in. You can go home if you want to."

Yes. Yes, go home. Go anywhere. Just don't go in there.

"Wait." Carissa went after her.

I shook my head; she couldn't be that gullible.

"Okay. If it means that much to you."

Tall Girl folded her arms and looked the other way.

So, she was the alpha of the group. What she said was law. And Carissa had fallen for it.

As she was crossing the sidewalk to go after her friend, a pair of shifters stepped out of a long, sleek, black car and walked toward the door.

I watched them warily.

"Hey, gorgeous," one of them growled, looking at Carissa. "What are you doing out here? You should be inside with me."

I wanted to rip his throat out and shove his designer sunglasses in the hole I left.

Slimy bastard.

Tall Girl, on the other hand, pounced on the chance to pull Carissa in with her. "She's a little shy," she purred, walking up to the shifter who'd hit on Carissa. "I think she needs a little coaxing."

He smiled, and his teeth flashed white in the light from the streetlamps. The smile of a predator. "Don't worry. I can do all the coaxing in the world." He slid an arm around her waist and left no question about whether or not she was going in with him.

I watched, barely holding myself back, as he steered her inside.

Her friends, as well as his friend, followed them in.

Never in all the years I'd been alive had I ever felt so useless. I couldn't step out of the shadows and save Carissa from the shifters. They would be on me in a minute—them, and all their friends. I couldn't follow her in, so there was no way of knowing what was happening.

I hoped she was as smart as I tried to give her credit for.

She wasn't smiling as she walked in, so she might call it an early night.

I could only hope.

I waited for her to come out. What choice did I have? I couldn't let her go. Her blood sang to me. I couldn't get the scent out of my head. I wouldn't be able to exist without knowing whether she was all right.

I saw one shifter after another walking in and out—and when they exited, they inevitably had a hot young thing on their arm.

Sometimes, the crowds outside the club were so thick, I could barely make out one face from another for all the moving, teeming bodies and their conflicting scents. Not that it mattered; I would've known her scent anywhere. It cut through all others.

When the redheaded friend stepped outside, giggling the way a girl giggles when she's had just shy of too much to drink, my senses went on high alert.

Were they leaving? There was hope yet.

A well-dressed shifter stepped out behind her and stroked her hair. She nearly swooned. They walked off together.

I checked my watch. It had been two hours. Two hours! I could hardly believe how time had flown. It didn't matter when I was waiting for her. All my senses were focused on one person.

The tall, dark-haired alpha girl stepped out maybe twenty minutes later with a beefy creature on her arm. She was practically draped over him—he nearly had to carry her, but not because she was drunk. He waited for a valet while she nuzzled him, arms around his neck.

My blood boiled. Had she left Carissa in there? Selfish. It was one thing to separate during the night if that was everybody's plan—I had done that enough times with my brothers when we were out at the club, and the disco before that, decades ago.

But when somebody didn't want to be there to begin with, it wasn't right to leave them.

I muttered curses under my breath as they got into a sports car.

The rest of her friends left the same way over the next half-hour. Even the bigger girl, who looked like she wanted to pinch herself as she walked hand-in-hand with a massive shifter whose thick, black hair hung past his shoulders.

But no Carissa.

I wasn't sure what to think.

She couldn't be having a good time in there.

I couldn't go in and get her—what would I say if I could? *I smelled your blood and need you to come with me?* Right. That would seem much less threatening than a bunch of shifters.

Suddenly, my problem solved itself when she hurried outside. Alone.

I could almost taste my relief, leaning against the cool, brick wall for a second.

She looked back and forth, maybe debating on whether to catch a cab or walk, before heading in the direction from which she'd arrived with her friends.

She had company.

Just as I was about to trail her, the double doors to the club opened and out stepped the shifter who had made a pass at her and ushered her inside. He looked furious as he took off in her direction.

I followed, almost running to catch up. I didn't reach them until he had already grabbed her arm.

"Hey, asshole! Let go!" She tried and failed to wrench her arm free.

"What's your problem?" he growled. "Don't you know when a guy's trying to show you a good time?"

"I can have a good time on my own, thank you. Let me go!" She tried again and let out a little whimper of pain when his hand visibly tightened.

"Let her go." I stepped up beside him, hands balled into fists. "She said she doesn't want to hang out with you tonight, friend."

His head swiveled in my direction, and his already dark eyes turned nearly black with hatred. "I'm not your friend."

"No. You're not. Now, let her go, or we both know you'll regret it."

Our eyes were locked.

I almost forgot about Carissa, I was so ready to fight.

That would've been catastrophic—and knowing it would be catastrophic was the only thing keeping me in check.

A public brawl between a shifter and a vampire? The last thing we needed.

"You're alone. You know I have a lot of friends across the street," he whispered menacingly.

"You wouldn't have time to get them out here," I promised. "Now, let her go. There are plenty of other girls in there for you to choose from."

His face contorted into a mask of disgust, but he released her. "This is war," he snarled. "Wait and see what we do to you for this."

I watched as he strode away, every muscle tensed with rage.

I relaxed then remembered the overwhelming girl standing just behind me.

I turned to find her staring up at me with wide, blue eyes and wondered what I was supposed to do with her.

❧ 27 ❧

GAGE

"What was that all about?" she asked, eyes still wide. "What did he mean by war? Who was he to you? And who are you, anyway?"

"A lot of questions." I grinned.

"Answer the last one first, please." I admired how self-possessed she was after what had just gone down. I guessed a girl as beautiful as her, living in a place as rough as New York, would have to learn to let things roll off her back.

"My name is Gage. I saw that guy harassing you and thought you could use some help." I shrugged.

"But what did he mean by war?"

"It's nothing. Don't worry about it."

We stood there, me with my hands in my pockets and her with her arms wrapped around her thin, easily broken body.

She had no idea how close she'd come.

"Are you all right getting home?"

"I guess so." She chewed her bottom lip and hesitated.

"Do you want me to walk with you?"

She shook her head then nodded. "I can't even think straight," she admitted, blushing. "Not that that guy bothered me all that much, but that club... I didn't have a good time. It's been a strange night."

"I know what you mean. I've had a strange night, too." Very strange.

For starters, I had never felt such a pull toward any human. She drew me to her without saying a word, consuming my entire being with the need to have her.

"Would you mind walking me?" she asked with a shy smile. She was so endearing.

"Of course." I let her lead the way—it wouldn't be a good idea for her to know I had been following her—and fell in step beside her.

It was still fairly early for Manhattan on the weekend, barely midnight.

"Were you out alone tonight?" I asked, reminding myself again I wasn't supposed to know anything about her.

She let out a hard laugh without humor. "I am now, I guess. It didn't start out that way."

I remembered the tall girl who'd manipulated her, and frowned.

"By the way. You never told me your name," I murmured.

She smiled that same shy, little smile. "Carissa. But you can call me Cari. Anybody who saves me from the clutches of a monster gets to call me by my nickname."

She had no idea how right she was, either. It was uncanny how sharp her instincts were.

Then again, what about the monster who is walking her home?

"Carissa. That's pretty."

"It sounds like something out of an old romance, one of those Victorian melodramas," she joked.

I wished I could tell her I was alive when those Victorian melodramas came out, and that, yes, her name would've fit in perfectly in that era.

A breeze blew past us and lifted her dark-blonde waves, sending her scent even more alluringly to my nostrils.

I gulped, fighting back the bloodlust raging all through me.

"So, Gage, what do you do?" she asked as we continued to walk.

Unlike the people going past us, we were strolling. Neither of us was in any hurry to get anywhere.

"For a living, you mean?"

"Of course," she smiled.

"I help run the family business. My father passed away a long time ago, so my brothers and sister and I keep things going." The image of Fane's face flashed before my eyes.

"Oh. I'm sorry to hear that," she murmured. "My father died a long time ago, too."

"He did?"

"9/11," she said, and we left it at that. No further explanation needed.

"What do you do?"

"I work for a magazine. Nothing special."

"What do you want to do?"

We waited at a corner for the light to change, and she turned to me.

"Huh?"

"What do you want to do?" I asked again. "Everybody wants to do something else, something other than what they're doing. Isn't that the whole point?"

She laughed. She had a great laugh. "I guess you're right! Between you and me, I would rather be working in one of the offices instead of sitting in a cubicle out on the floor. Writing or editing."

"You're a writer?"

"I wish."

"Do you write?"

"Yes."

"Do you like to write?"

"Sure."

"Then, you're a writer."

"You make it sound so simple." She smiled.

"It is when you boil it down." I took her elbow to help her across the street—not even thinking about it, just wanting to be sure she was safe when there were cars waiting to turn in our direction.

She didn't pull away.

"I should keep you around as my career manager," she joked. "If you ever get tired of your job, let me know."

"Eh, for me it's not that easy."

"I thought everything was easy when you boil it down." She winked.

I had to laugh. "For me, it really is different. It's more of a... family business."

Her eyes went perfectly round. "The mafia?" she whispered.

I burst out laughing so hard I had to stop walking for a second. I couldn't remember the last time I'd laughed like this, or if there was ever a time in my long existence when I needed humor relief. "No, no! Not at all." I laughed some more.

"I didn't think it was that funny," she said, but she was smiling.

"I'm sorry." I wiped a tear from the corner of my eye. "If my brothers had heard that, they would die. No, we're not that way at all. Think more... like the way certain positions are passed down from one generation to the other."

"Royalty?" She sounded skeptical this time.

"In a way. In a very, very loose way. And I think we should stop talking about it now."

Her eyes twinkled wickedly. "Am I being walked home by an actual Prince Charming, who saved me back there?"

"I see you're not willing to let this go."

"Okay, okay. I'll stop."

We walked to a pizza shop with a window facing out onto the street.

"Would it be ridiculous if I told you I'm starving right now?" she asked.

No, it wouldn't, because I was starving, too. But not for food.

It was everything I could do to hold a conversation with her when the pull of her blood filled my consciousness.

"Of course not. You're human. You get hungry."

She smirked. "Yeah, but girls aren't supposed to like to eat. Didn't you know that?"

"I might have heard something like that, but it doesn't mean I believe it."

"Oh, I like you." She grinned before turning toward the man leaning halfway out the window. "Slice of white, please."

I watched as she carefully dabbed off the excess grease with a handful of napkins before sprinkling salt and garlic powder—oh, the irony, vampires, and garlic, supposed to keep us away. A stupid legend with no basis in fact.

She folded the slice in half—it was almost as big as her head —and took a large bite. She closed her eyes and let out a little groan of pleasure.

I didn't know whether to applaud or kiss her.

Kiss her? Where had that come from? And yet I felt it.

"I'm sorry. Are you hungry?" she asked, pointing to the window. "I didn't mean to hog the space."

"I'm fine."

She took another bite, and we walked more slowly while she ate. Even after she was finished, we kept a slower pace, talking about whatever came to mind.

We couldn't seem to stop coming up with things to say. I knew I couldn't. She told me she was a Yankees fan in a family full of Mets fanatics, she had five siblings in all, and that her mom was a school teacher.

"And Dad was an investment banker," she quickly added, voice tinged with pain.

I marveled at how years could pass, but the pain was still there. I knew the feeling.

"I lost both my parents at the same time, actually. Years and years ago."

"Wow. Both of them?"

"Yeah. My brother and I, we're the oldest. Twins. We sort of had to keep everybody else in line. We weren't ready to take over the business, I don't think. But I wanted to, you know? He was older by around a hair's breadth, so he got the job. I wasted a lot of time being mad at him because of that. I got myself into trouble over it, too."

"We all make mistakes when we're young."

I held my tongue. She had no idea how young I wasn't.

"Anyway, I still remember the uncertainty and pain of those days. Sometimes I still feel it, in little bursts. You know?"

She sighed. "Yes! It's like sometimes, I almost forget it happened. It was so long ago. How is it possible I would forget after all these years of not being with him?"

"I don't know. A defense mechanism, maybe. Our brains want to keep us safe, and I don't know... Functioning, I guess. If we thought about the pain every day, all the time, how could we function?"

"I guess that's true." She smiled—a little sadly, but it was a smile.

My hand itched to take hers, but I didn't dare let myself do that. If I did, I would want more. I already wanted more.

And when did I go from wanting to taste more of her blood to wanting to hold her hand?

We reached a block of brownstones, and she stopped around halfway down, in front of a stone staircase. "This is me," she said, shifting her weight from one foot to the other.

I realized then that we'd been together for hours.

It was almost four in the morning—the newspaper trucks were driving past as we stood there, wondering what to do next.

"The whole house?" I asked.

"No! I wish. Just an apartment." She looked up the stairs then at me. "Do you want to come up?"

That surprised me.

For one brief, breathless moment, I was about to say yes. I was about to go up there with her and take her. I wanted to be with her, all over her, inside her. I wanted to compel her to let me drink her rich, sweet blood until she was at the edge of life and death—I knew I wouldn't be able to stop myself until it reached that point. I would drink my fill and let the blood flow through me until I quenched my thirst for her. It wouldn't be enough, either. It would never be enough.

I really wanted to go. I did. I came so close.

There was a loud noise down the street, like a car backfiring, and it shook me from my trance.

No way I could do this. If the league ever found out I was drinking from a human, I would never get away with it. Consorting was bad enough, but drinking from them was against our laws.

She spun around, surprised, searching for the source of the noise.

I took the opportunity and crossed the street, disappearing behind a minivan and then into the shadows.

I stared through the windows of the van and saw her looking around for me with her mouth hanging open.

No, I couldn't take a chance on being with her or drinking from her.

If we got caught, it wouldn't be just me who faced the league's wrath. They would kill her to keep her quiet, and I couldn't do that to her.

No matter how desperate I was for her.

No matter how sure I was she was meant for me.

❧ 28 ❧

CARISSA

Where the heck did he go? Was he a magician or wizard or something? One minute, I was going against everything I had ever believed about going to bed with a guy right after I met him. The next, he was gone. So much for trying to turn over a new leaf.

Did I scare him away?

I looked around, turning in a full circle.

He was gone. He really was.

My heart sank until it was somewhere in the vicinity of my sandals—sandals I was glad I'd worn that night, since it meant being able to walk for hours on end without wanting to cut off my feet.

Not that it mattered, because I would never see him again.

I thought there was something special between us. Was I that far off-base? Was I just kidding myself? I must have been.

He was so sweet, so gallant. I didn't even get his number—not like he'd asked for mine, anyway.

I guessed he figured he'd done his good deed for the night and could go home with a clean conscience.

I was fun to walk around with for four stinking hours, but that was all. Wasn't it supposed to be the other way around? Weren't guys supposed to sleep with a woman and then disappear? Not do something semi-meaningful, something that made a girl think she was bonding with somebody when she wasn't?

I was just about to turn toward my front stairs and drag my feet the whole way to my apartment—and that was when I spotted him, hurrying down the block on the other side of the street.

A car turned in his direction, and the headlights shone on his profile. Unmistakably him.

I took off after him before I could stop myself or even think about it, jogging until I turned the corner and saw him hurrying past a row of storefronts.

I kept my distance, hanging maybe a half-block back so he didn't catch sight of me if he turned around. I didn't want to come off as some desperate stalker, refusing to take the hint that he didn't want me. I knew girls like that. I'd had a few friends in college who were like that. I had made a vow a long time ago I would never be that girl.

You should be home, getting into bed, you idiot.

No matter what I told myself, I couldn't help it. There was something special about him. He got me, as strange as it seemed. And he was real. He didn't put on some fake macho BS act to impress me, even though he obviously had money and was pretty well-off. The family business. Whatever that meant, it bought him some pretty nice clothes and a watch I could've paid a year's worth of rent with.

The guys I met at the club had been equally well-dressed and flashy, but that was the difference in a nutshell. They were flashy. They had to show off, like it actually mattered they could afford VIP treatment and a bottle of Cristal. Big whoop.

Give me a guy who smiles indulgently when I tear into a slice of pizza any day of the week, thanks very much, I thought as I ducked behind a dumpster when he paused to wait for a light to change.

Who did I think I was? Nancy Drew? Hiding behind a dumpster. Jeez. But that didn't stop me.

I kept following him, darting between cars as I crossed the street. We definitely lived on different sides of town. He was heading into the heart of Manhattan, where all the high-rises were. Yet another thing to confirm how wealthy he was.

Where did he come from? He'd randomly jumped in and saved me earlier. I didn't know what I would've done without him. It could've turned out to be a very different night. I might have been running away from someone rather than running after someone.

I did not have a good feeling about that club, no matter how hot the guys were. Unlike Mathilda, I cared about more than what a man looked like. But there'd been no getting through to Maddy. She had been insistent I go in. But she was always pushy, wasn't she? I loved her, but she was a pushy broad. She was also a good friend—something I had to remind myself from time to time. Like when she'd left me on my own in the middle of a bunch of guys who were practically licking their chops.

I told myself that was why I was desperate to find out more about Gage. He was like a unicorn. Respectful and kind and funny and smart. He actually took my elbow when we crossed the street together, as though he was trying to protect me. He looked like he could kick some ass if he had to.

I had never known anybody like him. I didn't know men like him still existed. Hadn't men been chivalrous and protective of their women back in the old days? Hadn't those days passed? Not for him. It was sweet.

I wondered how the girls were doing. They'd all gone home with somebody, even Jenna. I was happy for her. She deserved a fun night. I only hoped she was smart about it—I had the feeling she was a virgin, and I felt sort of protective of her. She wanted so much to fit in with the rest of us. I made a mental note to call her first thing in the morning.

Oh, wait. It's almost first thing in the morning now.

It would be dawn in a little while, and I was still following Gage down half-empty streets, all the way across town. I wondered what I planned to do once I caught up with him, or if I wanted to catch up with him at all.

What if he walked into a brothel? Did they still have brothels? Or a drug den or something like that? What then? I wondered if I should maybe quit while I was ahead, cut my losses and get a cab. It would be better to believe he was a good guy and leave it there.

Finally, after what felt like forever, he opened the tall, glass doors of a high-rise and went inside. I was across the street when he did, and I craned my neck to look up, up, up. It seemed to go on forever. All glass, sparkling in the dim pre-dawn light. Very swanky. So, he lived there. Lucky him.

He wasn't the only one going in, either.

It was like everybody in the building had gone out that night and was just getting home. All of them were dressed roughly the same—club clothes, sort of like what I was wearing but more like what the other girls wore. Sexy. Fun. The clothes a person wore when they wanted to get noticed. I never could dress like that, no matter how many times Maddy or any of the others tried to convince me I should. I guessed I had the body for it. It was decent enough. I just never felt right, like I was wearing a costume that didn't quite fit. How could I have fun when I felt awkward and not like myself?

The sun was rising by the time I decided to head home. He wasn't coming back out.

I almost missed him, but I chalked that up to feeling tired and rumpled and disappointed. I didn't know him before I left the club, and life would go on without him.

I hailed a cab and climbed into the first one that stopped, leaning back against the seat with a sigh. Comfortable shoes or not, my feet hurt after all that walking. I guessed they would hurt no matter what I was wearing.

My friends from the gym would be impressed with all that walking—I wished I'd worn a pedometer or something to record how far I had actually gone. But pedometers didn't usually go well with dressy clothes. Even I knew that.

It didn't take long to get back home—dawn was the one time of day when traffic seemed to ease up a little. Not like I would've known that before then. I wasn't exactly the early bird going after the worm.

With heavy feet, I climbed the front stairs then went up another three floors. I half-hoped somebody would spot me and think I was doing a walk of shame. But no. For once, none of my nosy neighbors were around. Some people were actually asleep.

"Hey, Chloe. I'm coming." My kitty was purring away at the door as I unlocked it.

Poor thing would've been waiting for me all night—I never stayed out as late as I had. She wound herself around my ankles the second I stepped through the door. I didn't know whether she was being affectionate or trying to trip me as punishment for leaving her alone all night.

"It's not like I didn't leave food for you, you big baby." I pushed her out of my way before falling onto the bed without bothering to take off my dress first.

She purred and rubbed herself against my back until I had to smile. At least there was somebody at home who was happy to see me.

"Why didn't he want to at least give me a good-night kiss?" I rolled over to snuggle her. "I mean, a hug, even. Or a handshake. Anything. Why did he run off like he did?" I looked down at her, like she would give me an answer other than "Purrrrr."

"Maybe his girlfriend was coming down the street, behind me," I guessed. "Maybe he freaked out when he saw her coming along and thought he could run away. Or he's with Witness Protection. No, that's stupid. People don't move to New York to go into Witness Protection. They're usually moving from a big city, not to one. Jeez. I wish I knew."

I tucked one arm under my head and watched the cat play with a random bit of lint. I wished I had her problems. She had her food and water and a litter box, and she basically walked around the place like she owned everything and was being generous by letting me share her space.

His name was Gage.

That was all I knew about him.

I also knew he made me feel special, that I'd never felt that sort of spark with another guy, ever. Would I ever see him again? Would he even remember me? I hoped I would, and I hoped he did. Because I knew I would remember him.

I was still thinking about him as my eyes slid closed, imagining his face in my head, remembering how he'd laughed until he couldn't walk anymore.

❧ 29 ❧

JONAH

"I still can't get a hold of her. She turned her phone off. Did I tell you that? It used to ring, but now it goes straight to voicemail." Scott looked more and more desperate every time he tried, and failed, to reach Sara.

It was getting harder every time to tell him she was all right and sound convincing while I did it. Except, I knew that where she was, there probably wasn't any cell coverage.

I couldn't imagine there were any cell towers around where Allonic lived, and that was probably where he'd taken Anissa and Sara to meet with their mother.

I vaguely remembered hearing she had recovered there, back at the caves with the rest of the shades.

"She's all right. Who knows how far away they had to go?" I wished I could change the subject. I hated having to make things up to get him off-track.

He was too smart for that, anyway. And way too devoted to Sara. Not that that was a bad thing. I was devoted to Anissa, and she didn't even want me anymore. That didn't change my feelings for her, not a bit. So, I could sort of understand where he was coming from. It didn't help contain my frustration, however.

"I wish she could've let me know where she was going," he muttered before disappearing into his bedroom. I was almost relieved when I heard the door slamming. One less thing to worry about for the time being.

Gage came in from the balcony, and I reflected on how weird he'd been, too.

He wouldn't say what was up with him or why he'd disappeared from the club a few nights earlier. When we got home, he hadn't been here, but he came back just before dawn and went straight to his room. He was keeping secrets again. Hadn't he learned the first time?

"Where's Philippa?" he asked, going to the kitchen. He pulled some blood from the fridge and poured it out into a glass.

"Where do you think?" I made sure Scott's door was tightly closed before saying anything else. "She hasn't been able to stay out of the vault."

"I'm worried somebody will see her going in or coming out," he said.

"I know. But you know how she is. It doesn't matter how many times you tell her something, or how sensible it is. If she doesn't want to listen, she'll tune you out."

"She would refuse help if she was on fire," Gage agreed.

We smiled together, and, for a second, it felt like the old days. Back when we were friends.

I wanted to give him the benefit of the doubt, but it wasn't easy when he wasn't giving me much to work with. When he wouldn't tell me why he'd acted like somebody had killed his dog ever since we went to the club together.

"How's the brand feel?" I glanced at his arm.

"The same. There. Like it's been since it appeared. But it doesn't hurt, at least."

"Yeah. Same for me." I could tolerate its presence as long as it didn't bring pain or any surprises.

I turned my head at the sound of footsteps.

It was good to see Philippa walk in, even if her face was as sad and distracted as ever. She was going to waste away in front of us if she didn't get it together.

Gage poured blood from the bag and handed her a glass without saying a word. He was right. She needed to feed and get her strength back. She shook her head.

"What good are you to him if you starve to death?" he asked.

"I'm far from starving to death," she insisted.

"Even so. Drink."

She rolled her eyes but drank.

Gage always knew how to get through to her better than I did.

My phone buzzed.

For a second, my heart leapt with the thought that it was Anissa.

How ridiculous.

She had already told me she had no intention of being with me anymore, hadn't she? I was kidding myself to think she would go back on that so easily. Anissa was stubborn. She didn't change her mind that quickly.

It was a text: *Go to the roof.*

The sender was unknown.

I wondered what I was risking by going at all, and what I'd risk if I didn't go. Who would send me such a cryptic message?

I laughed humorlessly to myself. Who wouldn't at this point?

"What's up?" Philippa asked. Even so soon after drinking the blood, her color looked better.

"Nothing. Be right back." I slid the phone into my pocket.

"Where are you going?"

"The roof."

"Why?"

"Because that's where I feel like going right now. I want to be alone for a minute."

Her eyebrows knitted together when she frowned, but she let me go without argument.

I went outside into the darkness and asked myself again who would send such a message. My senses were on overdrive, trying to pick up any little trace of a person. Or a creature like myself.

The wind whipped around me, the way it always did so high up. I looked around me but saw nothing. Then, there was a shifting in the shadows.

"Hello?" I called, ready to leap if I had to.

"Hello, Jonah." Out stepped Fane.

"Oh, wow." I let out a deep breath and bent over, hands on my knees. "You could've let me know it was you who was texting me. Where did you get a phone?"

"Don't worry about that. I have my ways."

"Evidently. What's this all about?" My heart raced.

It was never exactly good news when Fane showed up out of the blue.

"We need to have a family meeting."

I bit back the slight hiccup of emotion that hit me when he said those words.

Exactly the way he used to say it back in the day, before everything happened. When we were just a family—an unconventional family, a vampire family, but a family nonetheless. Whenever it was time to get together and talk something over, be it about the clan or about where the family would take a vacation that summer, he would announce it was time for a family meeting.

And we would roll our eyes and drag our feet—those meetings could last a long, long time, depending on how many opinions there were and how deeply they contradicted each other.

I would've done anything, given anything, to go back to those days.

I shook off the memory. There was no time for that. "Are you talking about the entire family? Scott, too?"

"I think it's time for him to know the truth, yes. He's around?" His voice cracked.

"Yes. He's downstairs. At least, he was when I came up here."

He nodded. "Bring him, too."

"Where are we going to have it? Here?"

"No, not here. Someplace private. I'll take care of that."

"Yes. Great. He'll enjoy that."

Fane smiled. "Go get everybody. I'll be waiting here for you."

I nodded and went back down to the penthouse. Philippa and Gage would probably be glad to hear Fane was back, but Scott?

I dreaded what was about to happen.

Scott was with the others when I walked in, and Philippa was trying to make him laugh—unsuccessfully.

I cleared my throat and shot her a glance. "I think we all need to go to the roof," I said, feeling like a complete idiot.

"Why?" Scott almost laughed.

"It's important. Somebody up there wants to see us. All of us."

Gage and Philippa appeared stricken, and they both shifted their eyes toward Scott.

He was oblivious, too busy wondering why we would do something he thought was out of character for us.

"On the roof." He cocked his head.

"Yes. Come on. We have to go."

"Yeah, come on." Philippa took him by the arm. "I think it will be okay."

"You don't think this is weird?" he asked.

"Honestly? No." Gage exchanged a look with me before walking out.

Philippa and Scott followed, and I brought up the rear.

We climbed the short staircase leading from the balcony to the roof.

I came up on Scott's right while Philippa remained on the left. I thought our brother might need a little support when he saw Fane.

And I was right.

Just like he had with me, Fane stepped out of the shadows.

He stared at Scott with a mixture of pride and sorrow. "Hello, Scott."

Scott froze. His mouth fell open.

I remembered how I felt when I first saw Fane, that rush of conflicting emotions and thoughts. Disbelief, elation, confusion, even anger. The anger of knowing he'd been alive all this time.

"What is this?" he asked, glancing back and forth, eyes wide. He started shaking. "Is this some sort of joke?"

"No. It's no joke." I took his arm, in case he staggered. "It's all right, man. Just hang in there."

"Hang in there?" He shook my hand away. "You knew about this? You all knew about this? You're not even surprised to see him!"

"Yes, we all knew about it. I'm sorry. We didn't want to keep him from you, but there was no choice."

"Oh, spare me." He turned to Fane. "Dad?"

"No. Not Dad. I'll explain everything."

"Explain?" His bitter laughter cut through the wind blowing around us. "Yeah, you'd better explain. You show up after all this time and act as though it's no big deal? And the rest of these guys knew before I did? I wasn't good enough to know you were still alive? And you stand there and tell me you're not my father? Who are you, then?"

"As I said, I'll explain everything, but not here. There's no safety here."

"We're on a roof!" Scott bellowed.

I rolled my eyes and wished he could control himself a little better—even Philippa didn't freak out the way he was, and she had always been the dramatic one.

"Quickly," Fane said, and he threw a portal in the blink of an eye.

Gage moved Philippa aside and took Scott's left arm, while I took his right.

He wasn't going to shake me off again.

Scott was still yelling and cursing up a storm when we pushed him through the portal and into Duskwood.

He's in for a lot of surprises tonight, I thought as we went through.

❦ 30 ❦

JONAH

It was as I remembered, exactly as it always was. Dark, still, with fog that swirled around my feet.

Scott had stopped yelling and was stuck in a sort of stunned silence. I couldn't blame him. Again, I remembered how I felt the first time I found myself there. At least he had us with him. I would try to walk him through it as gently and carefully as possible. If Fane wanted to bring him up to speed, he was going to have to absorb a lot of information in a very short time.

"What is this place?" Scott whispered almost reverently. Like we were in a church or some other sacred place.

I could understand that.

There was something special about Duskwood. An ancient cemetery—wasn't that right? The writing on the tombstones in a language so ancient, no living creature knew how to speak or read it.

"It's called Duskwood. An alternate dimension." Philippa walked to him and placed her hands on his chest, with Gage and me still flanking him. "There's a lot we haven't been able to tell you, and I'm sorry. There were reasons, good reasons. You'll understand them all, I promise."

"You promise," Scott muttered.

"Yes. I promise. But you have to listen, and you have to keep an open mind. Okay? Please. It's so important you at least keep an open mind. Everything will be all right."

He hesitated, as though there was nothing he would like less, but nodded anyway. He could be stubborn, too, as stubborn as any of us. It was a genetic thing.

"Are you finished?" Fane asked.

I knew he hadn't meant to sound so cold and unfeeling. It was a way for him to distance himself from us. He couldn't afford to think of us as his children anymore—though there were moments when he obviously did, when he couldn't help it. Like when we saw Mom-not-Mom aka Nivia in my Mother's body, back in Sorrowswatch.

"How dare you?" Scott whispered in a tight, dangerous voice. "You show up after all this time, and you have the nerve to talk to us that way?"

The rest of us exchanged a look. It seemed like we had all gone through the same progression of emotion and shock and indignation.

"He'll explain everything, Scott. Trust us, all right?"

"I don't want to hear it from him." He stared at me with cold, narrow eyes. "I want to hear it from you."

"What?"

"I want you to tell me. Tell me what you know and why you couldn't be honest with me from the beginning."

"If you weren't always with Sara—" Philippa cut in.

"Don't you start that with me right now. Just don't." Scott glanced at her then glared at me again. "Go on."

"There's only so much I know," I said. "But what I know—what I believe—is there was a good reason for Mom and Dad to go away. We were all in danger. They left in order to protect us. That's the truth."

"Danger from who?" he asked.

"From Lucian. I know, it's a lot to believe at once, but it's the truth. He's been screwing with our family for years. He was the one who turned Mom, thinking he could force her to be with him instead of with us. He did it out of spite for Dad. He didn't know she would turn us, too. Like I said, it's a long story, and we don't have a lot of time."

"Why couldn't he tell us?" He faced Fane. "Why didn't you tell us?"

"It would've only made things dangerous for you. If you knew and he found out you knew, he would stop at nothing to find out where we were. I couldn't let that happen, knowing he would torture you to get the information he wanted."

"What about Mom?" He looked at each of us in turn. "Where is she?"

Fane spoke up. "That's another story, and why I brought all of you here."

"Where is she?" Scott asked again, like he hadn't heard what Fane said.

"We saw her," I murmured. "Not her, really. There was another being in her body. I know, I know," I said when it was clear he was about to ask another several hundred questions, "it's beyond anything we've ever encountered before. I know. But that's how it is. And it was a big shock."

"It was horrifying. Disgusting." Philippa shivered. "It was her body and her face, but it wasn't her. You're lucky you didn't have to see it."

"I disagree," Scott said. "You got to see her, at least."

"You can't unsee what we saw, or un-hear what we heard," Gage murmured. "If I slept, I would probably have nightmares about her. It was an abomination to her memory, Scott. You didn't miss anything."

Scott snorted. "I missed a lot. I missed a whole lot."

I wondered if he would ever be able to forgive us.

"While we're on the subject of your mother," Fane interjected, "she's the reason I called you all together."

"What about her?" Philippa asked.

I heard hope in her voice, and it nearly crushed me. She wanted so much for Mom to be Mom. Well, we all did, didn't we?

"I have to find her." He stared at all of us, his children. "I have to find your mother's body. We all deserve answers as to how Nivia ended up in there."

"Nivia?" Scott asked.

"The being inhabiting Elena's body," Fane said. "As far as I knew, your mother died. That's the belief I've had to live with for all these years. Now, I find out another being has inhabited her. I need to know how, and why, and what happened to your mother —your actual mother—during all of this. Is she gone or inside the body? Is Nivia too strong to let her out? These are all questions that must be answered. We need to know."

"I'll go with you," Philippa said, taking a step forward.

"Not so fast," Fane said, and I thought I saw a shadow of a smile tugging at the corners of his mouth. He had always admired her spirit, even when she frustrated him. Daddy's Girl. "I think we've already learned it's unwise to run straight into an unknown situation. We need to have a plan in place."

"This is Mom we're talking about," Scott argued, and his voice was stronger. Indignation was taking the place of shock. "We don't have the time to stand around here in this place, wherever we are, and come up with a plan. I've already been left out of enough. I want us to go after her, and I want to be caught up on all of this."

"Scott." Fane's voice was sharp, cutting through the confusion.

Scott's mouth snapped shut. Dad could always do that—he had the sort of strength and presence that made it possible for him to command an entire room. His children were no challenge. "I understand what you're going through. I do. I've had to live for years in-between worlds, never being myself again, always having to live as Fane."

"You're Fane?"

"Oh, no." Philippa rolled her eyes. "I forgot he didn't know that, either."

I stepped in. "Yes, he's Fane. And this is not to be discussed outside of us. Not Fane and not our father. Can we move on?" I glanced at Fane and nodded.

"As I was saying," he continued with a doleful look at Scott, "all along, I've blamed myself for her death. I've blamed myself for so many things. For earning Lucian's hatred, for bringing all of this on us. I hated myself for not being able to save her from dying. And now, there's a chance she's not actually dead. Trust me, none of you wants to understand what happened more than I do."

That was enough to shut Scott up, but it didn't do much for my peace of mind. I caught a glimpse of movement in the shadows and turned in that direction.

A flash of long hair, a white cloak.

Sirene.

Even as my hackles raised at the sight of her, I couldn't help but wonder how it made her feel to hear that Fane wanted to know what happened to his wife.

Sirene's eyes met mine, and her face was like a mask. It didn't reveal anything, but I understood.

She disappeared then, back into the shadows.

31

JONAH

"What does all of this mean? Are we going out to find Mom or what?" Scott looked around.

"Aren't you more worried about your girlfriend?" Philippa whispered.

"Not right now, Philippa." He glared at her.

"It doesn't matter what any of you are more worried about because I'm going on my own. This was not intended to be a family trip. I only wanted to let you know what my intentions are, so you'll know where I am and what I'm doing."

"That doesn't seem fair," Gage said. "I don't like the idea of you going out all alone to handle this."

"I don't remember asking you if you thought it was fair," Fane reminded him. "And the last time I checked, I'm the—"

"You're the what?" he asked. "The father? You set the rules? I thought you were Fane. I thought you weren't our father anymore. You should make up your mind about that."

"Stop it," I said, raising my voice. It still sounded muffled. The sound hardly carried at all, as though I was yelling in the middle of a padded room. "We won't get anywhere this way."

"Your brother is right," Fane said, still looking at Gage. "If we keep sniping at each other, we'll fall further apart. We need to come together at a time like this. We need all our strength, and we have to trust each other."

I bit my tongue on hearing that. I couldn't help but

remember how Gage had destroyed every bit of trust I ever had in him.

"Anyway," Philippa said, looking at Scott, "Sara's with Anissa. Remember? She's not out there alone, so maybe it's time to think about our family and our clan and less about theirs for a little while."

"She's not just with Anissa," I said. "She's probably with their mother."

"What?" Fane appeared stunned, and it took a lot to get that sort of reaction from him. "Did you say their mother?"

"Yes. Why?"

"Tabitha? Tabitha died in the Great Fire. I should know. I mean, wasn't I accused of setting it?"

Scott's sharp intake of breath revealed his reaction to remembering that bit of information. Maybe he would finally figure out this wasn't a joke, that Dad and Mom fled for a good reason.

"It's a long story." I felt like a broken record, repeating the same platitudes over and over.

"I have time," Fane replied.

"Maybe we don't."

"Talk," he ordered. "Please."

I sighed. "A shade saved her. She made it through the fire and found where the shades live, and one of them took her in. She was near death, from what I understand. It took years for her to fully heal."

He took this in, then asked, "Where did you hear this?"

"A Custodian told me the entire story."

"That's impossible."

"It's not impossible," I assured him. "And Anissa and Sara's brother is a Custodian as well."

"Their brother? They have a brother?" he asked.

"Yes. Half-vampire, half-shade. Didn't you pick up on it when we were all together?"

"What?" he asked.

"It's Allonic." For once, I knew something he didn't know. I felt a little smug about it.

"Allonic. I had no idea."

"I wasn't aware you knew Allonic," Philippa said.

"I wouldn't say I know him, but I'm familiar with him. We've crossed paths many times—you would be surprised how easy it is for those of our kind to cross paths. Maybe it's fate.

Who knows?" He turned to me. "I didn't know he was half-vampire."

"Yes. He has fangs, but he doesn't drink blood. Well... not usually." I vaguely remembered him drinking Valerius's blood back in Sorrowswatch, but everything from that experience was so fuzzy and foggy, it was hard to make sense of much of it. Almost dying would do that, I guessed.

"I never knew she was his mother," Fane murmured. "I never bothered to ask who his mother was. We don't know each other that well." He turned to Scott. "Your Sara must be fine, then, if she's with her mother. Tabitha wouldn't let harm come to her children."

Scott's forehead creased, and his mouth curved into a smirk. "I can't say I agree with that." But, to his credit, he didn't argue, either.

"Regardless of everything we've discussed, or how important it is for you to know where your mother is and what happened to her, there's clan business for you to attend to. You can't keep running off on these expeditions. I'll be doing this alone. It's better this way, and safer for all of you."

"I don't think so," Philippa argued.

"I do. Remember, this entire time I've been gone, I've gotten used to being alone. I know how to handle whatever comes at me."

"Yes. You're legendary," Scott said.

"Something like that," Fane replied, shaking his head.

"What about your other woman? How does she feel about this?" I couldn't help myself. I had to know.

"Wait. What? What other woman?" Scott asked. "You have another woman?"

"Tell him," I said. "Tell him about the happy new arrival that's on its way."

"Jonah. This isn't like you," Fane murmured.

"How would you know any more? It's been how long since you left? Besides, you know how I feel about this. I didn't lie when I first found out."

His face settled into hard lines. "Your brother is referring to Sirene."

"Who's that?" Scott asked.

"A witch," I whispered, still staring at Fane. "The witch who's carrying his child."

"This doesn't concern you, and I'm not discussing it with you," Fane snarled.

"I don't get this." Scott looked around, almost laughing. "You're telling me we have a sibling and it doesn't concern us? How can you say that?"

"I agree with Scott," Gage said.

"So do I," Philippa added. "I think this is something else we need to clarify. There are too many secrets. I'm sick of them."

She wrapped her arms around herself, and I saw, for the first time, she was shaking.

I put an arm around her shoulders.

She continued, "I wish we could go back to the way things were before, but I know that isn't possible. And that's fine. We can't turn back time. But we can start being a little more open with each other, a little more honest. We need to stick together. There are too many pieces in play right now for us to hold back from each other. Don't you get it? We're all on the same team. Aren't we?"

Her question hung in the air.

I didn't know how to answer it or whether or not I could. I had the feeling she'd directed it to Fane.

"Of course," he finally said, his shoulders falling. "We're all on the same team. All I ask is that you remember something. If there are secrets, if I'm keeping something from you, there's always a good reason. Just like you didn't know why your mother and I left. We did it for the right reasons, and it tore us apart inside. I mean that. We didn't do it willingly, but it was the only way. This is the same sort of situation—perhaps not as dire, but just as important. It's best that I keep certain things to myself for now. Not because I don't think you deserve to know about your sibling, but because it's for the best."

"Says who?" Gage asked.

"Says me." And that was the final word on the subject. He always had a way of making his point known in very few words. He looked around as if he was daring any of us to challenge him again. None of us did.

"Fine. That's how it is, then." I spoke for all of us.

They must have agreed because they didn't counter my decision.

"It's time for all of you to go home," Fane announced. "Come on. I'll walk you back to the portal."

I couldn't help thinking so much was left unsaid. Too much. I didn't particularly care for the feeling. We all dragged our feet going back to the portal—none of us wanted to leave things the way they were. Even so, I couldn't help but reflect on the fact we were all together. Finally, after so long. We were together.

Except for Mom. Her presence, or lack thereof, was deeply missed. She was always the lightness, the brightness, the breath of life in our family. She had always kept us laughing. And when we found ourselves in tense, tight situations, she was the one who held us together like glue. We needed her. I wondered if we would ever get her back. I told myself we wouldn't—it was reasonable, of course. I couldn't get my hopes up. Still, Fane's presence gave me a reason to hope.

We reached the portal and stopped. None of us wanted to be the first one to go through. We were all just as reluctant as the rest. Fane cleared his throat. "All right. Go back and take care of the clan, the way you have been all this time. They need you."

Gage nodded and squared his shoulders before striding through the portal and disappearing.

Philippa looked at Fane once more—her mouth opened then snapped shut. She followed Gage with her head hanging low.

"I still don't understand any of this," Scott said.

"I know." Fane sighed. "I'm sorry."

Seconds later, Scott was gone, too.

Fane faced me. "I'll get word to you as soon as I have something."

"All right. You know where to find me."

He smiled a little, and I decided that was as good a way as any to leave him.

Just like that, I was back on the roof. I wondered if I would ever get used to traveling via portal.

The rest of my siblings were there, staring at me.

Judging from the expression of shock on Scott's face, I had the feeling it was going to be a long night.

32

ANISSA

Funny. I was angry with Jonah. I'd been sure that taking a little space and figuring things out was the right thing to do. I was being strong, doing what was best for me. But when I stepped outside after leaving Jonah's penthouse, I felt alone. I didn't like the feeling very much. I wrapped my arms around myself to ward off the chill in the air, but that didn't do much to make me feel better. My spirit was about as low as it had ever been—which was saying something.

Wasn't I used to doing things on my own? I was, once. I could only rely on myself when Sara had been imprisoned. A one-woman army, something like that. Except, I got used to being with Jonah, relying on him to support me, to be there for me when I needed a shoulder to lean on. I needed him—or, I thought I did. That was my biggest mistake, telling myself I needed him. I had tricked myself into believing I couldn't get on without him—obviously, since I felt so lonely, standing out there on the sidewalk in front of the high-rise.

The feeling didn't last long. I didn't take more than three steps away from the building before my phone started buzzing. For a split second, I thought it might be him, trying to get in touch with me.

To ask me to come back.

I wouldn't. Maybe.

It wasn't him. It was a text from Raze.

Another funny thing, how Raze used to be such a huge part of my life, but I almost never thought about him anymore.

Everything had shifted so far, so fast.

Meet me at the coffee shop on the northwest corner, his text read.

I blinked, too stunned to move.

How did he know where I was?

I looked around and saw the coffee shop in question. What was he doing in this part of town? The library, sure, but out here? I had a lot of questions for him. I practically sprinted to the corner to meet him.

He was sitting at a small, round table, one of those high-top ones with the tall stools.

I hopped up onto one and glared at him. "What are you doing here?"

He flinched. "I didn't know there was an invisible fence I couldn't go over," he muttered. "And hello to you, too, by the way."

I didn't soften. "How did you know where I was?"

"What if I followed you?"

"What if I hit you right now, in front of all these people?"

"Come on, Anissa. Don't be this way. I've been searching for you. There was something very important you need to know about. And I didn't actually follow you—I was only kidding."

"Hilarious." I smirked. "What is it I need to know? And that still doesn't explain how you found me."

He glanced down at his coffee cup. "What if I told you Sara told me where to find you."

My eyes lit up. "Sara? Where is she? I was just on my way to find her."

"You wouldn't know where to look."

"Yeah, no kidding, but I've been sleuthing for a while now. I'm getting pretty good at tracking people."

"I don't even wanna know," he muttered.

"Good, because I don't even wanna tell you."

I would've liked to. I needed to unload on somebody—there was so much happening in my head and my heart, and a best friend would've come in handy right about then. But there was too much that could get Raze in trouble if he knew about it. I wouldn't put him in that position.

And I had the feeling he wouldn't want to hear about Jonah. Certain things I didn't need to be told.

"Where is she?" I asked instead of getting into my messed-up issues.

"I can take you to her."

Something about the way he was evading the question bothered me. On top of that, he had to take me to her—like maybe she couldn't meet up with me somewhere.

"What's wrong with her?" Panic rose in my throat. My hands started to shake.

"You'll understand everything when I take you. Believe me, it'll be easier if you see it with yourself than if I try to describe it." His eyes swept back and forth over the room, where people were enjoying coffee and pastries even late at night.

The city that never slept needed its caffeine, I guessed.

"Oh, man. You're not helping me feel better, Raze."

"We need to get out of here before you have a panic attack."

"We need to get out of here so I can see my sister," I hissed. I missed her so much—and I was terrified that something happened, that she was hurt. I had seen too many things, witnessed too much of what all the multiple dimensions held, to believe she was all right. The more I saw, the less I trusted that anybody I cared about would ever really be all right again.

We stepped outside, and the cool air helped calm me a little. It hit the sweat that had built on my forehead, on the back of my neck, when I'd thought about my sister in danger. I had been through enough of that—and so had she. She deserved a little peace. "I wish you would tell me she's safe, at least," I muttered as we walked side-by-side.

"She's safe. I wouldn't be taking you to her if she wasn't. Do you think I would lead you into a dangerous situation?" He looked down at me with a disapproving smirk. "Do you even remember me? I'm Raze. I'm the guy you've known for years and years. We used to talk about things. Remember? And you would tell me what was going on with you..."

"All right, all right. I get it. Call it some... What is it? Post-traumatic thing, what humans get when they go through something scary or stressful. I'm on edge, in other words. I watched her suffer in a dungeon." I glanced around when I realized my voice was getting louder and louder all the time.

None of the people shuffling past on the sidewalk seemed to hear me. If they had, well, it was New York. There were stranger things than dungeons.

Raze noticed my discomfort and did his best not to laugh, but he should've tried harder.

"Shut up," I whispered.

"Listen. I get it. Okay? You're worried about her because she's already been through a lot."

We headed down a narrow alley, and I immediately thought back to the night I met Jonah. The attack from the werewolves. If I had only known where that night would lead me…

"Yes. She has. I'm afraid she won't be able to take much more before she breaks."

"She won't break. She's strong. Like you."

I hoped he was right. I didn't have anything to hold on to but hope just then.

We walked for another five minutes or so, zigzagging through traffic and ducking down alleys. I wondered where he was taking me—but when the buildings started turning from high-rises and apartments over storefronts and became big, boxy warehouses, I got the idea.

She was hiding in a warehouse.

My imagination spun out of control, putting together all sorts of scenarios for what she was going through.

"Why couldn't she stay at the Bourke penthouse?" I asked. "Why here?"

"You'll see."

"Raze, I swear…"

"You will see, Anissa." His voice was sharp, sharper than he had ever sounded before.

I wasn't used to hearing him lose his temper like that. If anything, it made me respect him a little more. But just a little, since it was me he was losing his temper with.

I didn't say another word until we stepped inside a dark building with most of its windows broken.

The walls were covered in ivy, the chain-link fence containing it and separating it from the rest of the warehouses on the block held back an amazing array of garbage—bottles, cans, clothing. Clothing? It smelled, too. I wondered if there was a dead animal in there someplace.

And my sister was here.

"Could you have maybe picked a better place than this?" I asked.

"Sorry. The other abandoned warehouses were all booked up."

I followed him as he led me farther and farther into the darkness.

The air still carried the smell of death, mixed in with dampness and rot. What a beautiful combination. I wrinkled my nose in distaste.

"Watch your step," he cautioned. "It gets pretty rough."

"So I noticed."

Boards with nails sticking up out of them, rusty tools, rat nests—thankfully, without any rats. Animal feces. That explained some of the smell, at least.

There was a doorway on the side of the building which was propped open with a brick. Raze went to it and pulled it open.

The hinges screamed in protest.

"What's this lead to?" I asked, covering my ears.

"There's a set of tunnels connecting the four warehouses in this four-block square. I guess they were all owned by the same company, I don't know. Maybe one set of products were in one place, another in another, whatever, and they used the tunnels to transport things in bad weather." He chuckled. "I'm making this up as I go along."

"As good an explanation as any I could come up with." I shrugged.

We started down the tunnel, which was wide enough for us to walk side-by-side and still have room to stretch our arms out. I followed Raze's careful footsteps. It looked as though he had sort of cleared a path at some point.

"Here," he said. "There's a door hidden in one of these walls."

I kept my eyes trained on the wall, searching for a door. I would never have seen it if I hadn't known it was there, and I had to wonder why my sister was behind it. Was she that deep in hiding?

"Okay. We're going in. I want you to promise you'll keep your cool."

"You are scaring me again."

"Promise me. You'll see how important it is when you get inside... but, by then, it'll be too late for you to get it together."

My heart took off even faster than before. I could barely breathe. Sweat popped out again on my neck. For Sara's sake, I nodded firmly and told myself to hold it together.

He didn't look convinced, but he nodded and opened the door anyway.

The room wasn't large, but there was more than enough room for three of us. An old office, maybe, or a supply room. Three bare bulbs lit it, hanging from the ceiling, and I could see my sister sitting in an old, wooden chair.

"Sara?" I whispered.

She looked fine, like there was nothing wrong with her at all. That was a relief.

I had half-expected her to be missing an arm or something.

She turned to me and burst into tears.

I took a step toward her with my arms outstretched, but Raze's hand on my shoulder held me back.

In the blink of an eye, I could see why he had stopped me.

One of the lightbulbs above her head exploded, sending a shower of glass shards flying everywhere.

I jumped and shrieked softly—it was a natural reaction, something I didn't even think about. Maybe I should've held myself together.

Sara started crying harder, almost sobbing.

She lifted her hands, and I gasped in shock as sparks of electricity shot from her fingertips.

Raze's grip on my shoulder tightened—funny how I'd almost forgot he was there. It must've had something to do with the lightning bolts shooting from my sister's fingers.

"What is this?" I whispered, frozen solid. I could feel the electricity in the air. It made my hair stand on end.

As if she was answering me, Sara let out a sharp cry. Her arms started shaking, and the bolts branched out into intricate spider-webs of electricity. All of them were aimed at the wall, which I could see was burned and charred. So, she had done this before —a lot.

The entire room lit up in shades of blue and purple and white as the bolts spread even farther, climbing up to the ceiling, spreading like fire in a web of light and crackling energy. The lightbulbs glowed brighter, brighter, until I was sure they would explode, too.

"Stand back!" Raze called out over the ear-splitting snapping and cracking. Like a thunderstorm, only contained in a very small space. I covered my ears and let him pull me closer, away from the ever-expanding web my sister was building around her.

Soon, she was surrounded by light, sitting in the center. Still crying.

And just like that, it was over.

The room went dark except for the two remaining light bulbs, which had somehow managed to stay whole.

I realized I had been holding my breath through much of what had happened, and I took a gulp of air—which tasted funny after that strong electric charge.

Almost metallic.

I looked at her again, then up at Raze. "Can one of you tell me what's happening here?"

33

ANISSA

I waited for Raze to answer. Somebody needed to start answering, very soon.

All he did was shake his head and mutter a single word. "Elemental."

I waited for more. When he didn't continue, I said, "And?"

"And I don't know exactly what's happening. The two of us are the only people who know about it besides Sara. I can't ask anybody else—I mean, I don't know what they would do to her if they knew what she was capable of."

Sara let out a little whimper.

His head snapped around in her direction. "Sorry, sorry. I didn't mean to make you upset. Everything's okay." He talked to her like he would talk to a temperamental child, trying to soothe her.

He was afraid of her, I realized. I couldn't blame him. I was sort of afraid of her, too. But I was more afraid for her.

"She called me a couple of days ago," he explained. "She told me what was happening to her, that these... impulses... were starting to take over. She was terrified, since she couldn't control it. It was getting stronger every day. She was afraid she'd kill somebody, or maybe set the penthouse on fire. Once it started, she didn't know how to stop."

"It doesn't stop until I'm worn out," she whispered from where she still sat.

None of it made sense. "She's a vampire, but what you're describing is something an elemental witch would be capable of."

"Yeah. I know."

"There's no witch blood in my sister—and definitely no elemental witch blood." I looked at her then back at him. "Right?"

A few quick flashes of light burst from Sara's fingers, and I cringed against Raze.

She whimpered again. "I don't know anymore. I don't know anything." Sara tucked her hands under her armpits like she was trying to contain what was coming out of her. Her face was tearstained and smeared with dirt. Her eyes were swollen from crying.

"Just try to relax," I said, feeling completely useless.

What was I supposed to say to her? That it was cool? That there was nothing out of the ordinary about her being able to shoot lightning out of her hands?

"I'm trying," she said in a weak voice, so soft I could barely hear.

My heart went out to her. My poor sister. She had already been through so much.

Raze spoke up. "We've been talking throughout this whole time. The best I can figure out is she consumed contaminated blood at some point."

"Elemental blood?" That would explain it, to a degree. I was sure Sara was a pure vampire. I remembered when she was born, for Pete's sake. I remembered her father, my stepfather. He was a vampire, too. A pure-blood vampire.

He nodded. "I overheard something at school one day, not long ago. I was walking down the hall, going from class to class, and there was a group of guys behind me. I didn't recognize their voices, but I overheard them talking about blood. Something about European clans. The word *elemental* was thrown around, too. Of course, I didn't put anything together at the time because it meant nothing to me. I didn't think about it again until this happened. I was disinterested, so I didn't pay attention to who was speaking. I wish I had. I feel like I could've helped."

Same old Raze. He had the best heart of anybody I knew.

I touched his shoulder and stared him straight in the eye. "You've done more than enough. Without you, who knows what would've happened?"

I didn't want to think about my sister being on her own in this condition, suffering and hurting, nowhere to go, always in danger of somebody discovering her.

He appeared a little embarrassed and cleared his throat. "So, yeah. I'm suspicious. And it does make sense, since there's no other way this could've happened to her."

I looked at her again. Where would she get contaminated blood? The blood we consumed was synthetic, but it was always closely monitored. That was one of the many rules the humans had for us—and it made sense. It was actually for our benefit. If the production of synthetic blood was regulated, it meant we were safer and healthier. There would be less of a chance of a sick vampire running around shooting lightning bolts out of his hands.

"Who would do this?" I asked neither of them in particular. It was just something I needed to verbalize. Then, I asked her, "What's going on? Is there something you aren't telling me? Were you getting blood someplace you shouldn't have been?"

That was the wrong thing to ask.

Wrong by a mile.

My sister's eyes went almost scarily wide. She stood, slowly, raising her arms as she did. "I don't know what's happening!" she yelled. "It's not my fault!"

She flung her hands upward, toward the ceiling, and out of her palms jetted two crackling, zigzag lightning bolts—heading straight toward me.

"Duck!" Raze screamed.

My reflexes were always strong—I had needed to hone them when I was Marcus's assassin—and I managed to sidestep one and duck the other.

Only I didn't duck deep enough.

So much for my reflexes.

I screamed as one of the bolts hit my shoulder. The force slammed me into the wall. I didn't know which hurt worse—hitting the wall or the burning of my shoulder where the lightning struck me.

On reflection, it was the lightning.

I tried to move my arm and screamed again as agonizing pain ripped through me. I felt sort of buzzy, like my nerves were dancing. The sensation wore off after a moment or two.

Sara ran to me, babbling apologies, and I flinched away when she tried to touch me. Her face fell. "I'm so sorry," she whispered through even more tears. "I didn't mean it. I can't control it. I would never hurt you, Anissa. I never would. Tell me you believe that."

"Of course, I do," I whispered, still clenching my teeth against the pain.

Raze sank to his knees beside me. "It's all right," he said to Sara. "Be calm. We know you didn't mean to do it. Anissa would never blame you for something beyond your control." He looked at me, and his eyes were startlingly intense. "Would you?" he asked in a voice heavy with meaning.

"No. I wouldn't."

What else could I say? If I told her off for hurting me, she'd probably strike me again—maybe with even higher voltage.

I glared at him—probably because I was angry and hurting and couldn't glare at my sister. "What else do you know about this? There has to be something else, Raze. Come on. You're smart, you read a lot of books. You've never heard of anything like this before?'

He shook his head. "I already told you everything I know."

"Come on!"

"I know that's not what you want to hear, but it's the truth. You know, you're not the only one who's worried about this. It doesn't only matter to you. I'm the one who's been trying to protect her while you were—"

"All right," I snapped. I didn't need to get into that. Not then, not ever.

I heard a crackle and winced, and when I looked at my sister, she was shaking. Her hair stood on end, the way mine had, and the air started getting that metallic taste to it again.

"Sara! You need to calm down. Be calm." Raze turned all his attention to my sister. "Close your eyes. Take a few deep breaths. Come on. We've practiced this, right? I know you can do it. Come on, Sara."

He coached her through it as she did what he asked.

Slowly, slowly, the energy in the room lessened. The air began to feel normal again, and she stopped crackling.

For the time being.

Once it was clear she was over her excitement, Raze looked down at me. "The more excited or upset she gets, the worse it is."

"No fooling," I whispered, glancing back at my sister.

She'd never been good at controlling her emotions in the first place. And the worse she got, the worse it got. Which made her feel worse, which made the electricity worse.

On and on until we would all be burned to a crisp.

I told myself to get over my pain and confusion for her sake. "Hey. Nobody blames you for this, okay? I'm sorry if it sounded like I was blaming you before. I'm just as confused about this as either of you, and I'm worried about you. That's why I sounded the way I did. I hate that this is happening to you. I love you."

She gave me a weak smile. "Still?"

"Always."

"It just... It seems you've gone through so much for me already, and this is just another thing."

"But you're the one who kept us both alive when we were on our own. I'll never forget that. Besides, you're my sister. I'll never stop wanting to help you. Okay?"

"Okay." She seemed calmer than she had been since I walked through the door, which was a relief.

I could breathe without being afraid every breath was my last.

I took a moment to get my head together before I tried to stand up. My back ached, my ribs were sore from where I slammed into the wall. I didn't dare try to swing my right arm back and forth since it was more than my skin that had been seared. The burn went deeper than that, even though my skin barely looked harmed. My muscles ached and twitched. I could hardly stand it and had to grit my teeth to keep from crying out every time I moved it.

Only the thought of my sister losing control again kept me silent.

"All right," I said. "Let's figure out where we go from here." I leaned against the wall for support, taking deep breaths to keep my head straight.

34

ANISSA

Raze pulled a chair out for me, and I sat in it, trying to think through our next steps. I couldn't let Sara go on the way she was. There was no way she—or anybody around her—would survive with her shooting off lightning bolts every time she stubbed her toe, or somebody was rude to her on the street.

"We can't figure out how to stop this until we know how it started. So, we have to pinpoint when it began and what could've happened to you." I stared at her, and it was so clear she was struggling to control herself. I wished I could give her a hug, but I was too afraid to touch her.

Raze spoke up. "There's something else I noticed around the mansion. Some of the guys who came in for the league meeting a few weeks back haven't left."

"No? Where are they from?"

"Europe."

"Maybe that's who the guys behind you were talking about. European vampires with elemental blood. They brought it over with them. I can't imagine why, but maybe they did."

"They do seem sort of shady. They're always checking over their shoulders when they talk, like they don't want anybody to overhear them. They have that slimy sort of look to them, too, and when they smile, it's more like a snarl." He shook his head with a shudder. "Like, if I was walking down the street and saw them coming, I'd cross to the other side."

Raze was pretty well-built, too, and I had never seen him back down from a fight. If they made him feel that way, they had to be trouble.

"I trust your instincts," I said. "So you think they might've had something to do with it?"

"I wouldn't put it past them," he said. "Everybody knows they're bad news and wants to know why they haven't left yet."

I turned toward my sister. "Where have you been getting the blood you've been consuming since we left the mansion?"

Her expression was surprised, stunned, offended. "From the Bourke blood bank," she whispered.

"You're sure about that?"

"I'm positive." She nodded her head violently. "Only there."

I decided to stop asking questions while she was still in control of herself.

"All right. If that's the only blood Sara's been consuming, it means the Bourke blood is contaminated. What if there are other vampires in their clan who are going through this? I mean, it's possible, right? It's not as if any of the bags are marked a special way, so anybody could get any blood at all."

"True," Sara said.

"Let's follow this out to its logical conclusion," I said. "If there are others—and there probably are, since I doubt only a single bag was contaminated—there are higher odds of there being a cure for this. If not now, soon enough. I mean, this could become an epidemic. It's not the sort of thing that can be ignored." My shoulder ached like I needed a reminder of how dangerous my sister had become.

"Besides," I said in a softer voice, "there's no way a hybrid witch-vampire would be accepted. She would never be allowed to live among other vampires. She'd be ostracized."

She might even be put to death. I would never dare say it out loud, but it was the truth.

I shuddered to think about it.

"This is why she's here," he reminded me. "I knew she had to hide. Nobody can know about this until we know there's a cure. I had to come and find you, of course, and Sara told me where I could find the Bourke building."

"I'm glad you did." I gave my sister what I hoped was a genuine, reassuring smile.

"What do we do now?" she asked, looking at the two of us.

"I think we should tell the Bourkes. They have to know their blood is contaminated."

"Assuming they're not the ones who did this," Raze muttered.

"They would never do that," I snapped. "You don't know them."

"I've heard that before."

"It's true," I insisted, and it was only for my sister's sake that I managed to keep my voice at a reasonable volume. I really wanted to scream at him, maybe claw his eyes a little. With the one arm I could actually lift without crying out in pain, of course. "You don't know how he feels about her—one of the Bourke brothers. Scott. He would never, ever let something like this happen. He wouldn't even chance it."

"I'm sorry if I don't believe you," Raze said. "I guess I'm not as well-acquainted with them as you are. You'll have to introduce us sometime."

"Okay, fine, whatever." I shook my head—there was no way he would ever see things the way they really were, not while the Bourkes were our enemies. Or at least, the enemies of Marcus's clan—a clan I didn't plan to ever be a part of again. "It doesn't matter right now. What matters now is getting Sara someplace safe. This isn't a good enough spot. It's secluded, but it's not safe. I'm not saying it wasn't good enough in an emergency, but she's sitting in the middle of filth. And if anybody notices us coming and going, they'll figure out that we're hiding somebody or something here."

"You're right," he agreed.

"But we also can't be seen with her on the streets—no offense," I added, looking at Sara.

She actually gave me a little smile.

"What do we do, then?" he asked.

It was a mostly rhetorical question, I realized. But I still felt the need to answer it right away. I wished somebody could answer for me, for once. I wished I didn't feel like everything was on my shoulders.

Then, it came to me.

It was a long shot, but I had to try.

"Hang on a second. Just wait here." I stood and went to the door.

"Wait. Where are you going?"

"I'm not going far," I said, trying to calm Sara. "I promise, I'll be back shortly."

"All right." I glanced at Raze, who understood he needed to sweet-talk her into remaining calm while I was gone.

I hoped it wouldn't be for long. I hurried back through the tunnel, retracing the steps I'd taken with Raze until I reached the door propped with the brick. It was heavy enough, and the hinges rusted enough that I had to throw my weight behind it, which only made my sore muscles and aching bones hurt more. I could say I had been struck by lightning and survived it, though, and how many people could say that?

By my own sister, no less.

I stepped over the garbage strewn through the warehouse and made it outside, where the air was much fresher than it had been in that little room full of electricity and anguish. It was cool on my overheated skin, too. I wished it could help my shoulder.

"Here goes nothing," I whispered to myself. Then, only slightly louder, I whispered a single word. "Allonic?"

Nothing. I waited for a slow count of sixty with nothing to show for it.

"Allonic?" I whispered again, and again I counted.

Nothing.

I couldn't lose hope, but it started to drain out of me like water in a sieve.

"Come on," I whispered through gritted teeth. How much more was I supposed to endure? Why couldn't we get a break for once? "Allonic? Are you here somewhere? Can you hear me?"

After another minute, and then another, I wondered if I would have to course back to Sanctuary. I knew I could find it again if I had to, but I didn't want to take the time. My sister needed help immediately, and I was in enough pain I knew coursing would exhaust me.

Then, the answer to my prayers appeared.

It was like he materialized straight out of the shadows, out of pure, thin air.

A tall figure in a long cloak, the hood pulled over his head.

Relief flooded my body, relief I had never felt before.

"You took long enough," I snarled when I really wanted to

throw myself into his arms and weep from exhaustion and confusion. And gratitude.

He sighed. "You summoned me so you could give me a difficult time?" he asked in that low, gravelly voice of his.

"Sorry. I'm so glad you're here. We have a situation—a very dangerous one." I pulled at the collar of my tee and showed him my burned shoulder.

"That's quite a burn." He was very good at understatement, my brother.

"Our sister gave it to me."

He lowered his hood so I could see the slight smile playing over his face. "You brought me here for what? To settle a sibling fight?"

"I wish it were that simple. Come. Follow me."

As we walked through the warehouse, I explained the situation. His silence told me all I needed to know—he saw how grave the situation was. "I don't know how much more of the blood may be contaminated or if anymore was, but Sara is out of control. She has no idea how to handle this. She slammed me into a wall."

"Is she often emotional?"

"She's emotional, even fragile, but not violent. Not ever. She's not doing this on purpose."

We stopped at the door leading to the tunnels. "Here is what I don't understand. I've never heard of a case where a vampire or any other creature has been turned into an elemental witch, and I don't see how she could've gained these powers simply by consuming elemental blood."

"Mom developed certain... traits... from the shade who saved her, didn't she? Your father? I saw her in your memories. She didn't look like herself anymore."

"Yes, but that was after many years of feeding, of healing. She was little more than dead when she came to our Sanctuary, so her body was... compromised, I suppose. We're talking about one feeding, maybe two from the same bag in Sara's case. And taking on the traits of a shade is far different from gaining the powers of an elemental witch. It simply isn't the same situation."

I groaned and punched the metal door with my good hand on my good arm. "I'm trying my best to figure this out. I don't know where to start, all right?"

"I understand. I'm only trying to give you some of the insight you're looking for." His voice sounded gentler than usual, more compassionate.

"I know you are." I sighed, and wished I hadn't punched the door. Having one arm that didn't hurt was better than having two sore arms. It seemed my sister wasn't the only one who needed to learn a little self-control. "At any rate, that's not our biggest concern at the moment."

"Oh, there's more?" he asked. I guessed that passed for humor, coming from him.

"Yeah. We need to find a place to stash her while we figure this out. We need to hide her from other vampires. Imagine what would happen if even one of them got word of her existence. They would put out a call to have her dealt with. You know what that means."

"You don't have to tell me," he said in an almost dangerous voice.

Yes, he probably knew how unforgiving vampires were when it came to half-bloods and hybrids. Yet another thing we had in common.

Except a half-fae or half-shade wouldn't be put to death just for the sheer fact they existed. A half-witch, on the other hand? There were few creatures that vampires hated more than witches.

"Do you know of anywhere we can go?" I asked with my heart in my throat.

"I know just the place."

I lowered my head and drew a deep breath. For once, something was going my way.

"All right. Let's go get her." I led him through the door—he opened it for me—and down the tunnel to the door which concealed my sister.

No, I reminded myself, *our sister*.

I gave him the same warning Raze gave me when I first went in. It seemed pointless, like he already understood, but a warning couldn't hurt. Lightning, on the other hand, could.

We entered the room—Allonic had to duck to make it through the doorway—and immediately, Raze and Anissa asked, "Who is this?" in almost perfect unison.

"He's here to help. I called him." I didn't dare explain who he was or what our relationship to him was.

My instincts told me it would be a terrible idea to work her up—and Raze would need roughly an hour's worth of backstory to explain the entire thing. I didn't have that sort of time.

"I can throw a portal for you—but I can only take you and Sara," Allonic said.

"Wait. What?" Raze's eyes went narrow. "You're just going to go through a portal with this guy? You don't know what'll happen on the other side. And I'm not allowed to go with you? When I know everything that's been happening so far? I'm just supposed to forget everything and move on?"

"Yes. Please." I went to him, taking one of his hands. "Please. You have to keep all of this to yourself."

"What about you? What happens to you now?"

"I'll be safe, and so will Sara. That's what's most important right now, isn't it? Keeping her safe?"

"She's not the only one I care about, and you know it."

"Yes. I know." I squeezed his hand. "I appreciate that, and I appreciate everything you've done. You're my truest friend. I won't forget that."

He cleared his throat, almost like he was embarrassed. "And you know I would never tell anybody what's happening with Sara. You don't have to worry about it."

"Thank you," I whispered. I trusted him, which wasn't something I could say for just anybody.

"We need to go," Allonic said, still standing behind me.

"All right." I gave Raze's hand one more squeeze before going to Sara. She looked nervous.

"Are you sure this is okay?" she whispered.

"Sure. It'll be fine, and it's for the best. You won't have to worry about anybody finding you." I tucked a loose strand of her long, dark hair behind her ear. "It'll be okay."

She nodded firmly.

I turned to Allonic, who handed me his cloak.

"Here. Wrap this around the two of you."

He didn't have to tell me twice. I knew how important it was to follow his instructions when it came to going through a shade portal.

I wrapped the cloak around us and held it tightly closed. Sara's breath was coming in hard, short gasps. "Relax," I whispered. "It'll be over in a few seconds."

"All right," Allonic said. "It's ready."

He pointed, and we stepped through.

KEEP READING FOR AN EXCERPT FROM THE NEXT BOOK IN THE *League of Vampires*.

RYE BREWER

Retribution

LEAGUE OF VAMPIRES

Half-fae Anissa, a former vampire assassin finds herself embroiled in a new dilemma to save her sister Sara from a set of suddenly appearing elemental skills—a death sentence to a vampire.

Sara finds herself in a witch stronghold, surrounded by a hot sorcerer who's making her forget her boyfriend, while sparks fly between them. Real sparks. She needs help with her elementals skills. Now.

Interim clan leader Philippa is torn between spending her time guarding the body of the Ancient who possessed her former lover Vance, and following Vance so she can save him from the Ancient.

Gage can't get the blond human who saved his life out of his mind. The problem is, she can't get him out of hers either. And it's putting her in danger.

⚘

Sacred trusts, broken.

A legendary vampire wants more than absolution. He wants retribution.

Forbidden passions, foretold.

Forbidden trysts follow a forsaken twin vampire as he seeks out the human he shouldn't have feelings for.

Slighted ones, return.

Old enemies rise to new challenges, threatening treaties and alliances.

CHAPTER 1

ANISSA

As I had promised my sister, Sara, our trip through the shade portal lasted almost no time. It was much less frightening than my first trip. There was no way Sara could know how lucky she was, of course, but she handled it well. She only lost control of her elemental powers once, crackling a tiny bit of lightning a moment before the air around us changed, becoming warmer and softer. I bit back my frustration as I thought of the elemental powers that Sara now had. The ones she wasn't born with.

I could hear the twittering of birds, the rustling of leaves.

Where had our half-brother, Allonic, brought us? "We're here. You can take off the cloak." The cloak imbued with the essence of spiritwalkers. Which made crossing through shade portals possible. The only way non-shades could go through

I opened it and glanced around, squinting a little at first. It was night here—of course, or else we would've burned up—but even the moonlight was brighter than the almost complete darkness I'd gotten used to in the tunnels that Steward and Allonic called home.

Sara's reaction was stronger, since she had been in the tunnels much longer than I had.

"Where are we?" Her voice trembled dangerously.

"Calm down. Take a deep breath," I whispered soothingly, stroking her hair.

Tiny sparks jumped from her head to my palm, but I didn't jerk my hand away.

She nodded and did her best. After a moment, the sparks stopped jumping from her to me.

Only then could I get a good look around me.

It was beautiful. That was what I noticed first.

We were in a forest—no, the countryside. There weren't as many trees as in a forest. Much more open space. Rolling hills covered in lush, green grass, dotted here and there with trees and stone walls. What a charming place. Soothing. This was perfect for her. She needed a place like this, where she could see and feel safe.

There was a mountain range in the distance with snowcapped peaks. They glowed in the silver moonlight. I could've stood there and stared at them all night. A few clouds floated past, and the moon painted them, too.

Sara's eyes were wide as her mouth fell open. "It's so gorgeous," she murmured, awestruck. "So peaceful."

Peaceful. Good description. "Are we the only ones here?" I asked Allonic.

He nodded then corrected himself. "You're the only ones out here. Don't you recognize this place?"

I looked around again, more critically than before. Far off, toward the foot of one of the mountains, there was a small forest. I remembered a forest in the woods. "Are we where Sanctuary is?" Sanctuary held the Custodians—shades who were the keepers of all of Earth's history. Our half-brother lived with the Custodians but had always felt out of place, being part-vampire, part-shade.

He nodded. "This is ShadesRealm. This is what you stepped into when you first came to us."

"How? We didn't take a portal," I said.

"There's another portal which leads to the entrance of the cave that leads to Sanctuary from the outside world. That's the portal you took with Jonah. You didn't realize at the time what you were stepping through." That made sense. There was so much I didn't know back then.

"But that portal was different. I didn't need a cloak or to have a spiritwalker in me to enter it."

"True. That one serves a different purpose. It allows other types to enter."

"This is where shades live?" Sara sounded as naïve as I'd felt when I first arrived with Jonah.

Allonic gave her a nod. "Yes. You'll find that most non-human creatures live in realms of their own. Not like vampires and were-types, who try to live alongside humans. It's safer this way."

I swallowed hard at the thought of Jonah. It seemed a lifetime ago when we first met and fell for one another—he gave up being head of his clan for me. But then things went off-track, and he kept secrets from me. I told him I needed space to deal, to think things through. Of course, the thought of Jonah Bourke made my heart ache, and I wondered where he was right now. Was he okay? Did he miss me?

I chewed on my bottom lip then released it. "Now that we're here, I have so many things to tell you." Including telling Sara about Allonic's relation to us. It would be best to tell her in a wide, open place like where we stood. Less chance of me getting fried with her newly acquired electrical skills.

"Not here," Allonic warned, holding a hand up to silence me. His golden eyes swept over the surrounding area. "There might be shades around here."

"You think that's a problem?" I asked, suddenly wary.

"You remember what happened to you, don't you?" His eyes bored into me.

"What happened to you? Why don't I know about any of this?" Sara asked.

The spiritwalker. Like I could ever forget. "I'll catch you up." I turned back to him. "And yes, I do remember."

I would never forget the way they tortured me in that little chamber, making me crawl around like a worm on the floor.

"It's better for us to be someplace farther away, where prying ears can't overhear." He lifted one arm, and pointed a long finger in the direction of what appeared to be a tower climbing into the sky. We were so far away that, from where we stood, it was roughly the size of the span between my thumb and forefinger.

"Wow. Do you think we could get any farther away?" I asked.

He shook his head and scowled, before stepping between Sara and me, then wrapped his arms around us.

"We have to course there," he announced.

I didn't have the chance to draw a breath before we were on our way.

He practically lifted us off our feet and did all the work for us.

That was a relief.

I was exhausted, and I knew Sara was, too.

We slowed, then stopped at the base of the tower. It was much, much bigger than it had appeared from far away—almost the side of the Bourke high-rise where Jonah's clan lived, if not taller. Instead of glass, the tower was made of big, irregular stones of all colors and shapes, held together with what resembled mortar but which, on closer inspection, sparkled like glitter.

"What is this?" I asked in a hushed voice.

"Legend has it, the stones are held together with diamond and gold dust. I've never actually found out for sure whether that's true, but it makes a certain sort of sense. Diamonds and gold mean little to us. They're as good for holding stones together as they are for anything else."

I shook my head in amazement. The stones were cool to the touch and seemed to vibrate with magic. I could feel the magic moving up my fingers then across my palm.

I looked again at the vines which had wrapped their way around the height of the tower, vines covered in flowers of every color in the rainbow. I could imagine how beautiful they'd be in daylight—and imagining was all I did, of course. What with the whole thing of vampires and daylight.

"How old is it?" I asked, still marveling at its beauty.

Here and there, windows dotted the otherwise smooth appearance. They were narrow and tall, and all I saw through them was inky darkness. What was inside?

"Not sure, but some of the records I've found mention this tower as early as seven-hundred years ago."

"And it's still standing," I murmured.

Of course, it would be. It was probably enchanted. No way something so beautiful could exist for so long without an enchantment or some other kind of spell.

Sara craned her neck and stared straight up. "Don't tell me we're going to the top," she muttered.

"What if we are?" Allonic asked in a tone that was as close as he got to teasing.

"I would say you're crazy. The roof touches the clouds!"

"You're not afraid of heights, are you?" he asked in the same half-teasing tone.

"No. I'm afraid of falling from heights."

They glanced at each other and exchanged a shy smile.

My heart warmed.

"Come on. We can course up the stairs the way we coursed here. It will take much less time than taking them one step at a time, trust me."

Allonic led us inside, and I realized I was holding my breath as I stepped across the threshold and onto the stone floor.

It was just like the exterior. The interior walls, however, were framed in wood, and the stairs circling the inside in a spiral going all the way to the top were wood as well. It made me dizzy to stand in the center and look straight up.

Allonic took us both under his arms again and coursed to the top, which took longer than I had expected.

It really did touch the clouds.

By the time we reached the end of the stairs, which led to a wide landing and a closed door, the air felt much cooler and damper than it had on the ground. I took hold of the railing to keep myself steady as I adjusted to being so high. I couldn't even glance out a window to get an accurate idea of how far up we were, but just knowing how tall the tower was seemed to be enough.

I felt a little woozy at first.

Sara started to crane her neck to look down. "Don't do that," Allonic warned. "Trust me. You'll get dizzy."

"I believe you," she murmured with a shaky laugh.

"Why are we so high up?" I asked. "I mean, did we really have to go so far out of our way to be alone?"

Hundreds and hundreds of feet in the air, up thousands of steps? It seemed a little much.

"We aren't here to be alone," he said. "This is how our mother stays safe."

I let out a strangled gasp. For years, Sara and I had believed she'd died in the Great Fire. But after I'd found myself in Sanctuary and learned she'd survived, I'd dreamed of seeing her again. "Our mother?"

I'd had no idea he was taking us to her. I'd only thought he wanted to keep us safe.

Our mother.

My heart beat double time and rang in my ears.

Our mother.

He nodded. "Shades can't portal to the top of the tower and can't course, either, so she would be able to hear anyone who walked along the creaky stairs well in advance of their reaching the top."

"Except for you, of course," I added.

"Of course, since I'm not a full shade, and I can course."

In the middle of all this, I'd hardly noticed when Sara started to spark and sizzle. I should have been paying better attention to her.

It was so easy to forget sometimes she didn't know nearly as much as I did—and besides, I was too caught up in the thought that I was about to see Mom for the first time in so many years.

"Our mother?" Sara's voice seemed to crackle like the rest of her. "What does he mean by our mother?"

I gasped. "Sara. Let me explain."

She ignored me. "First of all, our mother" —she pointed to me then to herself, back and forth a few times— "is dead, and she has been for a long time." Then she turned to Allonic. "And she's not your mother."

Allonic didn't say a word.

"Sara, please. You have to calm down." I wondered if the wood all around and under us was flammable.

She was working herself into a massive emotional state. I would have warned her if I had known we were going here, to the place where our mother had been living.

I threw Allonic a dirty look as I tried to quiet my sister before she lost control again.

Suddenly, the door opened. Our heads turned in that direction—and the figure standing in the entrance.

"Anissa. Sara." That voice.

That same voice.

I couldn't believe it—I had seen Allonic's memories, and I knew they were true, but it wasn't the same as hearing her sweet, familiar voice. A voice that had soothed me when I was sick, a voice that praised me, a voice that rang out in laughter so many times I'd lost count.

It was her.

"Mom?" I forgot about Sara for a second and threw myself into my mother's arms.

She held me tight, and she even felt like Mom. I would know her hug anywhere.

"Sara!" Allonic's voice rang through the tower, echoing, bouncing off the walls.

I turned to see my sister shaking, twitching, with bolts of lightning running up and down her body until she collapsed onto the floor with her eyes closed.

She went perfectly still.

CHAPTER 2

ANISSA

"Oh, Sara!" I threw myself over her. "Sara, wake up!"

Mom sank to her knees opposite me and turned her head from side to side, patting her cheeks.

I touched her forehead.

Sara's skin was scorching hot, but she was breathing.

"Quick, get her inside." Mom rose to her feet and rushed inside.

I heard water sloshing around.

Allonic lifted Sara in his arms like she weighed nothing at all, and I followed him into the chamber.

There was a chaise lounge by one open window, which Allonic stretched her out on.

The air coming in was cool and fresh.

Mom hurried back and sat on the edge of the lounge, wiping Sara's forehead with a cool washcloth.

I still couldn't get over it. *Mom. Our mother. She was real.*

"Please, get me a bowl with more water from the tub," Mom said without looking up.

Allonic did as she asked while I stood there, rooted to the spot. I couldn't take my eyes off her.

With the moonlight streaming through the window and the glowing, dancing light from a few lanterns placed here and there, I got a clear view of her.

She was her, but not her. I couldn't get over it.

The Mom I remembered used to have very pale, almost translucent skin.

The woman sitting in front of me, however, had a deep tan. Not quite as dark as Allonic's skin, but much darker than what I was used to.

She bathed Sara's forehead with so much tenderness, my chest ached.

Dipping the cloth into the cold water, wringing it out, touching it to her cheeks, her neck, her chest. She ran it down the inside of her arms, her inner wrists.

"She's burning up," Mom murmured, and there was no question as to who she was when I heard her voice again.

"I guess it's from all the electricity," I uttered. "It created too much heat for her to bear."

"When did *this* happen?" Mom waved her hands around wildly. "How did it happen?" She glanced at me and did a quick double take when she noticed the intensity of my stare.

What was a frown turned into a soft, tentative smile on her face. The lines on her forehead smoothed out. "I know I look different now," she said, her voice low. "I'm sorry if that's a shock to you."

"It's all right," I whispered back, and I couldn't get my chin to stop trembling.

She blurred and doubled as tears filled my eyes then spilled over onto my cheeks.

Mom opened her arms, and I fell into them, weeping helplessly.

I knelt there in front of her, and she stroked my hair, rocking me back and forth the way she used to when I was a little girl.

She was humming the same old tune—I never knew what song it was, or if it was actually a song at all, but it was the song she had always hummed when she was rocking either of us.

I closed my eyes as the tears continued to flow, soaking into the soft, cream-colored tunic she wore. She even smelled the way I remembered her smelling. I breathed deep, wanting to capture all of her that I could.

"My baby," she whispered. Her hand on my head was like a balm on my soul.

I felt instantly soothed.

All the hardship and pain and questions, endless questions, of the last couple of months melted away as she stroked my hair.

I was afraid of holding her too tight, thinking I might hurt her, but really, I was just as afraid of letting go. What happened if I found out this was all a dream? What if none of it was real, or if she went away again? What if I never got another chance?

"Mom," I wept. "I missed you."

"I missed you, too. Both of you. Oh, you'll never know how much my heart has ached. How my arms ached to hold you again." She pressed her lips to the top of my head. "I love you so much. I've always loved you, every minute."

I pulled away and smiled up at her. She wiped the tears from my cheeks with her thumbs then took one of my hands as she continued to apply cold water to Sara's skin with the other.

"You look well," she murmured. "Beautiful, the way you always did."

"So do you."

"Even if I look different?" she asked, her eyes cutting to mine before moving back to Sara's face.

"Even so." I grinned.

I glanced around the chamber. It was comfortable enough, or seemed that way. Along with the lounge which Sara rested on were a pair of plush, soft chairs.

Off toward the back of the room was what I guessed passed for a kitchen, with a table and chairs, and a stove which vented out through the roof.

To the side beyond that was a bed with a chest at the foot. I noticed the drawing supplies on the kitchen table and wondered if she had been working on something when we arrived.

"Are you comfortable here? Are you happy?" I asked.

"As happy as I can be." She sounded the way a person does when they're trying to be diplomatic.

She wasn't happy, obviously, but she was making the best she could of the situation.

"You can't let anybody know you're here," I whispered.

"Sweetheart, I'm not even supposed to be alive," she reminded me. "But let's not talk about that now. What about you?"

"Oh. Maybe we shouldn't talk about that, either." I stared at the floor.

"That good?" Mom asked in her all-knowing *Mom* voice.

"Something like that, yes." My head snapped up. "I've met Gregor."

"You have?" Her eyes softened, and she smiled. "I always wanted you to." Her gaze held that faraway look. "I hope you understand."

"I do. He told me all about you and how you met and how you fell in love. And how you couldn't be together."

She patted my hand. "It was all a very long time ago. He was very special to me. I want you to know that—and to know why I couldn't tell you the truth. It was bad enough that many others already suspected my child wasn't full-blooded." Her eyes darkened, and her voice deepened. "So much prejudice and hatred, and for what?"

"I know."

I didn't want to share stories of how much worse things got for Sara and me once she wasn't around to protect us anymore. There was no need to make her feel worse.

"What do you think of your father?" she asked with a playful smile which wiped away her anger and sadness.

"He's... forceful," I said, trying to be diplomatic.

"That's a nice way of putting it." She chuckled. "What else?"

"He's protective. I know he only wants what's best for me."

"That will always be so," she agreed. "Even when he couldn't be with you, he wanted to be. And he loved you, just like I loved you when we couldn't be together."

"He protected me when things got tough."

"Tough?" she frowned.

Right. She didn't know about any of that.

"Oh, there's so much to tell you. I don't know if I want to get into all of it right now." I glanced at Allonic, who sat at the table.

He stayed quiet, letting us have our moment.

"We have time now, my girl—and your brother told me about a few of the challenges you've faced, though I'm sure you have more to share. You were always so strong and brave. You never backed down from a challenge—that worried me, sometimes, since we need to know when to turn around and walk away if a challenge is too great." She ran her hand over my head, down the side of my face. "You're so lovely. Both of you. My beautiful girls. My heart is so full right now, I can barely speak." She looked at Allonic. "All of my children, all together at once. It's something I never dared dream, but it was always hidden in my heart. I don't think I could be happier than I am right now."

"I know what you mean," I whispered, and the tears threatened again behind my eyes.

"What do you think of your brother?" she asked.

Nothing like being put on the spot, I thought. "It's nice, having a brother." I smiled at him. "I called for him tonight when I needed help with Sarah, and he came. I knew he would if he could."

Mom seemed pleased, the way any proud mother would.

Sara stirred, muttering something, and we turned our attention to her. Her skin had lost the flushed, sweaty appearance it had when we first brought her inside the chamber.

"She's getting better," Mom murmured, putting a hand to her forehead. "What happened to her?"

I looked again at Allonic, who nodded.

"I only found out about this tonight," I began. "She's exhibiting signs of being an elemental witch."

"An elemental witch?" Mom's eyes widened as she examined her daughter's face. "I don't believe it."

"It's the only explanation we could come up with. I mean, she shoots lightning from her hands, Mom."

"Can she pinpoint when it began?"

"Not long ago. She never said exactly when, but it hadn't been more than a few days since I last saw her. Maybe a week." Or more. I had lost track, hadn't I? "I sort of left her in the protection of a family of vampires while I took care of a few things. Including staying with Gregor for a little while."

"I see. Well, you're not your sister's keeper. You couldn't follow her around all day." She met my gaze. "You're not to blame for this, you know."

"I didn't realize I thought I was until you just said it," I admitted. "I promised I would protect her after I... after we left the mansion." I didn't want to get into the torture Sara had gone through or what Marcus made me do to save her life. I would've gladly forgotten all about it, too, if I could. "You know Sara. She's always needed protecting. She's my little sister. Of course, I feel responsible."

She shook her head, and her beautiful, wavy hair moved over her shoulders. "No. Things happen all the time—strange things, wonderful things, things we can't explain. Sometimes, they happen to us, sometimes they happen to others. We can't control them."

"I'm tired of not being in control. Things have been so confusing lately." I leaned against her knees, and she let me rest there.

It was nice, being able to rest, letting go of my burdens for a little while. It was nice having a mother to talk to again.

"I can imagine they have been," she whispered, glancing again at Sara.

She was still out cold, but her eyelids fluttered every so often.

"We're trying to understand how this happened to her," I said. "We thought she might have drunk contaminated blood, but Allonic doesn't believe she would possess these powers after feeding just once or twice."

"I think it depends upon the concentration in the blood," Mom replied. "I did a lot of studying when I was in the Sanctuary."

I noticed for the first time the stacks of books on either side of the bed, not to mention another stack behind where Sara's head rested on the lounge.

"Well, no matter how it happened. She's struggling with this. We had to get her out of sigh, before another vampire saw her and spread the word. I think a sparking, crackling vampire would attract attention."

"What about the one you found her with?" Allonic asked.

Mom gasped. "She was with someone else?"

I waved a dismissive hand. "Raze. You remember Raze."

"Oh, yes." She grinned. "He was always crazy about you."

"Mom." I blushed. I couldn't believe she was teasing me. "We're just friends like we always have been. Anyway, he'll keep her a secret. I mean, he didn't have to hide her, did he? But he did."

"I trust him." Mom turned to Allonic. "You were smart to bring them here."

"I had always intended to bring them to you, like we discussed."

It was still so odd, thinking about them having a relationship apart from the one Sara and I had with her.

They had their memories together.

I wondered if he knew the song she hummed, too.

CHAPTER 3

ANISSA

"I think I'll make us some tea," Mom announced. "She'll be all right. She just needs some rest now." She stood in an elegant, fluid movement.

I had always thought she could've been a dancer, she was so graceful. I loved watching her move around the chamber, soaking her in with my eyes. I had years and years of missing her to make up for.

While she was busy in the kitchen, I motioned for Allonic to join me by the window—if Mom noticed, she was discreet enough to pretend she hadn't.

"I have a few questions for you," I said in a soft voice, glancing back at Mom and Sara.

"Perhaps you could make it a little more obvious we're having a secret conversation right now," he muttered. "Perhaps we should whisper behind our hands."

I scowled. "All right. I'll let you have that one because I'm always giving you a hard time, but that's all. Deal?"

His chuckle was a deep rumble in his chest. "All right."

I grew serious. "You never did tell me why you drank from Valerius when we were in Sorrowswatch."

His smile, faint as it was, faded completely. "I thought I had."

"No. You said it had something to do with needing his blood. I'm sorry if I don't quite remember—it was a very hectic trip."

"A good way of describing it," he agreed.

"So? What was it all about?"

He gazed out the window, down, down, down to the world below.

It was overwhelming, being so far up.

I was sure I could touch the moon from where we stood.

Everything below us looked small in comparison, almost minuscule. Except for the mountains, which were just as majestic as they were from the ground.

When he spoke, his voice was softer than usual. "It's not easy, being an outsider."

"I know all about that."

"Then, you know what it's like to feel as though you're caught between two worlds. For me, I know I'll never be accepted by either side of my blood." He scoffed, shaking his head. "As far as my fellow shades are concerned, my position is tenuous at best. I'll never reach a position of authority, even though I should rightfully do so based on my parentage. If I were full shade, there would be no question. The only reason I'm kept around, in fact, is because of who my father was. If he were just some lowly shade living at the Sanctuary, I might not have a home there."

He took a deep breath. "And if that were the case, I wouldn't have a home anywhere, since we both know how accepting and welcoming vampires can be."

"Oh, yes," I growled under my breath.

"If I'm barely existent according to the shades, I'm a non-entity as far as vampires are concerned. I'm nothing. I have no position. I shouldn't even be here, according to the beliefs held by a good many of them. I have no claim to a name, no respect, no anything. I simply happen to have a vampire mother."

"But why feed on Valerius?" I asked, still not understanding.

"Because Valerius has power. Ancient, incomprehensible power. Power I would never have on my own, as myself."

"Power is that important to you?" I glanced again at Mom.

Her back was to us, and she was humming happily as she added tea leaves to a pot and poured boiling water from the kettle.

"Not power in and of itself. But when power can be used for protection or in times of crisis, yes. Wouldn't you prefer having power to the alternative?" He stared down at me with searching, questioning eyes.

He always seemed to be so collected and in control, it was

slightly jarring to watch him have reservations about the way he was.

"When you put it that way, of course. I would want to protect those I care for, or cover my back in case someone challenged me. Yes, I would take the power if I could."

He nodded.

I could tell he was relieved, even if he didn't want to speak the words out loud.

"When I saw my chance, I took it. I didn't think much about it. I've spent so long wondering if there would ever be a time when I would fit in or at least deserve a little respect. I don't worry about that as much from the shades as I do from the vampires, since I know the vampires actively hate anything slightly different from themselves. So, I took Valerius's blood."

I looked him up and down, noting how he appeared the same as he ever did. "Do you feel different?" I whispered.

"Not very," he replied in a hushed tone. "But I have this... this knowing. I know the power is there if I ever need to call on it."

I placed a hand on his arm. "For what it's worth, I hope you never have to call on it."

Strange, but true: I had started to become really fond of him, even outside the fact he was my brother. He was always there for me when I needed help.

He nodded, smiling a little. He needed to do more of that. He looked handsome when he did. "What about you?"

"What about me?"

"Are you going to tell the Bourkes about the contaminated blood? You should, and soon. What if there are others going through this same thing Sara's going through? That could be extremely dangerous."

"I know. This is all on my mind at once. Knowing what I have to do, knowing why I have to do it. Not wanting to do it." It was my turn to stare out the window, away from him.

"Why don't you want to do it?"

"Because I'm not sure I want to see Jonah right now—and yes, I know that's immature, and I'm only thinking about myself, but haven't I spent enough time thinking about everybody else? I mean, for years. I had to work to keep Sara alive. I had to protect her when I rescued her—and I would do it again, don't get me wrong. It hasn't been entirely about me for a long time.

Even with Jonah, I've been worried about him for almost as long as I've known him. Maybe it's time for me to be a little selfish. Just a little."

It was a long time before he spoke again. "I understand how you feel. I felt the same way when you first came to me."

"You did?"

"Yes. It was a big risk, taking you in. And then you ran off..."

"I remember," I said, wincing.

"But Anissa, this isn't simply one or two other vampires facing the possibility of getting... these powers." He turned toward Sara.

She was still resting. I wondered how much longer she would need to recuperate.

"There are thousands of Bourkes in that building. Any number of them might have gotten that contaminated blood."

"And one of them might have brought it to the clan," I added with a frown. "There's no way of knowing yet how it got there."

"Don't you want to know?"

"Of course, I do. But it's definitely not my place to walk into a clan meeting and start asking questions." I leaned against the stone lining the window and wrapped my arms around myself, still staring out across miles and miles of land that appeared silver in the light of the full moon. "I could talk to Jonah about it, though, and he could go to the clan. That's his job."

I turned away from the window and gazed up at my brother. Brother. The word still stuck in my mind sometimes.

"You're right. I'll figure something out, even if it's not to help them but to help myself. Because I do want answers. Who did this to my sister?"

"That's a start," he said, then added, "Our sister."

I smiled. "Right. Our sister."

Mom's voice floated to us from the other side of the chamber. "The tea is ready."

She practically glowed from the inside out.

It hit me this was the first time she had prepared anything for all her children at once. No wonder she seemed so jubilant, even if she was only pouring tea for us.

I breathed in the sweet, slightly spicy blend before drinking.

"What happened?"

The three of us turned to where Sara was sitting up, looking around with a dazed expression.

I hope you enjoyed Absolution! Out now, the next book in this series!

Sign up for the newsletter to be notified when it's released.

www.leagueofvampires.com

Put this in your browser window:
https://app.mailerlite.com/webforms/landing/k9z2k8

Made in the USA
Middletown, DE
03 April 2018